Holy Innocents

✠

A Novel By Bill Kassel

COMPANY PUBLICATIONS, INC.
ANN ARBOR, MICHIGAN & COLORADO SPRINGS, COLORADO

This novel is a work of fiction. Names, characters, places and incidents are either the product of the author's imagination or are used fictitiously. Any resemblance to actual events, locales, organizations or persons, living or dead, is entirely coincidental and beyond the intent of the author.

"A voice is heard in Ramah,
mourning and great weeping,
Rachel weeping for her children
and refusing to be comforted,
because her children are no more."

Jeremiah 31:15

The Principal Characters

Alan Kemp
Music Director at St. Mary's

Father Karl Muller
Pastor of St. Mary's

Sister Elaine Ryden
Director of Religious Education

Rev. Matthew Pell
Pastor of Bible Fellowship

Susan Pell
Pastor Matt's wife

Tamar Kittredge
Director of the Interfaith Counselling Center

Jessica MacNair
Nurse and Blood Drive Coordinator

Kyle Warner
WNT News Director

Marty Casten
Principal of the High School

Randy Burke
An English Teacher at the High School

Rosemarie Bolton
Secretary at St. Mary's

Deacon Richard Collinson
Diocesan Finance Manager

Ellie Conner
A Member of Bible Fellowship

Stanley Zubeck
Chief of Police

Jock Volmer
Police Detective Sergeant

Popeye/Elroy
The Savant

Chapter 1

The smell was faint but definite. Alan hesitated to put his weight against the heavy wooden door that still read "Boys," its metal push plate darkened by three generations of grubby little hands. Must be sewer gas backing up again. What a frustration for Pat, the janitor. He tried to keep Holy Innocents in good shape, even if the old school was mainly used just for parish offices, group meetings and religious education. As it was, he worked miracles with the pittance left over for maintenance from St. Mary's budget.

Alan considered the discomfort below his waist. It had been a long drive down from the chancery offices, and if he didn't use this room, he'd have to get the key to the church and walk all the way up the hill. He opened the door, and the putrid smell hit him hard in the face. It was clearly worse than ever before. Alan hurried through his business at the closest of the three urinals, trying not to breathe. He gave his fingers a cursory rinse at the sink that had the large chip filled in with epoxy, and hurried out of the room shaking his hands to air dry.

"Pat!" he shouted down the hall.

The janitor stuck his head out of the boiler room at the far end. "Whad ya want?" he asked.

"Have you smelled in here? Something reeks."

Pat walked up the hall in his characteristic side-to-side gait, his slow footsteps echoing off the hard surfaces of the corridor, and the handle of a ball peen hammer slapping his thigh where it hung from a loop on the side of his overalls. "Sewer gas again?"

"I suppose," Alan said. "But it's stronger than before, and it smells different." Pat opened the bathroom door, and his unruly mane of curly hair bounced as he shook his head. "Whoa. That's bad." He closed his eyes and sniffed the offensive air. "Doesn't smell like sewer gas." He walked over to the row of toilet stalls long without their doors. "Doesn't smell like sewer gas."

Alan could barely endure the stench, and he was half out into the hallway, holding the bathroom door open. Pat walked across to the sinks and sniffed again. "It's stronger over here," he said.

There was a white, metal trash can under the towel dispenser. The domed lid with the small, hinged trap door had always stuck when Pat would try to remove it to empty the trash, so he'd taken it off completely and relegated it to a dark corner of the furnace room. The can sat open on top, a plastic liner bag fastened around the rim with an elastic band.

Pat leaned over the can and sniffed. "It's in the rubbish." There was a grocery sack inside the can, rolled over and crumpled. Pat reached in, took out the sack, then set it on the floor and opened it.

"Jesus, Mary'n Joseph!" he cried.

Alan saw the janitor's eyes widen. "What's the matter?"

"Oh my God, look at this."

Alan let the door go and went over to peer into the open sack. The sight made him feel like he'd taken a punch that knocked the wind out of him.

"It's a baby," the janitor said. "It's a baby, and its head is all squashed. Oh my God, *look* at it."

"Get Father Karl, Pat. Leave everything alone. We've got to call the police."

✠ ✠ ✠

The sharp strobes of light from the police cruiser parked just outside the glass doors created bursts of glare in Stan Zubeck's glasses, which he found distracting. He sensed that the flashes were making his photo-gray lenses darken ever so slightly—or perhaps it was only his imagination. But he turned away, trying to put the light more to his back. The stocky, square-faced police chief flipped through the pages of a note pad, which annoyed Father Karl. The priest also found it annoying that Zubeck wasn't a regular at St. Mary's. The chief was as Catholic as he was Polish. But nearly two decades as a cop and an earlier one in counter-intelligence work had taken the edge off his piety.

"So, ah...Father. How often is this can emptied? Does the janitor–what's his name, Pat Foley? How often does he normally take out the trash?"

Why would the pastor concern himself with such a mundane detail of parish maintenance? Would this small-town police chief be aware of how often trash was removed from his squad room? Perhaps he would. "I'm afraid I really don't know. You'll have to ask Mr. Foley."

Dead baby in the trash can. What a tragedy. What would the bishop say?

Alan was sitting on one of the old wooden pews, left over from the renovation of St. Mary's back in the late seventies, which were placed along the green tiled walls of the hallway. The backs were much too vertical to have provided very much comfort to anyone who would have used them during Mass. Perhaps that was the idea–penance and worship all in one. The "Old Church." What must it have been like?

He watched the police photographer taking shots inside the boys' room, then shots of the boys' room door, then shots of the hallway itself. Alan knew the photographer, a local portrait guy named Marv Johnson. Marv had taken a course in investigative photography, which qualified him–more or less–to do assignments for the police and some of the local insurance brokers. It was a small town. Alan had seen him around, shooting car wrecks, but normally their paths crossed when Alan was playing music at weddings.

Another photographer, fat Charlie Dutton from the *Daily Herald*, was being held at bay outside the school building by a woman police officer. His reporter, Claire Shelby, and Kyle Warner from the local radio station had cornered the driver of a fire rescue van, and were pumping him for details. He had none.

What a scene, Alan thought. The old school hadn't experienced this much activity in years. And it *was* a school, wasn't it. A place which used to be filled with children. Alan considered this odd turn. A dead child. How strange.

Pat, the janitor, came out of the church secretary's office, where he had been trying to calm himself after his unnerving discovery. The secretary, Rosemarie Bolton, was behind him.

"Mr. Foley," Zubeck said, "how often do you normally empty the trash in the bathroom?"

"Ah...maybe once a week. There's not a lot of traffic through here, you know. I mean, before–when the school was going–there was rubbish every day. But now, with the building just used for offices and all, well, there's not usually a lot of trash." Pat was still keyed up. He felt nervous talking to the police chief.

"So the last time you emptied the can would have been when?" Zubeck flipped through his note pad.

Pat thought. "Well... I usually go 'round to all the cans first thing Monday morning, because pickup at the dumpster is Monday afternoon. Oh, they pick up Thursdays, too. But I don't empty the cans in the school more than once a week. Except the can in Rosemarie's office."

Rosemarie nodded. The expression on her round, grandmotherly face was somber.

"She usually has a lot of rubbish," Pat said. "And of course, there's garbage every day from the rectory. But that's Father's kitchen trash. He lives there, of course."

Zubeck was getting more detail than he wanted on the subject of trash. Alan watched the chief's broad face as its expressions registered whether each fact seemed useful or beside the point.

"So, the last time you would have emptied the can in the boys' room was Monday."

"Yep," said Pat. "About ten or eleven. Well...before lunch, anyway. Probably."

"Probably." Zubeck wrote in his pad some more. He became aware of the strobe light again and changed position on the pew where he was seated against the wall opposite Alan. "So this is Friday. Would Mr. Kemp have been the first person to use that restroom today?"

Alan's lanky torso straightened at the sound of his name. He brushed his hand along the side of his head, catching a lock of sandy hair that had escaped the rubber band holding his ponytail. He had let his hair grow long since leaving the Air Force three years before.

"Hard to say," Pat answered. "Hard to say. Rosemarie, did you see anyone in the building this morning before Alan came? Hard to say."

"I don't believe there were any gentlemen," said Rosemarie, "except Father, of course. He stopped into my office once today. Briefly. But then Father always uses the bathroom in the rectory."

The priest was annoyed at her revelation of this tidbit about his toilet habits. As if everyone wasn't interested enough in the personal lives of priests.

"Sister Elaine was here," Rosemarie added. "But she wouldn't have used the boys' room."

"And where is Sister Elaine now?" Zubeck asked.

"Oh, she's out making calls at the hospital and the nursing center," Rosemarie said. "She visits different places through the week."

"Out since this morning?"

"She left about nine-thirty."

"And why do you happen to be in the building today, Mr. Kemp?" More notebook flipping. "You said...you had come from the chancery office. Meeting up there?"

"Yes." Alan cleared his throat slightly. "I met with the diocesan liturgical director. I'm in charge of music for the parish, and we were going over songs for the confirmation liturgy–when the bishop will be coming."

The bishop coming. In three weeks. Dead baby in the trash can. Father Karl was more upset each time he thought of it.

Zubeck looked at Alan. "You play guitar out at Minnie's on the highway, don't you? The country band."

"That's right."

Zubeck checked his notebook again. "Good band."

"Thanks."

A uniformed officer came in through the glass doors and whispered something in the police chief's ear.

"I'll be out to give them a statement in a minute. And tell Dutton to keep his shorts on. He has plenty of time to get some pictures. He's already past his deadline for today." The officer went back outside.

"Now then, Father Muller," Zubeck said, "I know you haven't been at St. Mary's very long. What is it, six, seven months or so?"

"Five," the priest answered, a distressed expression on his long, gaunt face making him look even more severe than usual. Zubeck might know how long he'd been here–*if* Zubeck ever came to church.

"In that time, Father, have you been aware of any resentment here in town about the Church's policy on abortions?"

The Church's *policy* on abortions? Father Karl turned his head toward the square figure seated at the other end of the old pew. The Church had no *policy* on abortion–at least not in the sense that a diocese might have a *policy* on, say, how to apply to have a marriage annulled. Abortion wasn't an issue of *policy*. It was an issue of *morality*. The Church objected totally to abortion. Abortion was a sin. It was murder. It was the taking of a human life. Father Karl scowled at this Catholic policeman who never attended Mass. "I am not a political person," he said, straightening his boney shoulders inside his black clerical shirt. "I have never engaged in any public protest."

"You've preached on the subject?"

"Of course."

"And there was that incident of vandalism you reported, about–what was it?–about three months ago?"

"I do not believe that was anything more than simple anti-Catholic bigotry. This is a community in which Evangelical groups–" He found it difficult to call them churches. "–tend to dominate."

"A message painted on the door, wasn't it?"

"Yes." Father Karl spit out the words. "The pope is Anti-Christ."

Zubeck was still making notes. "Right."

Two paramedics emerged from the boys' room, one carrying a white bundle wrapped in a clear plastic bag. Alan watched as they walked down the hall and out the glass doors to the rescue van leaving a residue of the odor behind them. Fat Charlie Dutton began blasting away outside. Marv Johnson came out of the room with Dr. Sears. The police photographer began packing his equipment away in a case that sat open at the end of the hall, as Dr. Sears went over to Zubeck.

"You were right, Chief," said the physician, whose large, old-fashioned, black medical bag made him look very much the country GP. "The baby was aborted. Late term, pretty much fully formed."

Pat and Rosemarie glanced at each other, their faces screwed up into sickly expressions. Father Karl closed his eyes and shook his head.

"Who would do such a thing?" Rosemarie asked. "That poor child, here. A trash can, and on church property. My oh my..."

"People do very odd things," the police chief said, placing his note pad in the inside breast pocket of his jacket, which was well overdue for a pressing. "Father, I'd like to speak with Sister Elaine, when she returns. Please have her call me."

Sister Elaine. She'd just love talking to the police. A great respecter of authority, that one. "I'll tell her," said the priest, running his fingers nervously through his thin gray hair.

Zubeck started out to meet the press.

"Can I clean the boys' room?" asked Pat.

"After they've finished taking fingerprints." The chief stopped. "Incidentally, we'll need to have all of you fingerprinted–anyone who might have ever been in that bathroom–so we can see if there are any prints that can't be accounted for." He went outside, and a flash from Charlie Dutton's camera made him blink. He wished his glasses could turn dark at will.

Dr. Sears was looking grave. A member of St. Mary's, he was active in Right to Life. "This is horrible, Father," he said, "just horrible."

It *was* horrible. Bishop coming in three weeks. "Oh, uh...yes, Doctor. Shocking." A dead baby in the trash can was about the last thing Father Karl needed. The anti-Catholic feelings in this quiet, rural town were enough of a complication. He had hoped for a blessedly peaceful assignment easing into retirement. It was beginning to look like that plan was not working out.

But then, bigotry was nothing new. Father Karl had been a priest long enough to know that. He had been ordained in the late 1940s, and he remembered well the vague suspicion with which Catholics were viewed in some quarters even after the cosmopolitan experience of World War II. The hardening anti-Communism of the fifties didn't help, though ironically, the Church had been in the forefront of resistance to Red influence. So many Catholics had those long, unpronounceable, Eastern European surnames that smacked of subversion.

As long as bigots confined themselves to words–even hateful words painted on the front door of the church–Father Karl could handle the situation. A dead baby in a trash can, however, was a whole different order of concern. What would he have to cope with now?

Rosemarie was hesitant, but curious. "Dr. Sears...was it–" She felt strange asking. "Was the baby a boy or a girl, Doctor?"

The country physician, near retirement himself, looked at the secretary, his eyes heavy. "A boy," he said.

The same question had occurred to Alan, and he was struck by the absurd observation that at least the dead baby found in the boys' room was a boy. The most stupid things can come to mind at life's horrible moments. He reproached himself for even bothering to think about it.

"I don't suppose, Father," said Dr. Sears, "that the child can be buried from the church."

Such an idea. To draw even more attention to this gross event. "I–I don't know what can be done," said Father Karl. "I'll have to check with the chancery." The chancery. Bishop coming in three weeks. "Besides, we...don't know what the police will need to do with the child."

Would someone have to mutilate the little body still further? Horrifying thought.

"There's no need for an autopsy," Dr. Sears said. "I'm certain of that. We know the baby was aborted. Very close to delivery, too. Dilation and extraction–what's called a partial-birth abortion." He glanced back toward the bathroom. "Would have been a lovely little boy."

Father Karl thought about the dead baby and suddenly looked very sad. "Yes, Doctor," he said, shaking his head again, "I imagine we can bury the child."

✠ ✠ ✠

It was the duty of a pastor's wife to keep informed about the latest goings-on around town–and to keep her husband informed–and Susan Pell took to her duty with a dedication that was religious. One of the simplest ways of keeping up was listening to Kyle Warner's noontime news broadcast. Kyle was a member of Bible Fellowship and was someone Susan knew to be careful about getting his facts straight before he spoke of anything, whether in person or on the air. And WNT was one of those small-town stations for which no news is too trivial. A traffic ticket got your name read on the news.

Susan turned up the kitchen radio when she heard Kyle say that the body of an aborted baby had been found at the old Holy Innocents school. In a *trash can*. Could something like this really happen, *right here in town*? An appalling thing to hear on a lovely spring day, with the sun shining and the birds singing. May first. Unbelievable. *Unfathomable*. Susan had attended meetings of Right to Life in that very building. Of course, that was back in the days when Father Edward was encouraging interfaith cooperation. Back before Father Karl Muller came to town.

Not that Susan had much time for ecumenical sharing. She stood by her husband's view that cooperating on issues like abortion was one thing. Doctrine and scripture interpretation were something else. After all, Catholics are Catholics, and God knows, her husband's family had seen the fruits of Roman travesty close up. The Reverend Matthew Pell had inherited his father's congregation along with his father's tales of resentment over some harsh experiences in a Catholic orphan school.

The elder Pell, born Giuseppi Pellegrino, had been the object of special interest by a priest with a delicate touch and a vindictive nature. Fear-filled complaints to the school's principal brought only beatings and assignment to the most unpleasant and degrading chores. Giuseppi ran away at first chance, and chose the name Gene Pell as an escape from his former life, from his Italian immigrant ancestry, and from everything else that smacked of a cruel and hypocritical Church. Years later, he found both God and an evangelistic calling to which he brought a special, highly personal zeal. Such were the footsteps in which young Matthew Pell had followed his father into the Gospel ministry.

Susan felt sickened at the details in Kyle's report. She declined to imagine the details he'd left out. A baby, treated like that. She stood staring at the radio, which was mounted under the kitchen cabinets, picturing the old school building and making soft clicking noises with her tongue. Horrible. Just horrible. The sound of her husband's car in the driveway brought Sue's attention back to the tuna salad she was preparing for lunch. Pastor Matt came up the side steps and into the kitchen, a taut expression on his clean young face, and his wife sprung to her duty. "Did you hear what happened at the Catholic school?" she asked.

Matt was obviously preoccupied, and there was a pause before he answered. "Yes," he said, "I had Kyle on the car radio."

"Isn't it shocking? We've held our meetings right there. Imagine." She mixed some chopped celery into the tuna, then reached for a container of dried parsley on the spice rack. "Who could do a thing like that–I mean, even if you object to pro-life?"

"Satan has no scruples, Sue. You know that." He hung his sport jacket by the door, then went to the nook in a corner window bay.

"Oh Matt–but a baby. It's so...so..." She searched for a word to reflect the enormity of her shock and fell a bit short. "...well...disrespectful."

"It was disrespectful to abort it." Matt pushed aside a new copy of *Christianity Today* which had been left lying open on the bench, and sat down. "*Very* disrespectful."

Susan came over with the tuna and sat on the bench opposite her husband. There were two places set out on the table. She looked at Matt, her blue eyes framed by the blonde hair the young minister would normally bounce playfully when he greeted her at lunch. The two had been sweethearts since their sophomore year in the Christian high school Sue's parents had helped to found in a cluster of old stone buildings that had once been the county poor farm.

Sue believed she was born to be a minister's wife. She had been a constant presence at Bible Fellowship since giving her life to the Lord and her heart to Pastor Gene's handsome son. She was loved by her husband's flock, especially by the children, who looked forward eagerly to weekly Bible class with the gentle and pretty Miss Pastor Sue. And the very thought of anyone harming a baby chilled her to the core of her womanly being.

"Sometimes I can't believe people, Matt," she said. "The things that people do. Why, I told you about that terrible wife-beating incident. The Nazarene congregation is so upset." The travails of different churches around town were a field of special interest.

"That's Pastor Krug's problem, Dear."

"I honestly don't believe people," she said, opening a bread wrapper and taking out two slices. "There's going to be a chastisement, Matt. You've said so yourself." She dropped the bread into the toaster sitting on the table, and pushed down its handle. "How we must try the Lord's patience."

"The Lord will act in His own good time."

"A *baby*, Matt. Thrown away just like..." A shudder passed through her slim body.

Matt reached his hands across the table and clasped hers. Their eyes met, and they shared a feeling. Babies were very much on both their minds these days. They had been trying for quite some time now to get her pregnant–with no success.

"I know a thing like this means something special to you, Sue. To us. Try not to let it upset you so badly."

The merest sad smile broke across her lips as she looked at her husband. Matt smiled faintly in return. No matter what tragedies the young minister encountered–and pastoring Bible Fellowship, he encountered his share–he depended on his wife to help him keep things in perspective. There was something about her simple feminine goodness: her warm heart, her feeling for other people's pain–which he had to admit bordered on a love of gossip (he was working with her on that tendency)–and especially her unfailing knowledge of what was important in life. Susan was of the earth. And she brought Matt down to earth and kept him in touch with people and their real concerns, when he was inclined to see the philosophical side of things and soar off into theological speculations. He often said that his scholarly nature had made him a minister but Susan had made him a pastor.

He looked at her lovingly across the table. "Let's pray."

They bowed their heads, and Sue waited for him to begin. But Matt hesitated. "Perhaps I should call on Father Muller," he said after a pause.

She looked up. "Matt?"

"I'm sure he's very distressed."

"But he's been so unfriendly. And he has absolutely no time for Protestants. He's made that clear."

"You know my feelings about the Roman Church," Matt said. "But they've been our allies on abortion, despite Father Muller. An attack on them–like...this–is an attack on the whole pro-life movement."

"Do you think it was...feminists?"

"It was somebody with a point to make," he said. "And I don't think it can be excused, whether it was made against Catholics or anybody else."

He looked out through the window bay. Susan could read anger in the dark Sicilian eyes that punctuated his pale, boyish face. Then they both bowed their heads again.

"Father God, we thank you..."

✠ ✠ ✠

A trail of brown slime inched its way down the painted, cinder block wall. Marty Casten scanned the cafeteria and knew that even if he could spot who had thrown the chocolate ice cream, there would be no point in pursuing it. What a menagerie. Dim-witted town goons with multiple earrings and death-metal tee shirts. White farm boys trying to look like black rappers. Every variety of head decoration: shoulder-length, shaved, half-shaved/half-long, dreadlocks, bandanas, baseball caps turned around. Over-painted baby dolls with hair teased up four inches above the head, blouses open two inches down the cleavage and skirts hiked eight inches beyond the knee. The American high school. How the hell did we come to this?

Marty had started teaching back in the days when crew cuts were rebellious and white angora sweaters the edge of propriety. Back when students called you "sir" and slacking off was reading *The Catcher In the Rye* during study hall.

He shook his head in resignation, ran fingers through his wisp of thin, graying hair, scratched the side of a belly that had lost the firmness of the college athlete and high school gymnastics coach he had once been, and started back to his office. One pass through the cafeteria was enough lunch duty for him. It was a principal's prerogative to assign that onerous task to others. His own noontime plan was for a half hour of peace with an egg salad sandwich and the flavored, Swedish coffee brewing on his office credenza.

He could smell the aromatic liquid as he passed behind the long counter in the reception area. But his anticipation was broken by the voices of Brigitte Statterly, his attractive, young secretary, and Mavis Garner, the junior class guidance counselor, having lunch in the supply room. The women sounded upset, and after a brief hesitation and a quick glance in at his coffeemaker, Marty went to the supply room to see what was the matter.

"Is everything all right, ladies?" he asked.

Brigitte had her hand on the small radio that sat on a shelf above the copying machine. "Mr. Casten, have you heard? It's awful. Someone put an aborted fetus in a trash can at Holy Innocents."

"That is so sick," Mavis chimed in. "Can you believe it?"

"A trash can, in the men's room," Brigitte elaborated, "of all places."

This was the kind of information that takes a moment to process when you're mind is on egg salad, coffee and a half hour of peace. "Do they know who did it?"

"They're investigating," said Brigitte. "But according to the radio, they don't know much yet."

"Sick!" said Mavis. "Just sick."

A high school principal was accustomed to hearing about strange goings on. Marty had long since ceased being shocked at the varieties of human degradation that found their way to his office door. Dealing with the aftermath of child abuse, domestic violence, the occasional case of incest and other sordid aspects of contemporary, rural family life was part of his job. Still, he had to admit this situation was novel.

"A fetus in a trash can. At a school. Pretty revolting," he said, thinking about some revolting things discovered in the trash at his own school over the years. Then it struck him that, as outrageous as it was, the act of putting a dead body in a trash can had a certain juvenile quality about it. Had he come to hold teenagers in such low regard that the thought of some kid doing such a thing could creep into his mind like that? Maybe he'd just been in the business too long. Still, he wondered.

"Let me know if they find out anything else."

"All right, Mr. Casten."

Marty walked down the hallway that connected all the rooms in the administrative cluster, the two women chattering in the background about who could do such a disgusting thing and speculating on why. He sat down at his desk and thought for a moment, staring out the window. Then he got up, walked over to the credenza, and poured some coffee into a mug with a message printed on the side: "If you can read this, thank a teacher." He went back to his chair and placed the mug on his desk–without tasting the coffee–thought for another minute, and picked up the phone. He held the receiver in his hand and started to press the buttons on the key pad. Then he stopped and set the receiver back on its cradle.

He took a sip from his cup of coffee, distractedly, and was suddenly struck by the rich taste. Hazelnut.

✠ ✠ ✠

The petite frame of Sister Elaine Ryden sat behind her desk in the little cubicle that had once been the office of Holy Innocents' principal. The room wasn't more than ten feet square, if that, with one small window looking out on the street and another into the hallway. But it served her needs and somehow seemed to reflect her personality. Books, pamphlets and miscellaneous stacks of papers covered her desk and threatened to tumble off the shelves lining two walls. A poster with what appeared to be a Christlike figure walking through a lush, tropical forest loomed over the back of her chair. She was staring straight ahead, a pinched expression on her small face telling of the recent, distasteful chat with Police Chief Zubeck. Cops never change, do they. And police stations–even a small-town one–hadn't gotten any more pleasant than she remembered from her days of Gospel Action: out in the streets, marching against U.S. *imperialism* in Central America.

The scrappy little nun sat stiffly in her characteristic dark jumper, her short, straight hair slightly disheveled, and her arms stretched out on the desktop. The index finger of her right hand was tapping on the lid of her pyx, the small metal canister which looked like a cosmetic compact and was used to carry the host when she took communion to the sick. She glanced down at the container, remembering that it still held one piece of wafer which hadn't been consumed. Old Mrs. Cellini wasn't up to communion that morning. It occurred to Sister Elaine that her nervous tapping was hardly a respectful way to treat the Body of

Christ. The fragment should be returned to the tabernacle in the church.

As she walked up the hallway, she heard the sound of a guitar coming from one of the classrooms. She peeked in and saw Alan picking his way through some music spread out on a table.

"What are you working on?" she asked.

Alan stopped playing and looked up. "Oh. Hello, Sister. I'm just trying to learn a couple of songs the bishop wants us to do for the confirmation."

Elaine glanced down disdainfully at the music sheets. "I trust His Excellency isn't planning to burden us with too many songs about holy *men* and *sons* of God," she said icily.

Alan had experienced Sister Elaine's prickliness about language before. "I'm sure the bishop is sensitive to the feelings of women in his diocese."

"You shouldn't assume that," said Elaine. "Sometimes I think the good bishop slept through Vatican II."

"Right beside Father Karl?" Alan asked playfully.

"Don't get me started on Father Karl."

The arrival of Father Karl Muller at St. Mary's was a shock following hard on a loss. The previous pastor, Father Edward, had been young, energetic and tuned in to the shifting currents in the New Church. He was, for Sister Elaine, a dream pastor, calling constantly on her ample talents and letting her run religious education pretty much any way she liked. And what she liked involved a goodly dose of the self-revealing-transactional-therapy-hands-on-contact approach to personal catechesis–tinged with the woman-centered nature spirituality that had earned her order the nickname of the "Earth Mothers."

The petite nun's touch was particularly evident in the RCIA program–Rite of Christian Initiation of Adults–the yearlong process through which converts entered the Catholic Church. Elaine was a *people* person. She was good at making folks feel welcome and getting them to open up. Under her direction, RCIA had a definite *touchy-feely* quality, though she wouldn't have seen it that way. Still, the approach worked. St. Mary's convert numbers went up steadily, year after year. Father Edward had been delighted.

But young, energetic, tuned-in priests were just what was needed in the New

Church. Father Edward was on a fast track which many people assumed would take him from his first pastorate in this small, rural parish right up to diocesan headquarters–possibly, in time, to the bishop's chair. His leaving was a severe blow. The new pastor, on discovering Sister Elaine's interests and tendencies, made it plain that there would be no more pop psychology or eco-feminism at St. Mary's. Henceforth, the religious education program would stick to teaching that oldtime religion.

Elaine had said all she cared to about Father Karl. She turned with a sniff and walked out of the classroom, exiting the school through the fire doors at the far end of the hallway. She hurried up the hill to the church, unlocked the side door, and went into the darkened building. She made her way across the front of the sanctuary to the tabernacle in dim, colored light from the stained-glass windows. The two sets of small, bronze doors clanked open, one after the other, as she turned a key in the antique mechanism. She emptied the piece of host into a pewter ciborium, and closed the tabernacle doors again.

As she removed the key, Elaine noticed that some papers had spilled out of the back of the pulpit onto the floor. She knelt down to gather them up, when her eye was caught by a dark form in the back of the church. Clutching a handful of old announcement notes and Sunday bulletins, she stood up. "Hello?" She squinted to make out the shape, which now appeared to be a person kneeling in the back pew. "Who's there?" The church was locked, or supposed to be.

"Don't be frightened, Sister." It was Father Karl.

Elaine was relieved, and then annoyed at being startled by...*him*. "I'm sorry to disturb your prayers, Father. I didn't realize–"

"That's quite all right."

Father Karl stood and genuflected at the end of the pew. Then Elaine saw his long, angular frame moving up the dark aisle.

"We're all a bit jumpy after this morning," he said. "I found it difficult to concentrate at noon Mass."

"Of course, Father." Elaine replaced the papers inside the pulpit, and started across to the side door, eager to remove herself as gracefully as possible.

"Sister–"

The nun winced, ever so slightly, as she stopped.

"Have you any thoughts on who might have..."

"The baby?"

"Who might do such a thing?"

"Chief Zubeck seems to think it was a protest," said Elaine, recalling her morning's brush with civil authority.

"Do you agree with him?"

"I can't really say." Addressing this subject with Father Karl was beginning to make her tense. "Feelings about abortion can be very...strong."

Father Karl shook his head sadly. Could feelings be so strong? He had caught himself shaking his head several times throughout this very distressing day. "Such a desecration. A human life. A human body."

Elaine looked at him, her expression blank. She was clear about her feelings on abortion. Didn't she believe in the seamless garment of life? Life was sacred. All life, from beginning to end. It was a gift of God to be cherished and protected. Didn't she oppose capital punishment? Didn't she advocate the idea of animal rights? Wasn't she even a vegetarian?

But she was also a woman. And what could this priest know about a woman desperately pregnant who believes an abortion is her only hope? Elaine felt her stomach start to knot up. She understood that abortion ended a child's life. But she also knew how a woman feels about her own body. Father Karl would never understand such things. What man could? "People can feel...driven," she said. "They can feel at the mercy of forces beyond their control."

Father Karl stood in the dark church with his hands clasped in front of him, his head outlined against one of the stained-glass windows, and his face in shadows. He considered her words. "Yes Sister, there *are* dark forces. They come unexpectedly, and you can never know who will be drawn into the circle of evil." His eyes were turned down to the floor. "I suppose we shouldn't judge," he said. "But it's...hard."

What was it about this priest? Elaine got on well with pretty much everybody else in the parish. But Father Karl had seemed so weary and detached, from the first day he came to St. Mary's, which had made losing the energetic Father

Edward all the more painful. The old man took a long, slow breath, then turned away. His eyes caught some light from the window, and for the merest instant, it looked almost as if he might cry.

"You're right, Father," Elaine said. "No one should judge."

✠ ✠ ✠

"Chief, what's the push on this trash can thing?" Jock Volmer was as diligent a cop as any, but he couldn't see the point of Zubeck's long list of instructions. "I know this trick was damned offensive. But even if we can find out who snuck into the school–which I doubt we can–I'm not even sure what law they broke. Abortion is legal. What'ould we charge 'em on, littering?"

"I don't know," answered Zubeck, looking slowly at Marv Johnson's photographs, passing them from one hand to the other. "Malicious mischief or something. There's probably a regulation about improper disposal of body parts. Maybe breaking and entering, though it doesn't look like anybody broke in." He glanced up at his sergeant. "That's for the D.A. to call. But this stinks, Jocko, and I don't mean that poor, rotted baby. I saw enough appalling crap when I was in Baltimore. That's why I took *this* job, and I hate to see it happening here." He pushed the photos away and stood up. "Run it all down," he said, pointing to the list in Volmer's hand. "Especially the FBI. Find out if they've seen anything like this anywhere else. If there's something political going on, I want to know what to expect."

Jock shrugged and headed out of the chief's glassed-in office back into the squad room. Zubeck looked down at the shots again. The images made the tough cop's stomach sour. He gathered up the photographs, turned them over, and dropped them face-down on his desk.

Chapter 2

Alan pounded on the last chord of "Holy God, We Praise Thy Name" and held it out for an extended fermata. Finish big. Send 'em home humming. That was his philosophy. What was the point of a pipe organ if you couldn't be a little dramatic, especially on the final hymn? Perhaps it was the lingering influence of his Presbyterian upbringing. As the chord faded, he reached up and hit the button on the electronic carillon. The sound of bells resonated in the steeple: "The Church's One Foundation." He switched off the organ and P.A. system, gathered up his music and jacket, and closed the lid.

When he turned around and looked down from the loft, there they were, as usual. Mr. and Mrs. Nickerson. Lovely old couple. Ethel brought her hands together as if she were clapping in the air. Harold gave Alan a "thumbs up" sign. Eleven-thirty Mass every week, dependable as sunrise. They loved Alan's playing, whether on the organ, piano or guitar, and they never hesitated to let him know. He bowed broadly, sweeping one arm in front of his chest. They laughed and waved up at him. Delight at such small expressions of praise was his secret sin.

Alan varied his presentations from week to week. Sometimes he would play guitar and sing down front. One Mass each month, the choir would perform, rotating between the nine o'clock and the eleven-thirty. Occasionally, Alan would play the small spinet off to the far side of the altar. And from time to time, he'd even bring in his Alesis electronic keyboard. *That* he kept to a minimum. Father Karl wasn't convinced that guitars belonged at Mass, much less electronic instruments which he distrusted entirely.

Alan switched off the lights over the loft and started down the stairs. "Like the music of angels," said a voice from the bottom.

"Collie. What are you doing here?"

"I thought a drive in the country would be a nice way to spend Sunday." They shook hands.

Officially, Deacon Richard Collinson bore the title Diocesan Finance Manager. But as husband of the bishop's favorite niece, he functioned as Uncle's assistant (a touch of nepotism reflecting a time-honored, though oft-denied, Church tradition). Collie handled all the messy little chores that cluttered up the chancery and complicated Uncle's life. He was good at the job–smart, careful, discreet, politically astute, and sensitive to feelings and closely guarded interests wherever he found them, inside or outside the ecclesiastical structure. He was a friend of Alan's from as far back as elementary school days. In fact, it was his timely word to Father Edward which had made the connection for this job at St. Mary's, after Alan had come out of the Air Force at 33 and spent a couple of hard-scrabble years playing bar gigs in very bad rock bands.

Alan was pleased, if somewhat surprised, to find his friend. "You here to see Father Karl?" he asked.

"To see him," said Collie, "but not to talk to him."

"What do you mean?"

Collie looked around and noted that Father Karl had finished shaking hands out in front of the church and had disappeared into the rectory. "How 'bout brunch? Got any plans?"

"None in particular," Alan said. "You buying?"

"Sure. Where's a good place?"

They walked across the square in the sunshine. It was a pleasant day, warm with spring, and a young mother held on tightly to her little boy as he reached his hand to splash in a small fountain on the lawn by the county courthouse. They crossed the street on the far side of the square and went inside the Courthouse Inn. Collie headed quickly for the back of the room and chose a booth by the kitchen. Alan noted that his friend made a point of slipping into the seat with its back to the rest of the tables.

"No chance of Father Karl walking in on us here, is there?"

"Not likely," said Alan. "You hiding out from him?"

"Low profile," said Collie, taking a menu from the clip on the wall. "I stayed in the back corner at church, under the eighth station, and I didn't go up for communion."

"Why the cloak and dagger?"

Collie scanned down the entrés on the menu, then sat thoughtfully for a moment. He took off his round-rimmed glasses, which had been a trademark since high school days, and looked up at Alan. "The bishop is...concerned," he said, "about your pastor." He took a handkerchief from his jacket pocket and wiped the lenses carefully. "Father Karl is very...fragile."

Alan looked quizzical. "Fragile how?"

A waitress came and poured coffee into two mugs on the table. "Breakfast for you gents?" she asked pertly.

They ordered, and after the girl had gone, Alan asked, "What did you mean Father's 'fragile'?"

Collie took a sip of coffee. He folded the handkerchief and stuffed it back into his pocket. Then he put on his glasses and looked up at the walls, which were decorated with some not terribly professional murals depicting local scenes around the valley. One mural showed the square, with the courthouse in the foreground and St. Mary's behind it. "How much do you know about Father Karl?"

"Not much," Alan said. "He isn't a particularly open person, that I can see. Kind of 'Old Church.' Prefers traditional hymns. Doesn't think much of the newer, guitar stuff, I know that. But he's never really complained about what I do."

Collie nodded quietly. He seemed uncharacteristically guarded. Alan knew his friend had to play the diplomat in his work for the bishop, but the two of them had always been open and completely at ease with each other.

"Do you know how Father Karl happened to come to St. Mary's?" Collie asked after a moment.

"Well, from what I hear, he's close to retirement. So coming down here to replace Father Edward makes sense, I guess. It's a small parish. Not all that many demands on a priest, I shouldn't imagine. Frankly, I think Father Edward was getting bored. He was always involving himself in diocesan projects."

"Yeah, Ed's a live wire." The deacon sipped from his coffee mug.

"Sister Elaine pretty much ran the parish," said Alan. "At least that's the way it looked to me."

"What do you know about Father Karl's background?"

"I know he had other parishes."

"Much larger ones."

"And I heard something about a school."

"He was once headmaster at St. Francis Academy."

Alan made a low whistling sound. "St. Francis? That's pretty uptown. Big boarding school. Good name. Kind of expensive, too."

Running a highly regarded school like St. Francis would have been a plum assignment. Alan was impressed. "Our shepherd must be a bright guy."

"Karl Muller has some reputation in Catholic educational circles," Collie said. "You're right about his basic attitude. He *is* very 'Old Church.' He's expressed his reservations–rather deep ones, actually–about the direction the Church has taken since the reforms of the Second Vatican Council. He wasn't against Vatican II, but he thinks some of the new forms have been abused. Frankly, he has a point. Anyway, he was a superb educator. He never showed his personal uncertainty to his students or let it interfere with the work."

"None of that sounds very 'fragile' to me," Alan said, stirring a teaspoon of sugar into his coffee.

Collie glanced around at the murals again, then his eyes came back to Alan. "The last assignment–after St. Francis, that is–was...difficult. Father Karl was sent to St. Ann's parish. The bishop asked him, specifically, to take that spot, because of his recognition as an educator. By then, Father Karl, himself, felt it was time for a change. And he's always respected the bishop. So he took the job. But it was hard. St. Ann's school was on its back, and everyone knew it. There was no shortage of students. In fact, quite a few families depended on that school. But costs had gotten out of control. The parish hadn't been able to afford it for a long time, and the bishop didn't need a charity case with no end in sight."

Alan leaned back against the wall on which the booth benches were mounted and brought one foot up on the seat, his leg bent. He leaned an elbow on the raised knee and ran his fingers through his ponytail. The deacon went on with his story.

"Blessed Sacrament was within busing distance and had much better facilities," Collie continued. "But, of course, people love the parish school. There had to be a consolidation, and the bishop figured the bad news would come better from somebody who had solid educational credentials. It would look less arbitrary."

"So Father Karl was the hatchet man," said Alan.

"Exactly. It took two years preparing for the transition. Some bloody fights with parish council, parents' board, lay teachers' union. Every knock-down, drag-out confrontation you can imagine, every ugly name called." Collie took another sip of coffee, then picked up the butter knife from his place setting on the table and examined a small stain on one side. "Karl Muller had a nervous breakdown. The bishop sent him to a retreat center out west for over a year. When Father Edward was to leave St. Mary's, it seemed like a natural step to help Father Karl back into ministry. Back into life."

Alan reached for his mug and drank some more coffee. "So the bishop's afraid this dead baby episode will send Father out west again?"

"The bishop has the utmost regard for Father Karl," said Collie. "And, yes, quite frankly he's worried."

Alan motioned to the waitress, who came over with refills. "Breakfast'll be up in a minute," she said, flashing her perky smile.

"Father Karl seemed okay this weekend," Alan said, after the girl went away. "He's not a dynamic preacher–certainly not theatrical like Father Edward was. But he seemed as *on* as he ever is. Last week, of course, he was kind of subdued. But that was the first weekend after we found the body. Everyone was a little shaken."

Collie nodded. "I would appreciate it, Alan," he said, "if you could...keep an eye on Father Karl. Let me know if you observe anything...erratic."

"Like what?"

"Just...erratic. Off stride. I don't know. Anything that looks like special stress."

Alan shrugged. "Well, I'll watch out. For what it's worth. Of course, I don't see him much through the week."

"And...another thing," said Collie, his eyes turned down toward the table top. There was a pause. "Here's where you work off this breakfast, Alan."

"What do you mean?"

Collie smiled self-consciously. "Alan, you did some investigative work in the Air Force."

"Yes, base security, mainly. A little criminal stuff. Drug enforcement, AWOLs. Nothing flashy."

"How about when you were with the I.G. in Washington?"

"That was administrative stuff," he said. "Following up on discrimination and disciplinary complaints. Double-checking evidence reports. Pretty routine."

Alan had been assigned to the military police, and later to the office of the Air Force Inspector General. But even in Washington his duties had been decidedly unglamorous. He'd been a non-com staff member whose work was strictly supportive, and he had never considered himself a real *investigator*. "What's my Air Force history got to do with Father Karl?"

Collie looked straight into Alan's eyes. "My old friend, I need your help. The bishop wants to know what's behind this business. I've spoken with him about your background. I've explained that, as a professional musician, your work schedule is...flexible. You've got time during the day that someone with a nine-to-five job wouldn't have. And you're single, so your evenings are your own to–"

"Only when I'm not playing," Alan interrupted. "Don't forget, I've got the band out at Millie's three nights a week. And there are other gigs, when I can get them."

"You're far more flexible than most people," Collie continued.

Alan nodded in agreement.

"Anyway, the bishop would appreciate it–and *I* would appreciate it–if you could...follow up. Check around."

Check around? Alan hadn't lived in town all that long, and the one thing he had learned from his duties in the Air Force was that investigative work takes contacts–connections developed over time. "The police are on the case, Collie."

"I've spoken with Chief Zubeck," the deacon said. "He seems sincerely interested. But he– How can I put it? This is a small town, Alan. I know it's something of a backwater in the diocese, and it probably seems like the chancery doesn't pay much attention to what goes on down here. But believe me. We are aware of...conditions. There's a history here. Feelings about the Church are very complicated. It may be that the police would be operating under...inhibitions–factors which wouldn't necessarily constrain someone working...independently."

Alan started to speak, but Collie held up a hand to stop him. "Understand, Alan, we're not concerned with prosecutions," he said. "Evidence is not the issue. We want to know if anti-Catholic sentiment is growing in this part of the diocese, or if we should expect future difficulties over abortion. And we want to protect Father Karl. A few quiet inquiries might give us all the information we need."

This was certainly an unexpected turn. Conduct an investigation for the bishop? "I don't know how to react to this, Collie."

"It's a little out of the ordinary, I realize."

"I've never done anything quite like–"

"You're a perceptive person, Alan. You think about things, and you understand people. You can sense their emotions. I've seen you perform. You're very good at reading an audience–what people feel, what's motivating them."

"That's showmanship, Collie, not police work."

"It's *sensitivity*, Alan."

Alan appreciated the deacon's confidence in him. They had been friends since childhood. Collie did know Alan, perhaps better than anybody knew Alan. And the investigations he'd been involved in–even as peripheral as his role had been–were some of the most interesting parts of those years in the Air Force. Still, this whole thing struck Alan as very much *off the wall*.

Certainly, he couldn't dismiss the startling effect of finding that poor baby. It was revolting, and it had shaken St. Mary's deeply, as a parish community. No doubt, it had caused upset throughout the diocese. Hell, he had been pretty stunned by it himself. He was *there*, after all.

But, disturbing as the incident was, could the bishop be making too much of it? It was an *unborn* child, after all–and yes, Alan knew that the Church recognized it as a fully human being with a soul and a right to live–and yes, Alan agreed with that understanding. Still, was it reasonable to infer some larger pattern of anti-Catholic bigotry from one shocking incident?

Alan eyed his old friend across the table. He could see that Collie was taking this very seriously. Well, maybe there *was* more here than there appeared. Maybe this was an opportunity to learn something about the town–though maybe something not too pleasant. Or perhaps there was a small service to be rendered to the Church.

The Church.

The Church had gotten Alan through a very hard time in his life. Sheila. A painful divorce. He had liked the Air Force. It had provided him with a measure of order and stability a musician's life usually lacks. He might still be there. But everything had fallen apart. Father Karl would have been leaving St. Francis Academy around the time Alan was leaving the Air Force.

Alan turned his eyes down at the table and considered Collie's request. Then he looked up at his friend, who–he remembered at that moment–was responsible for his having the job at St. Mary's. "I suppose I could...poke around," he said. "I don't really know where to start, but...I'll figure something out. Just don't expect miracles."

The waitress brought two plates of eggs, and the men thanked her. Alan's were over easy with Canadian bacon. Collie's were sunny side up with sausage patties. The deacon broke off a piece of sausage with his fork, dipped it in the yolk of one egg, and put it in his mouth. He washed it down with a sip of coffee. Then he glanced playfully at Alan and flashed a winning smile, his eyes sparkling through the round glasses. "That's all right, my friend," he said. "Deacons don't *do* miracles. Those arrangements are made higher up."

✠ ✠ ✠

It wasn't the hard edge that made Tamar Kittredge so interesting to Sister Elaine. Indeed, the nun had often thought that if she could only bring her friend back to the Church, some of that crust might come off and Tamar could feel a little more at ease–more trustful, perhaps, more free to reveal the genuine warmth Elaine knew was behind all that brusqueness and cynicism. But conversations about religion always came to a quick end with Tamar.

"I'll come back to the Church when they're willing to make you a priest," she would say. "Frankly, Elaine, I don't know how you can function in such a stifling, sexist environment. You're a competent person, and there's no way they're going to recognize your true worth."

How do you describe a calling of the heart? What words can you use to explain faith to a worldly and practical person?

But it was that very practicality which Elaine so admired in Tamar–the ability to set priorities, stir people to action, get things done. Tamar had taken over the Interfaith Counselling Center when it was very near to closing its doors. The three churches that provided most of its funding–Methodist, Presbyterian and Lutheran–were quarreling over programs. A critical state grant was in danger of being diverted elsewhere. And the previous director had let an important support initiative, begun by a group of local business people, flounder for lack of direction.

It was the perfect challenge to Tamar, who at that moment, was very much in need of a challenge. Her divorce was final, and her experience working for a major foundation was still fresh enough. She wasn't all that enamored with moving to a little, jerk-water town. But it was a job and her entré back into her own life. A life without Mister Corporate Hot-shot. A life without putting her own needs on the shelf for a husband set on conquering the business world one secretary at a time.

Tamar had been rather surprised that no one representing any of the three supporting churches had asked about her religious beliefs. If they weren't asking, she felt under no compulsion to mention the agnosticism or atheism or whatever it was to which this one-time Catholic had come. Anyway, the job was to run a facility that provided counselling and basic assistance with a broad range of living needs. It was street-level social work, not very glamorous and not very spiritual.

The center's clientele consisted mainly of battered women, abused children, pregnant teenagers, and young couples one step ahead of the bill collector. Tamar, her four-member staff, and a handful of volunteers performed a kind of social triage on the walking wounded of rural America. They offered encouragement where possible and made referrals to different service agencies as necessary.

Sister Elaine enjoyed helping out at the center, and she'd become close to Tamar, which surprised her as much as it did everyone who knew of their friendship. They were an odd pair, one had to admit: the idealistic, back-to-the-earth nun and the prickly, no-nonsense administrator. But they shared a certain edgy feminist outlook–both convinced that women face an uphill battle–and they felt the kinship of women who, each in their own way, have to fight that battle alone.

There was one aspect of their relationship which made Elaine uncomfortable, however. She knew that Tamar handled the pregnant girls herself. And while such counselling was cloaked in confidentiality, Elaine suspected her friend was making referrals to the women's clinic up in the capital. That most of the girls who took Tamar's referrals would eventually have abortions was a probability Elaine didn't like to dwell on.

She had examined her conscience as to whether she should associate herself with the center if there was indeed any connection with abortion. It was a difficult question–which she had, quite pointedly, neglected to discuss with Father Karl. But in the end, she decided that perhaps this was an opportunity to be the Lord's witness, to exercise what influence she could. Besides, she was fond of Tamar. Even if there was an element of spiritual risk, her friend was worth the effort.

They were on the Interstate approaching the exit for the highway that used to be the main route from the capital. Tamar slowed down. She had a tendency to overshoot this particular exit, since it came up just beyond a curve through a wooded area. Her headlights flashed quickly across the reflective lettering on a not-all-that-prominent exit sign, and she pulled off down the ramp. A right turn at the bottom set her in the direction of the valley.

"I can't believe I ate that much," said Elaine, patting herself on the belly.

"I can't believe you talked me into a Thai restaurant," said Tamar.

"Now wasn't it good? Admit it, Tam, you enjoyed the cooking."

"Good, yes. But–*whew!*–the spices. Lift the top of your head right off."

Elaine laughed. "It is tangy."

"Tangy!"

"But they do wonderful things with vegetables. That's why I like it."

"Well, it's certainly popular."

"It's a favorite with the students at the university–located right across from the campus and all."

"Yes, the place was packed with them. I felt like everybody's great aunt."

Elaine chuckled again. "Time marches on, doesn't it?"

"Well, I don't know how nuns feel about the passage of time. But we civilians feel old."

"Oh, you shouldn't worry, Tam. You're a very attractive lady. I'm sure if you wanted, you could marry again."

Elaine's assessment was correct. Tamar had shed the nearly thirty pounds which had come with all the eating that served as consolation for a poor marriage. She was tall and slender, and she carried herself with dignity gained at a cost. If her face had lost the soft cuteness of youth, it had acquired the mature beauty of eyes that had shed their tears and lips that had learned to smile again.

She flashed her high beams to signal an oncoming driver to lower his lights. "Please, Elaine. Spare me any thoughts of marriage."

"You wouldn't want a man in your life again?"

Tamar smiled from the side of her mouth. "It's not for me to shock someone in Religious life. But I didn't say I'd sworn off men. I'm just not interested in marriage. Not for a long time, anyway."

Elaine's eyes fell into her lap. "Well...all that's outside my area."

"Don't lose any sleep over my moral state." Tamar laughed. "I have nobody leading me into temptation just now, I can assure you."

This line of discussion seemed to present an opportunity Elaine had been hoping for. "Tam...there's something I've been thinking about."

"Hmmm?"

"About the center." Elaine felt she had to approach her subject gingerly. "I've been wondering if there might be... Well, if we shouldn't do more for the girls that come in." She was fidgeting with her purse. Tamar noticed her twisting the strap around a finger. "These girls really ought to know more about the alternatives that are available to them–you know, before they do anything out of desperation. There *are* alternatives, of course."

Tamar glanced at her friend's face. "We're talking about alternatives to abortion."

"Well...yes."

"I don't push abortion, you know. I give them the facts. An abortion's no cake walk. I don't want anybody to be misled."

"I'm sure you're very caring."

The atmosphere in the car had changed. A certain seriousness now hung between the two women.

"But I do insist the option should be available," said Tamar. "I'm sorry, Elaine, but that's essential. I won't deny any woman that choice."

Elaine was looking straight ahead, watching the painted lines shooting through the headlight beams on the surface of the road. "I'll agree to disagree," she said.

"Fair enough."

"But I do believe we could place a bit more emphasis on *other* choices. I thought perhaps I could develop a workshop that discussed the various adoption services available. I'm sure you discuss adoption with them, Tam, but perhaps they could use a bit more detail. I hate to think of any girl taking extreme measures because she assumes there's no one to help her with anything else. Actually, the Church has numerous services to–"

"Hmmph!" Tamar's expression was tight. "Elaine, I wouldn't object to providing more information about adoption. But excuse me if I'm a little bit skeptical about how helpful the *Church* can be in such a circumstance. It seems to me that the *Church* is far more likely to point a condemning finger than it is to reach out and help some poor girl in need."

Elaine knew there wasn't much to be gained by trying to dispute Tamar on any point regarding Catholicism. Whatever had caused her break with the Church, the feelings were bitter and still very present.

"I'll put some ideas down about a workshop," she said. "Then you can decide how you want to go."

"All right," said Tamar.

They drove in silence for a time, both feeling uncomfortable. Abortion was clearly a problem between them, but they both valued their relationship, and neither wanted to jeopardize it. Tamar tried to lighten the mood. "Those hot pepper things–whatever they were called–they were the *worst*."

Elaine smiled.

Chapter 3

When Father Edward had been in residence, the rectory buzzed with activity. Teenagers would crowd into the living room for Catholic Youth Organization meetings. One weekend each month, on a regular rotation, a Sunday school class would come up for doughnuts and what Father called his "sermon on the porch" (though in inclement weather, the sessions were held indoors). There was a steady stream of visitors–many young priests, friends of Father Edward from seminary. And several times a year, parish council would meet around the rectory's grand dining room table, with business followed by a sumptuous buffet dinner.

Father Edward loved to entertain, and was known as a gracious host. But the resource that made dinners at the rectory really noteworthy was his mother, Martha, who would drive in from upstate for the occasions. She was an affable woman, an excellent cook who delighted in feeding people and doted on her only son. Her name was a source of amusement, as she fussed about the kitchen. "If the Church taught reincarnation," Father Edward liked to quip, "I could see my mother fixing matzo-ball soup for the Lord Himself."

Under Father Karl's regime, the rectory was a very different place. His spartan mode of living quickly found its reflection in a more solitary atmosphere. He never entertained. He took his meals in the kitchen. And soon after moving in, he had Pat, the janitor, dismantle the grand table and carry it down to the school for use at parish council meetings in one of the old classrooms which Father had converted into a sort of *official* office. (His *unnofficial* office, the one he actually worked in, was the study he'd set up in the former living room of the rectory.

The dining room Father Karl had turned to other purposes. The far end consisted of five long, floor-to-ceiling, arch-top windows set in a large bay which faced south and received strong sun throughout the daylight hours. Father filled the bay with plants–hanging baskets and pots of all sizes, placed about on the floor, on individual stands and on a large, glass étagère. Karl Muller loved plants. He found them a source of peace. He relaxed while watering, feeding and shaping them. And he lost himself in prayer on a kneeler which he'd had Pat bring over from the church and position right in front of the windows.

Father Karl was in the second decade of his rosary, when the door chime sounded in the front hall. Annoyance displayed itself on the old priest's face. Who could *this* be? Certainly no one on the church staff. Rosemarie knew to guard Father's mid-afternoon prayer time. She answered all his phone calls, with strict orders to take messages for everything except the most dire emergencies–and, of course, the bishop. All mail and deliveries went to the school. Confession times were posted and strictly adhered to. And most parishioners had gotten the message early that this was not the kind of pastor one dropped in on unexpectedly.

Father Karl tucked the rosary into his pocket, opened the front door, and was taken aback by the visitor he found there. "Reverend...Pell," he said.

"Good day to you...Father Muller," said Pastor Matt, with obvious hesitation in his voice. "I've wanted to come by and...see how you were faring...after the...shocking incident and all." He stood awkwardly on the front porch. "If this isn't a bad time."

Father Karl stared at him, then suddenly realized his lapse in hospitality. "Oh. Yes. Of course." He pushed the screen door outward to admit the minister. "How kind of you to be concerned. Please do come in."

Matt stepped uneasily inside the hallway. "You've no doubt been badgered by police and news people," he said, glancing around with the utmost curiosity, trying not to be too obvious about it. "I waited for awhile...not to add any more distress in this difficult matter." He had never been inside St. Mary's rectory before. In fact, he had never been inside the church. Even when Father Edward had been so active promoting Right to Life, Matt had conducted all his dealings with Catholics in the school building.

Father Karl showed his unexpected guest into the study. "Please do sit down...Reverend," he said. "There has been quite a bit of...well, activity, I suppose you'd say, surrounding this most unfortunate affair." *What could this Protestant want in coming here?* "And quite a few curiosity seekers too." *Was he indulging some morbid interest?* "But things have rather settled down."

Pastor Matt seated himself on a low settee. He nodded his head. "Oh. That's good," he said. There was a moment of strained silence, neither man quite knowing what to say next. Matt glanced nervously around the room. His eye was caught by a crucifix on the wall and lingered for a moment on the corpus. The idea of displaying the cross with the body on it had always been repellent to him. Protestants worship a *risen* Lord. "Uh, Father..." he said, turning his glance back to the priest. "I read in the paper that the baby has been buried. Forgive my curiosity..."

Curiosity.

"but does the Roman rite–"

Roman rite?

"permit its sacraments–

Sacraments?

"to be offered under such circumstances?"

"Well..." Father Karl could see that a bit of instruction was sorely needed. "Actually...Reverend...*burial* is not a sacrament." *What did these people learn in their so-called seminaries*? "The Catholic Church offers the anointing of the sick and dying—what was once known as *extreme unction*. That's the sacrament. The dead may be anointed also, though that's appropriate only within a reasonable time after death. A few hours. I...unfortunately...could not anoint the child. But he is interred in St. Mary's cemetery. We had a private service."

Not private enough, as it had turned out. Fat Charlie Dutton was there blasting away for the paper. Insensitive baboon. The media. Even in a town this small, the media think they can trample on anything.

"I see," Matt said. "Was it a Mass?"

Mass! Father Karl cleared his throat. "No. It wasn't a Mass. The child, naturally, couldn't have been baptized."

"Of course." Pastor Matt was feeling very uncomfortable and had begun to wonder if this call was such a good idea. He flexed his broad shoulders to relieve some tension. "Well, Father..." he said. "I really don't want to keep you, but I..." He felt himself floundering, suddenly realizing that he had no idea at all what he wanted to say to this priest and feeling a strong urge to be somewhere else. He swallowed and composed himself. *You'd better say something*, he thought, and then he just started speaking. "Well, that is, I want you to know that...those of us in the pro-life movement...here in town...we stand behind you, Father. One hundred percent. We've always appreciated the leadership role which the Catholic Church has taken in the struggle against...the evil of abortion. It's been an inspiration to us. And if this incident does bode any future difficulties for St. Mary's, I hope you know...that you can count on us to help in any way we can."

Now, where had all *that* come from?

Father Karl was struck by the nervous, almost childlike, sincerity in the handsome face of this young minister. "Why, thank you, Reverend."

Pastor Matt was struck as well. He realized that he had just made a much more fervent statement of Christian unity than he'd intended. Not that he knew what he really had intended. Was this the Holy Spirit at work? Matt stood up and held out his hand to Father Karl. They shook. "Well, I'll be going now, Father. Thank you for your time."

Father Karl held onto Matt's hand for a moment and looked at him, examining his dark eyes and feeling surprisingly touched. "Yes. Well...bless you." he said.

The visit was over as quickly and awkwardly as it had begun. The two men turned away from each other self-consciously. Father Karl showed Pastor Matt to the door. He stood looking after, fingering the rosary beads in his pocket as the younger man departed. *What could one make of all that? Strange. Very strange.*

✠ ✠ ✠

Sister Elaine recognized Pastor Matt as he came down the front steps, off the rectory porch, and headed toward where his car was parked at the curb. Odd. What would he be doing with Father Karl? Local Catholic-Protestant relations had been completely in the deep freeze since Father Edward's departure.

Elaine was carrying an antique wooden music stand which it was her habit to borrow from the choir loft. She borrowed it frequently, to use when conducting her religious education classes–much to Alan's annoyance. She *borrowed*, but she didn't *return*. More often than not, Alan would find the stand in her office, heaped with notes and pamphlets.

She carried the stand into the school building and set it down by the door to one of the classrooms, when she spotted Jessica MacNair waiting in front of her office. "Hello, Jessie," she called. "Sorry to be so behind. I'm setting up for my Monday-night RCIA meeting this evening, and I've been all over town today getting things put together for confirmation next week. The bishop always wants such a big deal."

She hurried down the hall to her visitor and touched Jessie's arm, which was straining around a large bundle of brochures and forms. The other hand held the cord grips of a large, craft shopping bag stuffed with more printed materials.

"Come into my office, and we'll get started."

Jessie followed her into the little room.

"Just put all that stuff on my desk," Elaine said, and Jessie complied gratefully. "I haven't seen you around the laundry room lately." It happened that Elaine and Jessie had apartments in the same building and ran into each other occasionally on laundry days.

"I've been on the run," Jessie said. "Coordinating the blood program takes a lot of time, on top of regular shifts at the hospital and all the other running I do."

"Nurses are busy people." Elaine was looking over Jessie's brochures. "I can hardly believe it's blood drive time again. It seems like we just folded up all those cots and carried them out of the community room."

"It does come around," said Jessie.

"Of course, you collect blood throughout the year. I suppose one drive site is the same as another for you." She picked up one of the printed pieces. "New Red Cross flyers this year, I see."

"Actually," said Jessie, "St. Mary's is especially good. Since I've been handling local collections, St. Mary's has been among our best sites. We were number one in the county last year."

Elaine smiled. "Oh, you just provide a little extra motivation, because you're a parishioner. You know how to apply that old Catholic guilt."

Jessie smiled. "It does please me that we do so well," she said.

The two women were discussing details of the blood drive, which was to run for three days starting tomorrow, when Alan stuck his head in through the office door. "Sister, Rosemarie's not in her office. Do you know if my package has come from Liturgy Suppliers?–" He stopped when he saw that Elaine had a guest. "Oh, I'm sorry. I didn't realize you were in the middle of something."

Alan looked at Jessie and noticed her honest-to-God nurse's uniform: cap, white dress, white stockings, even an old-fashioned nurse's cape. He had seen her dressed that way before in church–though he had never met her–and was always taken with the uniform. It had occurred to him that, with the increasingly casual manner in which health care professionals dressed (especially nurses, in pants, running shoes and multi-colored duty smocks), this was the only nurse he had seen since leaving the Air Force who actually wore traditional garb. Even when she showed up at church out of uniform she had caught his eye. Perhaps it was the long, chestnut hair, which at this moment was pinned demurely under her cap.

"You know Alan, don't you Jessie?" Elaine asked sociably.

Alan held out his hand. "I don't believe we've actually met," he said.

Jessie returned the greeting.

"Oh. Well then..." said Elaine, "Jessica MacNair, Alan Kemp."

"I enjoy your music at Mass," Jessie said.

"Why thank you."

"I haven't seen any of today's mail," said Elaine. "What is it you're expecting?"

"Choral music," Alan answered, still looking at the nurse, "an arrangement for one of the songs the bishop requested. I'm running out of time to work it up with the choir before confirmation."

"Ah, the bishop again," said Elaine with a hint of exasperation.

"Father Karl just wants everything to go right."

"Father Karl," Elaine sniffed.

"Now now, Sister."

Elaine let out a long, tense sigh. "I don't know. I ask you, Jessie, from a parishioner's point of view–" But she caught herself before saying anything regrettable.

Jessie frowned and turned her eyes down to her lap.

"Well," said Elaine, "sometimes I just don't know."

It seemed to Alan that it wasn't entirely appropriate for Sister Elaine to vent her feelings about the pastor before a member of the parish, even in so guarded a way. Elaine was part of the pastoral staff, after all. Indeed, Jessie appeared rather on the spot. Without looking up, she said, "I suppose we all miss Father Edward."

There was a moment of uneasy silence. Finally, Alan said, "Well, keep an eye on the mail, Sister."

Jessie was still looking down.

"By the way, Miss MacNair–" Alan had made note that Jessie was wearing no wedding ring. "–we could use some extra voices up in the loft."

"Oh, I'm not much of a singer," Jessie said with the merest suggestion of a blush.

"Don't worry about that," Alan replied. "It's not much of a choir."

It wasn't. In a parish the size of St. Mary's, Alan was happy to scrounge up what voices he could, whenever he could get them together. "But what we lack in capability we make up for in–" Alan suddenly realized that there wasn't much they made up for it *with*. "Well, we try, anyway."

"I'm sure it would be fun," Jessie said, smiling once again. "But my schedule is so unpredictable. I work different shifts all the time, and I never even know which Mass I'll be able to attend in any given week."

"Ah, too bad," said Alan, genuinely disappointed. "But I suppose I should leave you ladies to your business. Very nice meeting you, Miss MacNair."

"Please, call me Jessie." They shook hands again, and Alan walked out of the office feeling that it *had* been very nice to meet this attractive nurse.

Ever since Sheila, Alan had kept his distance from women. He enjoyed looking. And playing out at Minnie's, the looking was frequently well rewarded: plenty of bouncing bosoms hardly contained in low-cut, flounced, country tops, long legs protruding from short, ruffled skirts or showing their curves through skin-tight denim. It was no fluke that country line dancing had swept the nation. But that had been pretty much it, as far as Alan's social life was concerned.

Well, there *was* Barbie. Barbie. What a name. She had worked for a time as a waitress at Minnie's and was always hanging around the band between sets, turning those big eyes up to Alan. Her eyes weren't the only things that were big, and–mostly at the jestful urgings of the guys in the band, who found her quite outrageous–Alan had taken her out once for something to eat. The dinner conversation had about as much depth as her name, and when Alan returned her home and she quite overtly offered dessert, he excused himself and left with a most gentlemanly goodnight peck. For the rest of the time Barbie worked at Minnie's, she speculated that Alan must be gay, which became a source of great amusement to the band.

Alan walked down the hall and noticed that Rosemarie was back in her office. He stuck his head in to check on the mail. "Rosie, has my package come in from Liturgy Suppliers?"

"Sorry, Alan," she said with a shrug. "I got this morning's deliveries. There was no music."

"Damn!" He was hoping to pick over all the parts before Wednesday night's choir rehearsal.

"It might come UPS," Rosemarie hollered after, as Alan started up the hall. "They deliver in the afternoon sometimes. Shall I call you at home if it comes in?"

Alan took note of the antique music stand where Elaine had left it and shook his head. "That's all right, Rosie," he said. "I can't do anything with it now. I'll check with you in the morning." And he was out of the building, heading across the square. Though Minnie's was closed tonight, he'd promised to go out later to work up a couple of new songs with the guys. So he decided to catch a sandwich at the Courthouse Inn.

In the afternoon, the Inn's customers consisted mainly of civil servants: clerks and secretaries on late break from the courthouse and the county building, mail carriers just finished up with rounds, and the occasional police duo. Time was when the Courthouse Inn would have had a bustling afternoon trade in ladies with parcels and flowered hats. But that was in the old days, before the strip center out on the highway had sucked most of the business out of the courthouse square. Now the downtown shopping area consisted of Reilly's drugstore, as well as a small franchised catalog outlet, Springer's Hardware, and a handful of odd shops like the Christian bookstore and the co-op organic grocery. Among those still loyal to the old haunt was a group of teachers from the high school, who stopped by most afternoons. The Inn had only kept up a beer and wine license. But a frosty mug, or even a simple cup of coffee, was a blessing to these tired veterans unwinding after a day of skirmishes along the educational front lines.

Alan noticed a familiar face among a group in the far corner. It was Jack Compton, the high school's young instrumental music teacher (and one of its most gifted graduates from six years earlier) who also played sax out at Minnie's. Jack glanced up, spotted Alan, and gestured for him to come over. He introduced him to the others at the table, and Alan exchanged handshakes in succession, lingering on the hand of a very pretty brunette whom Jack introduced as Brigitte Statterly. Alan recalled that Jack had mentioned he was seeing–and, in fact, was getting quite serious with–the school secretary. The guys in the band had all urged Jack to bring his girlfriend out to Minnie's, to which he had replied that he planned to keep her as far away from Minnie's as possible. Alan could see why.

There was a lot of casual chatter about the day's atrocities at the high school, which it would appear were pretty much average in the lives of these local pedants. Alan was amused. He was more than a few years out of school and much removed from developments on the secondary education scene. Jack mentioned that Alan was music director at St. Mary's, which elicited a raised eyebrow on the face of one of the teachers.

"St. Mary's, huh?" Grover Hutchins, a portly history teacher with an inquisitive disposition, seemed keenly interested. "Tell me, Alan," he said, leaning over the table, "any truth to the rumor that St. Mary's is planning to reopen the school?"

That was a rumor Alan hadn't heard. "Not that I'm aware," he said.

Grover sat back in his seat. "Hmmm..."

"Where did you hear that?" Alan asked, quite bemused at the idea.

"It's around," Grover said, eyeing Alan with a suspicious squint. "It makes sense, doesn't it? I mean, that priest of yours has quite the reputation as a big-time Catholic school master. It just makes sense."

Alan was at a loss. "Well, no one's said anything to me. Not that I'm in the loop about such things. I just make music."

Grover continued giving Alan the look. "Hmmm..."

"Don't mind him, Alan," Jack said. "Grover keeps his ear to the ground."

"Not the easiest thing to do, either, with that belly of his," quipped Frank Tansley, the boys' gym teacher sitting at the far end of the table."

Grover shot him a glance.

"Nothing Grover likes better than a good rumor," Jack said. "That's why he keeps so involved with the union."

Grover let out with a "harrumph," which set his belly to jiggling. "You young punks'll come to appreciate the union, one of these days," he said tartly. "Wait till some private school tries to steal our state allotment per student. That's what they're trying to do, you can bet on it. The Catholic schools know where the butter is. And there are more than a few scabs in the legislature that want to give it to 'em. You'll see. They want our kids, that's what. And the money that goes with 'em."

"Is that why you think Father Karl was sent here?" Alan asked, intrigued by Grover's speculation.

The portly figure shifted in his seat and looked at Alan with a set to his eyes that was both comic and determined. "It's as good a reason as I can think of," said Grover, "as good a damned reason."

First Interlude

A lake in the upper corner of the valley was drained by a small stream whose five branches grew into rivers of modest size and some importance throughout the central part of the country. The largest of the rivers, which was called the Jordan, widened out enough within the valley itself to be navigable by small vessels, and in the late 1840s, a group of enterprising farmers had an idea that this waterway might provide a practical means to get grain and other farm products to the market center some thirty miles east. They tested their theory and found that short, flat-bottom boats could negotiate the twists and turns carrying about a wagon load of goods, guided by two men with poles, one in the bow and one in the stern. The loading point they established where a bridge crossed the river attracted drummers and tradesmen. A warehouse and a small cluster of shops soon formed the beginnings of a village.

The would-be canalmen had gotten their idea a generation too late, however. Railroads were already underpricing most waterborne transport and beating it on delivery time. Within five years, a track stretched across the valley and a depot had become the hub of activity in the little trading village on the river. The town grew, eventually becoming the county seat.

Some of the Irish workers who had built the rail line settled in the valley, bringing their wives, their children and their fervent Catholic faith. Their spiritual needs were met at first by traveling priests from a missionary order, and the occasional, open-air Masses were a curiosity to the local farm folk, mostly German Lutherans with a sprinkling of Baptists and Mennonites. But novelty turned to discomfort when the first stones were laid for the foundation of St. Mary's and the

Catholic presence in the valley became highly visible and permanent.

The passing of years, of good times and hard times, saw growth in the parish and expansion of the church. A fire destroyed the original building in the 1870s, and the rebuilt structure, with its higher, more elaborate bell tower, became the pride of the Catholic community and a statement of Catholic success in the town. Indeed, some of the wealthiest families in the valley, the owners of several key local businesses, were mainstays of St. Mary's. And for the most part, interaction between Catholics and non-Catholics was as easy or awkward as anywhere, depending on the individuals involved.

In the period between the world wars, things began to change. A great revival swept rural America in reaction to the disillusionment of World War I and the rise of disturbing new ideas like evolution and Bolshevism. In that charged atmosphere, the valley saw a flurry of religious activity. Several new churches sprouted up, preaching a spare and determined message of Bible-centered faith and emotional conversion called *Fundamentalism*. It was a vision that dismissed traditional Protestant denominations as flabby and complacent. And it reached deeply into the harsh, sectarian language of the Reformation, branding the Catholic Church as the *Whore of Babylon* and the *Bride of Satan*.

Such talk had its effect. There were occasional clashes between Catholics and Protestants–mainly fistfights in the schools or when drink fanned religious fervor among intemperate souls of either persuasion. At one point in the 1920s, St. Mary's pastor had to seek police protection after threats and several small acts of vandalism by suspected members of the Ku Klux Klan. The local newspaper condemned the actions and the spirit of parochialism behind them, and the danger passed without serious harm. But something was different. Parish members no longer felt quite as comfortable in the valley. Some even speculated about the fire that had destroyed the original church more than a half-century earlier–a blaze whose cause had never been fully determined.

Chapter 4

Minerva Johnson was the matriarch of the Coleman clan, one of two black families in the valley, and the proprietress of Minnie's Roadhouse. She was a large woman of good nature, strong presence and indeterminate age, and she had raised five children with little help from a ne'er-do-well husband named Ralph who hated work as much as he loved women. Ralph had been a periodic resident of the county drunk tank until he disappeared one day with a flat-chested, white manicurist named LuAnne and a weekend's receipts from the cash drawer at his wife's establishment. Aside from that short-term loss, the overall effect of Ralph's departure was an improvement in the profit margin at Minnie's, since the drain on the liquor inventory had ceased.

Over the years, Minerva–whom everyone usually called Aunt Min–had provided advice, care or employment to just about all of her two dozen or so family members spread around the county, and had taken in numerous others from out of state. She seemed to have more than her share of relatives in need of help. And she was always ready to provide it, with the single requirement that whoever dwelled under her roof had to accompany her to Sunday Mass at St. Mary's. That was a particular burden for those who came from branches of the family cut off from Aunt Min's Louisiana Catholic roots. Of course for many, attending Mass was less a trial than having to endure the country and western music–what Aunt Min called *white soul*–which was the bill of fare at the roadhouse.

It was her big-city relations who generally found those sounds most grating. One such was a nephew, Howard Hansen, actually the son of Aunt Min's second cousin, Camille, who had sent him from the south side of Chicago in the hope that he might avoid the life of the street gangs and live to finish high school. Cousin Camille took that hope to her grave, when she was cut down in crossfire between two rival groups fighting over drug turf less than a month after putting her son on the bus. Howard did stay in school, and his mulatto good looks and muscular build earned him the nickname "Handsome Howie." He had a natural charm and became highly popular, enjoying a sort of special status as the high school's resident exotic: the big-city, black street kid. He never lacked female companionship. And if any of the local farm boys objected to his involvement with white young ladies, the street fighting skills honed in Chicago quickly softened their racial attitudes.

Howie stayed on with Aunt Min after graduating high school, working at the roadhouse as a kind of host/bus boy/bouncer–even coming to tolerate country music–and taking advantage of every opportunity he could to hustle a few extra bucks which he was laying away for college. Aunt Min granted him complete flexibility so he could take whatever jobs might present themselves. He was on hand most nights, but seemed to come and go irregularly. Alan and the other guys in the band had noticed that Howie would sometimes be gone even on Thursdays or Fridays, two of the busiest nights, but they thought little about it.

Alan had just arrived at Minnie's for Monday-night rehearsal, and was parked by the kitchen. He had the trunk open, removing his guitar case, when he noticed Howie coming down the back stairs from Aunt Min's apartment. The young man headed across the parking lot, out to the corner where the Old Valley Road cut off from the highway at an angle. Alan was checking to be sure his effects pedal was in his gig bag, when he saw Howie jump back to avoid a small truck sweeping carelessly around the corner.

Howie was obviously all right. He shouted an obscenity, then looked around to be sure there was no other traffic, and continued across the road. As the trunk lid slammed, Alan saw Howie disappear through a gap in a tall hedge surrounding a stately old house that had once been a residence but was now some sort of professional location. Alan had been by the property, which backed up to the highway and had its entrance on the Old Valley Road, many times. He thought it was a doctor's office and wondered what doings Howie might have there at this time of day. Even in small towns, evening hours–like house calls–were a thing of the distant past for doctors.

The band had rehearsed for about an hour and a half, when Aunt Min brought out a pot of coffee from the kitchen and suggested a break. Most of the time had been devoted to working up an arrangement of the old Juice Newton hit, "The Sweetest Thing," for bass player Art Spiecer's daughter, Nicole. The sixteen-year-old was not particularly pretty. In fact, she was on the chubby side, and her braces had to put forth valiant effort to correct a fierce overbite. But she had striking, long, black, Crystal Gale hair and a voice that suggested Anne Murray. In any event, Aunt Min liked her and thought she had talent, so she permitted her to sing with the band from time to time.

Alan poured himself a cup of coffee and sat down with Jack Compton, whose saxophone was lying on the table before him. "Your fiancée is lovely," Alan said, and took a sip from the cup. "I was very impressed this afternoon."

"Well, she's not really my fiancée–not yet anyway," Jack said. "We're talking about marriage, but there's nothing official."

Alan set the cup on the table. "I wouldn't wait too long to nail things down," he said. "She's a doll, and you wouldn't want her getting any second thoughts." He ran his right index finger around the rim of the cup. "By the way," he continued, "that guy this afternoon–what was his name–Grover. Do you think he was serious? I mean what he said about St. Mary's reopening the school. That's a pretty wild idea, but he seemed really upset by it."

Jack leaned back in his chair. "I've heard a few rumors around the high school," he said, lacing his fingers behind his head. "I guess it does seem like a long shot. But there is a movement to provide state funds for private schools, and some of the older teachers–especially guys who brought the union into the district–they have strong feelings about all that."

Alan rubbed his chin, then leaned both elbows on the table, picked up his coffee mug, and held it between his hands. "How do you think feelings would split between the Catholics and Protestants who teach in the district?"

"Over state funding?" Jack asked. "Well, I don't know. I never thought about it, but I guess the Catholics wouldn't object as much. Of course, there are plenty of *Christian* schools–non-Catholic I mean–and they'd benefit, too. I really don't see the old-timers any happier about that." He crossed one leg over the other and brought his hands down around his raised knee. "Take Grover. He attends Bible Fellowship, same as I do, and I don't think he'd figure it's okay for some Evangelical academy to go pulling students out of the public schools. It all comes down to money with him."

"Grover strikes me as something of a crank," Alan said, and took a sip of coffee.

"You've got him right there," said Jack. "Still...there are some others whose opinions I would take more seriously. Let's just say Grover isn't the only one who's concerned."

Alan set down his mug and ran his finger around the bell of Jack's saxophone. "Concerned enough to do something?" he asked, diverting his eyes.

"Do what?"

"I don't know," Alan said uncertainly. He felt rather foolish pursuing the idea, but a thought had taken hold in his mind, and he had to ask. "Maybe just...let their anger out...some way."

Jack looked at Alan with a twist to his eyebrows that showed confusion. "I can't see what anybody would do," he said. "The union has plenty of lobbyists working the legislature. And that's where the action is."

Alan nodded. It was a foolish idea. "I'm sure," he said.

✠ ✠ ✠

Susan Pell lay with her head tilted back over the pillow and her eyes closed, and let out a long, satisfied breath. "That was nice, Matt."

"You think it took?" her husband asked, lying beside her?

"I think that if the Lord didn't want me pregnant tonight, He wouldn't have made it so beautiful," she said.

"Well, let's not presume on the Lord, Dear. If He wants you pregnant, He'll arrange it in His own good time."

They had been trying to conceive for nearly two years, ever since Matt's father had withdrawn completely from ministry and retired to Arkansas, leaving the church, the congregation and all the pastor's benefits to his son. Their lack of success at getting Susan pregnant had become a frustration. And they were close to acceptance of what appeared the Lord's will that they should never be parents when Louise Robertson, a member of Bible Fellowship and one of Sue's closest friends, suggested that they consult a new OB/GYN in town. He was an Indian who had studied in England and had introduced her to some promising techniques involving diet, more sophisticated monitoring of bodily cycles, and a restrained and selective schedule of lovemaking. It had worked for Louise and her husband, Brad. She was carrying twins. After Matt and Sue had begun seeing Dr. Singh, they started to feel hopeful again.

The only drawback was the part about selective lovemaking. The pastor and his wife had a good marriage, and they approached its physical aspect with particular relish. Their intense drives had prompted them to marry young, while Matt was still in college. And the debt incurred getting him through school and ordained, then sending her for an associate's degree, was the primary reason they delayed trying to have children. The pleasure they shared they took as a gift of God, though they sometimes felt the slightest bit of self-consciousness living the fishbowl existence that life can be for a clergyman and his family.

"I'm glad I'm not a Catholic priest," said Matt, lying on his back and smiling.

Sue turned her head and looked at him quizzically. "So am I. But what an odd thing to say."

Matt laughed. "I wouldn't have a passionate wife like you."

"I don't suppose you'd have any wife at all. And then what would you do?"

"A lot of praying."

"Matt, you're wicked." But she couldn't help laughing. "What would our congregation say if they knew what an animal you are?"

"Me? And what about you? One of the Lord's hot-blooded female creations."

Sue pulled the pillow out from under her head and whipped it around at him. "Ooo, you–" And her husband was on top of her, kissing her again, until they both broke into giggling. They settled down into a warm cuddle, with Sue's head on Matt's shoulder, and lay quietly.

"You know, I saw him today," Matt said after a time.

"Saw who?"

"The priest."

"Father Muller? Where?"

"I went over to St. Mary's. The parsonage–or the rectory–whatever they call it."

Sue got up on one elbow. "What happened? What did he say?"

"I think I took him by surprise." Matt thought back on his strained conversation with Father Karl. "He didn't really know what to say to me. And to tell you the truth, I didn't know what to say to *him*. We were both kind of uncomfortable."

"Well, what *did* you say?"

"I just told him that I was concerned about the incident with the baby–and that all the churches were behind him, in case he was under fire about abortion. I think he appreciated it."

Susan looked at her husband with a feeling of pride, and nodded her head. "That was very giving of you," she said, and patted him gently on the chest. "But I just wonder how many churches would be behind him. Not everybody is so charitable as to minister to a Catholic priest the way you did. It was a *witness*, Dear, a *testimony*."

"It was just a small kindness, that's all."

"But Father Muller is a priest, Matt. And this is the Roman Church we're talking about." A certain look came to her pretty face–the look she got whenever she was intensely interested in something. "Ellie Conner gave me a fascinating article, Matt. Did you know that there's an inscription on the pope's crown? It says 'Vicar of the Son of God.' Of course, it's in Latin. Well, you know some of the letters are the same as Roman numerals, so they have values like numbers. According to the article, if you add up all the letters that stand for numbers, the total comes to 666. Can you imagine that? The *sign*–Satan's own sign, right out in front for all the world to see."

This information struck Matt as rather contrived. He glanced up into his wife's earnest face, a smile breaking on his lips. "I don't know anything about the pope's crown, Sue."

✠ ✠ ✠

The band had packed up a little past eleven. Alan loaded his guitar case and gig bag in the trunk of his Tercel, and headed out toward the highway, when his headlights fell on Howie walking across the parking lot. "Hey, what're you up to this time of night?" he called to the young man.

Howie waved back. "Hi, Alan, what's happenin'? The guys rehearsing tonight?"

Alan pulled the car to a stop and leaned out his window. "Yeah, we had some material that needed polishing. How come you're stalking around in the dark? Sneaking out of some young lady's boudoir?"

"I only wish," said Howie, giving a smart slap to the roof of the Tercel. "Sometimes I do stuff for Dr. Fowler and Dr. Singh."

"Who are they?

"Over in that big old house. I'm pickin' up a few bucks."

Alan looked off in the direction of the house, the peak of its roof showing above the tall hedge. "If I'm not too curious," he said, looking back at Howie, "what do you do for them at eleven o'clock at night?"

Howie laughed, beaming his broad, personable smile. "Oh, they conduct secret experiments. I rob graveyards and bring them bodies in the middle of the night." He started off, waving. "See you around, man." And he hot-footed it across the parking lot and up the back stairs.

Chapter 5

No matter what he hung over those three tall windows at the east end of the flat, there was no keeping out the sun when the sky was clear. Every time the light woke him, Alan swore he was going to put up solid, wooden shutters or heavy, lined, velvet drapes or something equally dense and expensive. Then, it would occur to him that, to do the job properly, he should really treat all 12 windows in the large loft apartment. That was out of the question on his current earnings. Perhaps, if he could get some private students to supplement his income. He had thought about it, and had even been approached by some people at church who wanted their kids to learn piano. But he would need a decent instrument–a baby grand, preferably–and a respectable studio.

His loft was hardly that. It was basically one large space on the third floor over Reilly's pharmacy, about thirty by sixty, with fifteen-foot ceilings and exposed brick walls. It had once been a karate studio with two workout sections. In the middle sat a kind of boxed-in area enclosing the stairwell that came up from below, along with a small room that had been the karate instructor's office, and a bathroom containing a toilet, sink, shower stall and a bank of six small, metal lockers. All the accoutrements of living, including Alan's bed, bureau, television set, a couple of upholstered chairs and what passed for a kitchen, were on the east side of this "island." The old office Alan used as a closet, and a stack of cartons heaped on top of the rafters over the boxed-in part created a pyramid effect. He had once thought of moving his bed to the west side, where the pyramid would help to block the morning light. But that side was where he kept all the instruments, amplifiers and assorted electronic gear acquired over years and essential to the modern, switched-on musician.

The sun shining through his very inadequate, narrow-slat blinds had pulled Alan out of a dream that seemed to involve a woman in a white dress. Perhaps the attractive nurse he had met in Sister Elaine's office? He sat up in bed, rubbed his face, and took note of the time on his clock radio–not quite eight-thirty. He went through his normal morning ritual: bathroom, set up the coffeemaker, shower, get dressed, cup of coffee with toasted frozen bagel.

As he was savoring a first few sips, Alan's thoughts went back to the conversation with his deacon friend two days before. He felt unsure of how to proceed with the *following up* and *checking around* Collie had asked him to do. Where do you begin with something like this dead baby business? Could the rumor about Holy Innocents School reopening lead anywhere? It was an absurd idea. A bunch of public school teachers get angry about a Catholic school in town, so somebody puts a dead baby in a trash can? Nonsense.

The only fact Alan was aware of that seemed in any sense relevant was that someone had once sprayed some anti-Catholic graffiti on St. Mary's front door. He remembered it plainly enough. Everyone at the church was upset. Father Karl had Pat repaint the door as quickly as possible. People expected more trouble to follow. But nothing happened. Nothing until the baby.

Were the two incidents even related? Father Karl didn't think so. Had there ever been any other attacks on St. Mary's? None when Father Edward had been there–at least not since Alan had come. But Father Edward had been pastor at least two years before Alan arrived. Had anything happened during that time? What about before Father Edward?

Alan cleared away the breakfast debris, and went into the bathroom to shave and brush his teeth. It was too early for Rosemarie to have received the morning mail, so there was no point going over to the church to see if his choral music was in. He put on a light jacket and stuffed a small note pad and a pen inside his pocket, then locked up the flat and went down the stairs to the street. Where do you start an investigation? You begin with basic research. If St. Mary's had ever borne the brunt of anti-Catholic bigotry, what had happened and when? Was there any kind of pattern?

The office of the *Daily Herald* was a two-block walk, down to the corner of the courthouse square and around to the left past the masonic lodge. The receptionist led Alan into a windowless room filled with stacks of back copies and a wall lined with metal cabinets containing microfilm spools. She explained the system by which the decades of old issues were organized in various metal drawers, showed him how to thread the spools into the microfilm reader and focus the image on the screen. Then she left him on his own.

Alan started scanning the old issues of the *Herald*, beginning with the period of Father Edward's pastorate prior to his own arrival at St. Mary's, and worked back through the years into the 1950s. His travel back through time was interesting, offering some glimpses into the history of the town. He learned, for instance, that there had once been a music store on the courthouse square, two doors from the entrance to his flat. It had sold pianos and organs as well as guitars and a full line of band instruments. There had also been a rather elegant department store–elegant by small-town standards–and a good-size dealer in televisions and home appliances. It was clear that the whole downtown area was once a bustling center of trade and town life.

He was amused by the forty-year-old fashion advertising, chuckling over one lingerie ad in particular. The full-page panel featured models posing in formidable-looking undergarments with rapturous expressions on their faces, as if they were listening to romantic poetry in their corselettes and midriff-hugging brassieres. The ad must have pressed the limit of taste in its time.

There were many reports of church events through the years–all denominations. And there were articles about activities at Holy Innocents School. Alan read the coverage of Holy Innocents' closing thoroughly. It looked to him like the pastor who oversaw that process–one Father Gerard–had received criticism not unlike that which Father Karl got when he folded St. Ann's. But in all the reporting, going back to the early post-war years, Alan saw nothing that represented any kind of parallel to the graffiti incident, and certainly not to the dead baby affair. There was coverage of a burglary at the school, back in the late 1960s, in which several hundred dollars worth of audio-visual equipment had been taken. But the stolen property was recovered from a pawn shop in a town outside the county, and the perpetrators–two teenaged boys–were caught and punished.

Alan realized that he had been scanning microfilm for nearly two hours, and his eyes were feeling the effects of tracking fuzzy, gray type on the bluish projection screen. *That* was enough of *that*. He refiled the last spool of microfilm he'd had in the reader, and headed out to the street. Surely, there could have been things that happened which weren't reported in the paper, he thought. Rivalry between churches was nothing new. But if there had been vandalism or some other acts of conflict, who would know about it? As Alan came to the corner of the courthouse square, the answer stood before him–or rather slouched before him.

Popeye.

Popeye was a fixture in town, an old character who divided his time between drinking hot chocolate at Carl's Doughnut Shoppe, stalking around the downtown area on what seemed almost like regular patrols, and lounging on the stone benches in the courthouse square. Alan knew that his name was really Elroy, but he *thought* of him as Popeye. The old man's puffy jowls, his signature pipe and an odd, stooped-over walk, in which both of his legs seemed always to be out in front of his torso, put Alan in mind of the famous cartoon character.

While he was slightly retarded, Popeye's disability appeared to affect only some of his mental functions. He would be hard-pressed to reason through a puzzle or to reach a conclusion based on facts that had to be related one to the other. But he was a font of local knowledge. He had the unique ability to remember the name of every person he had ever met, and he never forgot an event that he had witnessed or been told about–not that he particularly understood the significance of any of this vast store of information.

Alan trotted across the street and caught up with Popeye as the old man was lowering himself, in his very methodical way, onto a curved bench by a piece of light field artillery from World War I. "Elroy!" Alan called out. "How're you doing today, buddy?"

Popeye looked up at Alan, and his brain began the laborious process of matching faces and names which was slow but never failed to make the right connection. "Alan Kemp," he said at last. "Alan Kemp."

"You're right, Elroy," said Alan. "You're always right." He sat down beside him. "I'll bet you've met everyone who ever set foot in this town, and you remember them all. It's amazing."

"Oh yes. I always remember," said Popeye with a touch of pride in his smile. He lifted the green baseball cap that bore the logo, "John Deer," a fixture of his bald head, and scratched nonchalantly behind his ear. "I always remember. I always do. People like it when I remember their names. And I always remember them."

"You certainly do," said Alan, leaning back with one arm on the backrest of the curved stone bench. "And you know what else amazes me? I'm always amazed at how much you know about what has happened in town. You're a real historian, Elroy. You're an expert in local history."

Popeye wasn't entirely sure what it meant to be a "historian," but Alan could see that the old man had taken it as a compliment, so he pressed on. "I've always enjoyed it when we've talked, Elroy, when you've told me about things that happen in town. You like to talk about those things, don't you, Elroy?"

"Oh yes. I do like to talk about things that happen. People like it when I talk about those things."

"I know they do, Elroy. *I* certainly enjoy it."

"Sometimes I talk to you over at the church," Popeye said, pointing toward St. Mary's.

"That's right, Elroy. We usually run into each other by the church. It's amazing how you remember those kinds of details." Alan felt foolish addressing a grown man in such a patronizing way. But he had chatted with Popeye often enough to know what he responded to. "Speaking of the church, Elroy," Alan said, trying to appear off-hand, "I was wondering if you can remember any time that somebody might have done something–oh, I don't know–something *damaging* to the church. You know, if somebody messed it up or broke something over there. Do you happen to remember anything like that, Elroy?"

Popeye looked at Alan blankly, not quite understanding.

"Think about it, Elroy," Alan urged gently. "Can you recall if anybody ever did something damaging–something bad that would have made a mess–over at St. Mary's?"

"St. Mary's?" Elroy asked, struggling with the thought. "St. Mary's is the church." And he pointed in that direction again.

"That's right, Elroy. St. Mary's is the church. *My* church. Can you remember anything *bad* that happened over there?"

Elroy sat blankly for a moment, then his eyes lit up. A connection. "Oh yes. I remember the letters. Big letters. On the front doors of the church. Someone painted letters on the front doors."

"That's right, Elroy. I remember that myself. Someone did paint big letters on the doors–"

"Big letters, right on the front doors." The valve was open, and the details came pouring out. "The letters were white, and they were big. And Father Karl Muller was mad about the letters. Father Karl Muller was very mad. And the police came. There was a police car with lights on top. And Father Karl Muller talked to the policeman right out on the street in front of the church. The policeman was... Officer Jim Schultz. It was Officer Jim Schultz. And Father Karl Muller was mad, and he talked to Officer Jim Schultz. And Pat Foley painted over the letters and made the doors brown again. But you could still see the letters a little bit. And Pat Foley painted over them again. Pat Foley painted over the letters three times to make them go away. And–"

"Yes, yes, Elroy," Alan interrupted. "I remember that, too. That's very good. It's amazing how you can remember all that."

Alan had experienced Popeye's tangents before. You had to rein him in quickly, or the conversation would seek its own direction–and God knows where. He patted the old man on the shoulder. "But I was wondering about...well, about other times."

"Other times?"

"Yes. I was wondering if there were any other times when anybody did anything bad at the church."

"Not the letters?"

"No, Elroy, not the letters. Did somebody ever do anything else that was bad? Did anybody ever break a window or something like that?"

"Break a window?"

"Yes, Elroy. Did anyone break a window?"

"Oh yes. Someone drove a car through a big window."

"A car?"

Popeye nodded his head earnestly. "Oh yes. Sorrell Baxter drove a car through a window. And all the glass broke, and some lawn mowers broke, too." He pointed toward Springer's Hardware.

"Oh, no, Elroy. That was the hardware store," Alan said. "I don't mean that–"

"Sorrell Baxter likes to drink alcohol. Sorrell Baxter drinks a lot of alcohol, and he drove his car into the window of the hardware store, and it broke. And Jonathan Springer was very mad. And the police came and took Sorrell Baxter away to jail."

"I see, Elroy." Alan couldn't help laughing. Popeye's chain of memories and associations was totally unpredictable. "That's very interesting," said Alan. "I'd never heard about that, but–"

"Jonathan Springer was very mad."

"I'm sure he was, Elroy–"

"It was a Buick."

"Pardon me, Elroy?"

"Sorrell Baxter drove a Buick through the window." Popeye took pride in the details.

"Elroy," Alan said, trying once again to bring the conversation back on the right track, "please think about this, now. Did anybody ever break a window in the church?"

"The church?"

"Yes, Elroy. St. Mary's Church. Did anyone ever break a window at St. Mary's Church?"

Elroy looked toward the church. "No," he said. "No one broke a window at St. Mary's Church."

Alan was beginning to think this exchange was not going to yield any useful information. But he figured he might as well make one more try. "Okay, let's forget about windows, Elroy. Did anybody ever break *into* the church–I mean did they go inside and do anything in the building? Can you remember anything like that?"

"Anyone go inside the church?"

Alan saw the immediate need to clarify. "I don't mean just anybody."

"A lot of people go inside the church all the time," said Popeye.

"I know that, Elroy. But I don't mean people going to church. I mean like in the middle of the night, when nobody *should* be in the church. Do you remember if anybody ever went inside the church in the middle of the night and did something bad?"

Popeye sat fingering his pipe, searching his memory deeply. "I saw someone go inside–" And he stopped and thought again.

"In the middle of the night, I mean, Elroy."

"I saw...someone..." Popeye looked actually pained. He seemed to be trying desperately to make a connection that just wasn't coming together.

Alan sat patiently while the old man rifled through his memory. Popeye's intense expression was interesting. His eyelids twitched, and his lips curled up, trying to form words that weren't quite there. Finally, Alan decided his assumption that Popeye wasn't going to be of any help was confirmed. There was no point making him suffer. "Well, Elroy," he said, patting him on the shoulder again, "that's okay. I enjoyed talking to you." Alan stood up and started away from the bench. "You have a good day, Elroy. I'll talk to you another–"

"The back part," Popeye said just then.

"What's that, Elroy?"

"I saw someone go inside the back part."

"What do you mean?"

"The back part of the church." Popeye's eyes were closed, and he moved a finger in the air as if he were drawing a picture on some invisible blackboard. "Down the hill. I saw someone go inside the back part of the church down the hill."

"The school building is down the hill, Elroy. Do you mean the building behind the church?"

"Behind the church," Popeye said, opening his eyes. "I saw someone go inside the building *behind* the church, down the hill."

Alan sat down on the bench again. He put one hand on the backrest and leaned in toward Popeye, looking intensely into the old man's face. "When did you see someone go inside the school building, Elroy?"

"I saw someone go inside the school building in the middle of the night," Popeye answered. "I walk around at night. I keep an eye on things. I walk around at night, and I saw someone go inside the school building in the middle of the night when I was walking around."

Alan knew that Popeye did walk around at night. He had often spotted him lumbering along in his odd, stooped-over manner, making his nightly patrols, when Alan was coming home from Minnie's. "Who did you see go inside the school building, Elroy?"

"I don't know," Popeye said vaguely. "I...don't...don't know..." He was still searching that deep, black well of a memory.

Alan scanned the old man's puffy face and figured the conversation had reached an impasse. But then...

"It was a lady."

"Elroy?"

"I saw...a lady...go inside the school building in the middle of the night."

"When did this lady go inside the school building?"

"In the middle of the night."

"I don't mean that, Elroy." Alan didn't want to confuse him. Popeye had a very weak perception of time, Alan knew. He could rattle on with stories about things that happened in town years before, as if they were the latest news of the day.

"Think now, Elroy. Was it a long time ago that you saw a lady go inside the school building, or was it recently? I mean was it...like, just a few days ago or last week, maybe? Or was it years and years ago...when you were young?" Alan could see that Popeye was struggling. "See if you can remember, Elroy," he said slowly. "Was it a long time ago, or was it just a *little* time ago?"

Popeye closed his eyes. "It was..."

Alan didn't know if he could push him any harder.

Popeye opened his eyes and looked at Alan with a smile of certainty. "It was a *little* time ago," he said. "I saw a lady go inside the school building in the middle of the night when I was walking around, and it was a little time ago."

Could this be the person who left the baby in the trash? Could Popeye have witnessed it? "Elroy," Alan said, leaning toward him again, "was the lady alone, or was there anybody with her?"

Popeye thought. "She was alone. I saw a lady go inside the school building, and she was alone."

"Nobody was with her?"

"Nobody was with her."

"Elroy, did you see if she was carrying anything? Can you remember if she had a package or anything?"

"A package?"

"A package or a bag."

"A bag?"

Alan was pushing too hard, and Popeye was getting confused. "Just think for a moment, Elroy," he said soothingly, patting the old man on the shoulder again, trying to help him relax. "You just take it easy now, and try to remember. Was the lady carrying anything?"

"The lady was carrying a bag," Elroy said. "Ladies always carry bags."

This was probably as much as Alan was going to get. But whether this mysterious lady was carrying a handbag or a sack containing a dead baby, Popeye had seen a woman go into the school building in the middle of the night. Alan accepted that at face value. What Popeye told you was always correct–as long as he stuck to the facts and didn't have to interpret them.

The only question in Alan's mind was: What did "a little time ago" really mean? Was it yesterday that the old man saw this lady, or was it ten years earlier? With Popeye, there was no way to be sure.

Chapter 6

No union reps. Absolutely none. Superintendent Adolph Schloesser had insisted on it, and he had enough experience in the careful stroking of political operatives to know what he was talking about. All the contract school districts had been asked either to send delegations to the capital to visit the offices of their state senators and assemblymen or else to host the elected officials or their key staffers back at the schools. It was all part of a carefully managed, statewide campaign to massage the reform proposals working their way through the relevant legislative committees.

Superintendent Schloesser had arranged a perfect educational experience for Kay Albright, State Senator Ben Dillard's legislative assistant: a tour of the district's five schools, luncheon at the Courthouse Inn, then an afternoon roundtable with the five school principals, a couple of school board members and a small, carefully selected group of teachers. But no one from the union office. This was to be a spontaneous exchange in which the selfless tenders of the academic vineyard shared their sincerest hopes and dreams for the young minds placed in their care. Schloesser had spent a week coaching his people for this session, and he wasn't going to have any wing-tipped union slicks lousing up the spontaneity.

Kay Albright, a very sharp, very attractive, very professional-looking woman in her late twenties, was listening attentively as Madeleine Cooper held forth on how the changes in small-town life were impacting the schools. Madeleine explained how she had to spend more and more time tending to the physical needs of her third-graders. She was teaching such basic skills as combing hair and proper toilet hygiene to children who got themselves off to school in the morning and returned to unattended homes in the afternoon. So often, Mom was working long hours in the local flour mill or one of the small assembly plants out in the industrial park, then earning what she could–and Lord only knows how–after hours. Of course, Dad was nowhere to be found, the illegitimacy rate in the county starting to resemble that of some big-city ghettos.

Kay nodded her head and whispered something to her very sharp, very attractive, very professional-looking assistant, Carin, who was taking notes. High school principal Marty Casten watched the two young women interact in their very professional way. Seated directly across from them, he couldn't help letting his eyes wander from their earnest faces, framed in businesslike, mid-length, hairdos, down their well-tailored suits to their shapely legs. It occurred to him that his view of these two political angels was the high point of what long before had become a tedious day.

"Teachers aren't their students' parents," Madeleine said, wagging her finger as she might do in the middle of a lesson. "We're playing catch-up. We're being asked to do *now* what mothers and fathers should have been doing years ago. Consequently, more and more of our real work–the teaching we were trained to do–is simply not getting done."

Kay nodded again. "We're hearing the same thing from schools all over the state," she said sympathetically. "I really do appreciate your concerns."

"We've tried to address the issue in some fairly innovative ways," said Superintendent Schloesser. "We've had volunteers–some mothers who serve as classroom assistants–help the children who need special, basic care. But nowadays, there simply aren't very many mothers who are free during the school day. And of course, we're asking them to do things that are often quite unpleasant. Some of our volunteers have told us they've had enough of such basic care with their own children. And who can blame them?"

"Certainly," said Kay.

"We've devised a plan," Schloesser went on, "that involves trained, basic-care counselors who can handle the children's needs and free the teachers for more actual teaching." It was a setup for a money pitch–one of several he'd made during the day. "And we have hoped that any new budgeting systems being proposed could allow for greater discretionary funding to encourage innovations of this type."

"There's a fierce budget battle going on, Dr. Schloesser," said Kay, noticing Marty Casten's gaze lingering on her legs from the corner of her eye.

"I realize that," said the superintendent. "But we do hope the senator appreciates the challenges we face, even in small-town America. This just isn't the pristine heartland anymore."

"Oh, the senator has great sensitivity for the problems of our rural communities," Kay said. She slid her hand inconspicuously down the side of her leg and adjusted her skirt. "You know, he was raised on a farm himself."

Marty chuckled quietly to himself, both at Kay's subtle maneuver and at this load of barnyard nectar she was dumping on behalf of her boss. The senator was raised on a farm, all right, a horse ranch in one of the wealthiest suburbs in the state. Fact was, Ben Dillard–or "*Dullard*," as Marty called him–was a pure carpetbagger. He was a partner in a prominent capital law firm, who had set up a branch office and a legal residence in this rural district when old State Senator Chick Slocum was nearing retirement with no strong successor on the horizon. Dillard had ambitions toward the governor's mansion and enough money behind him to grease his way into the state house as a first step in that direction. He slipped easily into Slocum's seat, and was now trying to ride this education-reform hobby horse, making himself the champion of rural schools. What a joke. Dillard's own two kids never did move out to the district with the good senator and his lovely wife. They were still at the same private, out-of-state boarding school they had always attended.

Now these two angels seated across from Marty were out seeking the will of the people. More to the point, they were calculating how the champion of rural schools could pander to the property owners and the teachers' union at the same time. That was the key: finding a formula for lightening the school-tax burden while throwing enough candy at the schools.

The day's discussions had been wide ranging, and Schloesser was satisfied that he had been able to cover all the points on his list–all but one. Like many members of the legislature, State Senator Dillard had been intrigued by the idea, being pushed hard by the governor's office, of financing schools on the basis of vouchers for each student attending. Those vouchers would cover the average yearly cost of educating a student in the state, and could be redeemed at any school in which parents chose to enroll their child. The point was to set up a healthy competition between schools in the hope that educational performance would improve overall and the districts would become more attuned to the needs and interests of their residents. Under the governor's proposal, currently in committee, the vouchers could be redeemed at *private* schools as well as public ones.

Dillard was playing it coy. He had made known his interest in the proposal, but hedged on whether he felt non-public schools should participate in the voucher plan. He knew that the union was obsessively opposed to anything that threatened to weaken its influence over the contract school districts, and giving parents the power of the purse surely did that. At the same time, the champion of rural schools saw small communities all over the state caught in a vice between steeply escalating educational *costs* and steadily declining educational *results*–which put a damper on development and, consequently, on tax revenue. Somewhere in that conflict Ben Dillard perceived an opportunity.

What the senator's true feelings about the voucher idea really were Schloesser could only speculate. He knew that Dillard not only had his own children in private school but was the product of private education himself. Of course, in these populist times, such a personal advantage could, often as not, be a political liability. Still, being keyed into all the rumors about Dillard's aspirations to higher office, Schloesser also knew that the senator was currying favor among certain groups for which the idea of state funds going to private schools had great appeal–particularly Catholics, and *most* particularly the considerable Catholic communities in the state's larger urban centers. The senator enjoyed a natural advantage in such circles: he was Catholic himself.

Kay Albright looked at her watch and whispered something to Carin. It was getting late, and the two women would be eager to start back to the capital, so Schloesser made his approach to the *big* question.

"Well, we've certainly been delighted you could join us today, ladies," he said. "I hope this experience has provided some useful insights which you can take back to the senator." He leaned forward in his seat and assumed an attitude of intense seriousness. "Before we adjourn, though, I do want to express a concern we've all had–and I *am* certain I speak for everyone involved with our local schools..."

Kay knew what was coming. She'd heard it at every meeting they'd had in every school district they'd visited.

"We have grave reservations about the voucher proposal," Schloesser continued.

"No one is more motivated than educators to find ways of improving the performance of our schools and delivering educational services more effectively. We're talking about the future of our children, after all." Not exactly true in the superintendent's case. School district administrators are often viewed as the bureaucratic equivalent of migrant workers, and not without reason, since they tend to move around a lot. Schloesser's own children had long ago completed school in a district far away.

"Now, there may be some merit in ideas like magnet schools or allowing increased flexibility of school choice–that is *within* individual districts. A little competition can be a good thing. Keeps us on our toes." This he said with a smile which was mirrored by the members of his staff.

"But at a time when budgets are as over-stressed as they are today," he went on earnestly, "and when taxpayers are demonstrating such resistance to increased millages and bond issues–and of course, we're all taxpayers, so we understand the problems our citizens face–" Another smile. "Well, the idea of diverting public funds to private schools could pretty much spell the death of public education as we've known it."

Kay listened attentively to Schloesser's speech, as she had each time she'd heard it in every other school district. *If public education, as we've known it, were doing its job, there would be no need to fear competition from private schools.* That's what she *thought*. What she *said* was, "I can assure you, Dr. Schloesser, the senator is considering every possible implication of this proposal. He holds our state's education system in the highest regard and certainly wants to be sure we do everything possible to strengthen our public schools."

"But now, ladies and gentlemen," she continued, standing up, "Carin and I must be on our way." And the two political operatives made their gracious exit with many thanks and much chatter about the wonderful things they'd seen and how State Senator Dillard would be delighted to hear of the stunning progress being made even in the face of so many formidable challenges and how everyone could count on him getting behind the most effective solution to the problems of our rural schools, about which he cared so deeply.

When they had departed, Schloesser and the others held a post-mortem on the day's events. The superintendent told the group he felt generally positive about the way things had gone with their visitors, but was still wary of Dillard's position on the voucher question. Would he hold the line, or would he sell out to the private-school backers? One of the teachers, trying to be reassuring, pointed out that Dillard's was just one vote in the state senate. But another countered that Dillard wasn't the only one who was squishy on the question and that when you counted the legislators who were actively behind the governor's plan, the squishy ones could make the difference.

Marty Casten was becoming annoyed with this speculation, all of which he found pretty much pointless. "Perhaps we should just leave it to the union," he said, looking up at the clock and wanting very much to bring this long day to a close.

Schloesser sat back in his chair. "Maybe you're right, Marty." He raised his hands to signal a general dismissal. "Thank you, people. I appreciate all your help with this."

As the participants started getting up to go, Randy Burke, an English teacher at the high school, leaned over to Marty. "Well *I*, for one–" he said in a playful tone which the principal always found irritating, "*I* think someone should *really* let the noble senator know how we feel about all this Catholic-school bull poopoo." Randy always spoke in an exaggerated, theatrical manner, with gestures that were flamboyant and somewhat effeminate.

"What would you suggest?" Marty asked.

Randy brought the back of his hand up to his mouth with a broadly conspiratorial sweep. "I say we get that Catholic priest over at St. Mary's, put him in a bag and dump him in a trash can in State Senator Dillard's office. Whatcha think,

Prince? That the way to make a statement?"

Marty looked sideways at Randy with one eyebrow raised. He didn't much care for the tastelessness of that suggestion, after all the upset surrounding the dead baby, and he always disliked the way Randy contracted the title "Principal" to "Prince."

"I get the feeling you're not a daily communicant over at St. Mary's, Randy," said one of the other teachers from the high school.

"Oh, I gave that up years ago. Used to be an alter boy, believe it or not. I looked so cute in my little alb. Or was it a chasuble? No, that's what the priest wears. Well, who can remember. Anyway, you won't catch me involved in that stuff again."

"I don't think State Senator Dillard would appreciate your little statement, Randy," the principal said with a hint of annoyance. "I understand he's Roman Catholic himself."

"Oh, and I'm sure he's a good one." Randy gave Marty a wink. "All right then, Prince. In that case, what say we get those two dollies back, tie them up in their own pantyhose, and hold them?"

"For ransom?" Marty said flatly.

"No. Just hold them." Randy winked again, slapped Marty on the knee and left, fluttering goodbyes to his colleagues as he went.

The principal shook his head. Randy. What the students saw in him Marty could never understand. Some dismissed him as a fairy, to be sure. But not most. Randy was one of those teachers who had the power to attract a certain kind of kid–and to make them into disciples. He had energy. He dressed in a flashy, artsy manner and was always flitting around, spouting fragments of poetry. He had that edge of irreverence that appeals instantly to teenagers convinced that the world, and especially their parents, can't possibly appreciate their deep insights and tortured intellects. Marty hated to admit it, but Randy was a very good teacher and the best yearbook and literary magazine advisor the high school had had in a long time. His student publications had won several statewide awards–which was what had qualified him to participate in today's festivities. Personally, Marty couldn't stand the little jerk.

Superintendent Schloesser leaned back in his chair, trying to stretch the day's tensions out of his back, which tended to knot up. "What kind of impression did you get from our two guests, Marty," he asked with a yawn.

The yawn was catching: Marty's own mouth opened widely, and he took in a large gulp of air. "Frankly, Dolph," he said after the yawn had passed, "I figure we were just paying union dues today. Dillard will sell to the highest bidder, you know that." He stood up, shrugging out some stiffness in his own shoulders. "Those two angels were just sampling the market. The lobbyists will make it or break it in the back rooms of the capitol."

The superintendent nodded his head. "I guess you're right," he said. "We'll just have to wait and see how strong the Catholics really are."

✠ ✠ ✠

Liturgy Suppliers was going to hear from him, Alan thought. Their order fulfillment had really fallen off. Well, at least he had the music in time for his Wednesday night choir rehearsal, though with little enough margin. The UPS truck had rolled up just as Rosemarie was about to close the office that afternoon.

Now if Alan could only get the Westhover sisters to sing their lines on key. This was a nice little song, a contemporary piece written by one of the hot, new-wave liturgical songwriters whose works were filling up all the Catholic hymnals. It was about God calling us by name to achieve our full potential, filled with images of making the blind see and the lame run free. The bishop apparently liked it. But to Alan, this song illustrated some of the problems common to much of the current music being developed for use at Mass.

For one thing, the melody was very flowing–airy and delicate–with long sustained notes. It was a pretty tune, but Alan knew it would pose special challenges to some of his singers, especially Edith and Helen. Whatever potential God might be calling those two charming maiden ladies to achieve, it clearly didn't involve music.

The song also had long breaks at the ends of the stanzas. The final note of each was held for two measures, then followed by two full measures of rests. Alan could see the congregation standing in their pews, fidgeting about, waiting for the next verse. Of course, this structure wasn't as problematic as that of many modern liturgical songs, which often contained breaks right in the *middle* of the verses. Such empty spaces were terribly disconcerting to people not trained as singers.

Alan frequently pondered those kinds of musical rough spots. Having come to Catholicism in adulthood from a Protestant background, he had a different perspective on church music, and he was always struck by a glaring contradiction: In the years since the Second Vatican Council, emphasis had been placed on involving congregations more fully in the act of communal worship, so singing had assumed a position of special prominence during mass. But far too much of the music that had been created in the post-Vatican years did not encourage congregational singing. Indeed, much of it was plainly unsingable, with very loose musical structure and, in most instances (worst of all, to Alan's mind), lyrics that didn't rhyme.

Why couldn't modern liturgists and Catholic composers understand what made the classic hymns great? Were they too influenced by pop music? It might not be easy to write a great, enduring hymn–Alan certainly knew that, having tried and failed to do it himself more than once–but the elements were obvious enough. A great hymn contains strong ideas, expressed in strong words, sustained by strong musical phrases. Perhaps his outlook was still too "Protestant," but it didn't seem a difficult idea to grasp: If you want people to sing, give them good songs.

It was typical of Alan to analyze the problem that way. He was analytical by nature, and the Church was no less an object of his ruminations than any other aspect of life. In fact, he was particularly prone to ponder the idiosyncrasies of religious practice. He had found consolation in the Catholic faith; continuity and common sense in the Church's teachings; and a surprising degree of fulfillment in the role he played in the worship community–as song leader, bringer of music, lifter of hearts in chorus. He recognized his work as a ministry, and he appreciated its value. But it was evident to him that he didn't have the outlook of other converts. He was not *swept up* in the way people seem to be when they've made the often wrenching emotional passage from one church to another, or from no church at all.

Perhaps it was the circumstances under which Alan had joined the Church. He missed the ecumenical spirit he had encountered in the Air Force. In the military one moved much more easily back and forth across denominational lines. When he was involved in the chaplaincy music program he frequently played for Protestant services as well as for Catholic Masses, along with many interfaith events. Civilian religious life was much more compartmentalized. Alan knew, for instance, that there was a ministerial association here in the valley. But it had never held any of its meetings at St. Mary's, and he didn't think that Father Karl belonged–or Father Edward before him, for that matter. Had the two priests set themselves apart, or were the Protestant ministers reluctant to accept them? Even as open as Father Ed had been, it seemed that the only ongoing contact he maintained with other clergy in town was through pro-life activities.

Then again, perhaps the roots of Alan's attitude went even deeper. More than just a former Protestant, Alan was an only child in a family whose religious identity was, frankly, not all that firm. His parents had come from different faith backgrounds. His father had been a Catholic of tenuous conviction, and his mother had been a Methodist who dismissed the symbolism and ritual of the Catholic Church as so much superstition. The religious compromise that made their relationship possible called for very little religion at all. When they finally decided that Alan would benefit from a modicum of religious education and the chance to sing in a choir, the local Presbyterian church suggested itself as most convenient.

Musically, Alan's church experience had been beneficial. Spiritually, it just reinforced his sense of himself as an only child. Throughout his life Alan had always felt *the odd man out*–keeping his own counsel, judging things on his own terms. In pre-convert days he had been an uncommitted Protestant, amused at what he saw as dressed-up Sunday piety. Now he was a Catholic who viewed the Church through former-Protestant eyes. It was a perspective that helped him make good music. But it left him kind of lonely.

When all the choir members had arrived for the evening's session, Alan warmed them up with some vocalization exercises and a chorus of "Hail, Holy Queen," a song they had down pat and sang with gusto. The group rose to full voice on the final "Salve Regina," with even the Westhover sisters finishing on key. Now *that* was a hymn. Point proven once again.

The sound of someone clapping echoed through the church. Alan turned around and looked down from the choir loft. It was Jessica MacNair standing in the center aisle and wearing her nurse's uniform.

"That was very good," she called. "Are you going to do that one Sunday?"

"No. It's just a warm up," Alan answered, pleased to see her. "Are you planning to come up and sing with us?"

"I'm afraid not," she said, with an expression that struck Alan as charmingly shy. "We have our blood drive going on down in the school. I was just coming back from my dinner break and heard the singing."

"Oh. Too bad." He was genuinely disappointed.

"If anyone wants to donate, we'll be going until nine."

"We'll be wrapping up about then," said Alan.

"Well, we may run later," Jessie said, "depending on how many people show up tonight. And I can stick around for awhile, if...anyone wants to come down. St. Mary's has been the best collection site in the county. We do have a reputation to maintain."

Alan looked down on the smiling face accented by the pert little nurse's cap, and mused to himself that this was an extremely attractive woman. "I'll work everybody especially hard," he said. "Maybe we'll all build up a few extra corpuscles for you."

Jessie laughed. "Great," she said. "I'll hope to see as many of you as can come." She started to go out, then stopped and turned back up to the loft. "Oh, older folks might not want to donate, and that's perfectly okay. Twenties through forties are the best age range."

Alan watched her glide out of the church, following the graceful motion of her walk. He figured *his* age was just perfect.

✠ ✠ ✠

Carlton Fitch was a likable old lush–which was the problem. Every Wednesday night, the men's circle would pray to free him from the bondage of alcoholism. He would experience the deep conviction that he had been touched by the Spirit of the Lord, and know that his life had been renewed. That conviction would be alive in his heart all day Thursday and last until about 3:00 o'clock Friday afternoon, when it would begin to waiver. At 6:00, he would be at Minnie's, and by 9:00, he would be a slave of Satan again. Frankly, the men in the circle were tired of it–none the least Pastor Matt. But Carlton's Wednesday evening experiences were so sincere, and he was just so likable.

"'Where two or three are gathered in My name,' says the Lord. 'there am *I*,'" intoned Matt. "And we *call* upon the Name of Jesus. Drive out this spirit of wickedness."

All the men in the circle responded, "Amen!"

"We *agree* in the Name of Jesus. Give our brother, Carlton, the *victory*, Lord."

"Amen!"

"In the Name of Jesus, we *bind* you, Satan."

"Amen!"

"We *rebuke* you, Satan."

"Amen!"

Carlton had tears in his eyes, as usual.

"Father God, we know that You have called our brother, Carlton, to be Your very own. We know that You have washed him in the blood of the Lamb and set him free. His soul was purchased by the suffering and death of Your Son, Jesus. And nothing–not the gates of *hell*–can stand against Your saving power."

"Amen!"

"Thank You, Jesus."

They all repeated, "Thank You, Jesus."

Once again, Pastor Matt: "Thank you, Jesus."

And again the others: "Thank you, Jesus."

"Amen and amen," said Matt, drawing the prayer to a close.

Carlton wiped his eyes. One of the men patted him on the back, encouragingly.

Matt looked across the long, plywood-paneled basement room, whose walls were strewn with the crudely drawn but gaily colored pictures of Jesus produced by the children in Susan's Sunday school class, and saw that his wife had finished praying with the women's circle. "Well brothers," he said, "I think the ladies have prepared their usual pleasing treats. Let's break for a few minutes, and get a little something to eat. Then we'll take a look at tonight's lesson."

Everyone crowded around the refreshment table to poke over this week's fare. Louise Robertson's fruit tarts were the object of particular interest. Louise had been honing her baking skills since she had become pregnant and quit her job. Her husband, Brad, joked to the other men that, with all the baking Louise was doing, it was a race to see who would have the larger belly by the time the twins arrived.

The ladies were eager to hear how Louise was feeling carrying two up front. She reported that her back was taking quite a bit of strain, but otherwise, she was feeling fine, and Dr. Singh had said that everything seemed to be progressing as it should. Louise and Sue exchanged a glance in quiet confirmation that the pastor and his wife had high hopes for Dr. Singh's methods themselves.

One of the older ladies asked Louise if Dr. Singh used "that sound picture gizmo" to check on the babies' progress.

"Ultrasound," Louise said. "Yes, I had one yesterday during my checkup. You can watch the babies move around and everything. It's just fascinating."

Someone wondered how you could possibly make a picture out of sound. Brad, who was an engineer, tried to explain how the sound waves are interpreted by a computer which constructs the image. But after attempting, with some difficulty, to offer a simple explanation of the process, he had to admit that it was kind of hard to understand, but rest assured, it really did work.

"One of the marvels of God," said Carlton Fitch, who was still feeling touched by the Spirit. "One of the marvels of God."

"It certainly is," said Pastor Matt.

"Well, it's a marvel of God that's been mightily abused, you can bet," said Ida Franklin. "Turned to evil purposes, as I see it. Why, it's that sonagram and those amniocentesis tests that determine whether babies have any imperfections." Ida was an energetic, grandmotherly type who was deep into the pro-life movement and thoroughly familiar with the literature. "Now, I don't criticize anyone who's suffering over a child with some birth defect. It's a heartbreak. Believe me, I know. My Gerald has that foot problem, and I know it'll never be right. It just tears a mother's heart in two. But we're called to accept the will of God. We bear our crosses as best we can, and we don't select out those children who are less than perfect and rip them from their mothers' wombs. Why, did you know that in India, sonagrams are used to tell if babies are boys or girls? And if they're girls, more often than not they're aborted right then and there."

Someone observed that selective abortion was practiced commonly enough in this country as well, and that (God help them) those poor little Indian baby girls would probably just be drowned or have their throats slit after they were born anyway–not that this was any excuse for abortion.

Someone else asked if Dr. Singh wasn't from India.

"Well yes," said Louise, "but he studied medicine in England."

"The best of inventions can be used for evil," said Matt. "Still, we have to recognize progress when we see it. God has given man the intelligence to create the most marvelous things. But it's an ongoing struggle to keep the good things in life out of Satan's hands."

"Amen," said Carlton.

The conversation bounced back and forth between the delicacy of the crust in Louise's tarts and the evils of abortion. Someone commented on the recent news about a law proposed to outlaw the partial-birth abortion procedure. "Can you imagine? They actually stab a baby in the head while it's being delivered."

"Monstrous!"

"Unthinkable!"

"Infanticide," said Ida Franklin. "Infanticide pure and simple. Clear, unadulterated murder. No question about it."

A collective shudder passed around the room.

"God help us," Brad Robertson said, shaking his head sadly, "but perhaps it takes something that hideous to get enough people really outraged. Maybe then the tide will finally turn."

"We can only pray," said Matt, gesturing for everyone to sit down so he could begin the week's lesson.

The young minister frequently used these Wednesday-night Bible studies to float ideas and refine his thoughts for Sunday sermons. A good portion of the congregation attended the sessions off and on, but there was a core group of about a dozen people who came on a regular basis. They considered themselves Pastor

Matt's "think tank," and enjoyed having a part in framing the message of Bible Fellowship. They were forever suggesting topics, clipping articles, and bringing up experiences or conversations they'd had about religious issues with friends, relatives or co-workers.

One of the most aggressive of this group was Ellie Conner, who always had some tale to tell of a confrontation with an agnostic, an atheist or–worst of all–a Catholic. There was a definite edge about Ellie, and not without reason. She had been a rebellious teenager who took a Jack Kerouac-inspired trip to the West Coast in the early 1970s, did much experimenting with drugs and even more with sex. She came back to her hometown sadder, wiser and with an illegitimate child in tow, but found that her parents took no particular delight in the return of their prodigal daughter and even less in their half-Asian grandchild. There followed a dreadful marriage and eventual abandonment by an ill-tempered husband who left her after two more children and a miscarriage that nearly took her life. At least she had claimed it was a miscarriage. Actually, it had been a horribly botched abortion.

As Ellie lay in an out-of-town hospital, recovering from what the ER physician had described as a "butcher-shop job," she surveyed her life and realized she could no longer go on as she had. The choice before her was salvation or suicide. She decided to try the first option, knowing she could always fall back on the second if things didn't work out. She called a neighbor who attended some "Bible-thumping church," and the neighbor introduced her to Pastor Gene Pell, Matt's father.

Bible Fellowship gave her a new life. She felt welcome. She found solace and companionship among people whose faith was sincere and uncomplicated–many of whom had stories to tell as painful as her own. She soaked up Pastor Gene's strong, direct preaching. His words gave her hope and encouragement. They also gave her a perspective that seemed to explain much of the hurt in her life, especially that inflicted by her unforgiving parents.

It was all so simple. Her mother and father were Catholics–albeit not good Catholics. Truth to tell, neither of them had set foot inside a Catholic church in years, and they had certainly never troubled themselves to raise Ellie or her two sisters in the faith. Nonetheless, they were mired in Roman hypocrisy.

For Ellie, this insight was a sort of epiphany. She could see the whole sad story of her life as in a bright light. And it fired her with a sense of mission. She became a fierce apostle, quick to shower the Good News on anyone she felt was in need of the saving Word. Her special mission field was among Catholics, particularly young Catholics. She encouraged her three teenage children to bring their friends around, and took every opportunity to proselytize.

Ellie was never happier than when she came upon a book or tract that revealed some Catholic apostasy she hadn't considered or shed new light on papist mischief. And tonight she had come to Bible study loaded for bear. In her plump lap sat a nearly 500-page tome titled *Roman Catholicism*. She had run across it on a bottom shelf way back in the reading corner at the Christian bookstore downtown. It had obviously been left there, dust-covered and overlooked, for years. A quick scan through its table of contents convinced her she had struck the mother lode. Here was every conceivable criticism of Catholic belief and practice, and she was beside herself with eagerness to share it with the group.

Pastor Matt opened his Bible to the letters of Paul, intending to explore the great missionary's insights into justification through faith in Jesus Christ, when Ellie raised a hand. "Pastor," she said. "Before we begin, I thought you might be interested in a book I found recently." She held it up. "It's by a man named Boettner, and it's just amazing."

Matt recognized the book. It was a work that had occupied a place of prominence on his father's bookshelf and from which Pastor Gene had drawn much inspiration. Matt had read the lengthy volume at his father's insistence, and he knew it was a virulent attack on the Catholic Church, one-sided and poorly documented. While he certainly had his own disagreements with Catholic views, Matt prided himself on a certain fair-mindedness.

"I'm familiar with that book," he said, eyeing the volume with a twist to his lip.

"Well, it's just amazing," Ellie enthused. "It just blows the Roman cult right out of the water."

Someone asked what kinds of things were in the book.

"Well, it shows how false all the Catholic claims really are," she said. "For instance, Catholics say the pope is *infallible*–you know, what he says can't be wrong? Why that's the biggest laugh of all. The pope is supposed to speak *ex cathedra*. That means 'from the chair.' It refers to the chair of Peter, who was supposed to be the first pope, you know? Well, it's just a *laugh*. The chair that the pope sits on is only about a thousand years old. It couldn't possibly be the chair of Peter, because it would have to be two thousand years old. So the whole claim is false, don't you see? If speaking from the chair of Peter is what makes the pope's word infallible, then the whole thing's a *fraud*."

Some of the people in the room found the argument vaguely plausible, and the sound of "Hmmmm" was heard. Others were skeptical, and looked over at their pastor for guidance. Still others silently said to themselves, "There goes Ellie again."

Matt stirred uneasily in his seat. "I think," he said, "that Mr. Boettner might be interpreting the idea of speaking 'from the chair' a bit too literally. The phrase *ex cathedra* doesn't really have anything to do with a particular piece of furniture. It refers to the Catholic Church's claim that the pope inherits his authority from the Apostle Peter." The group listened attentively to their young pastor. "It's like saying that a judge makes a ruling 'from the bench,' which means *in his official capacity*. Now, I personally question the Catholic Church's claim on the question of lineage, and I think Rome is open to attack on that point. But the pope's chair really has nothing to do with it."

As was generally the case, everyone was impressed with Matt's argument. They had long realized that he was far more measured in his thinking than his father, and most members of the congregation appreciated that–much as they may have admired Pastor Gene's fervor in the pulpit. Those who had been taken with Boettner's observation about the insufficient age of the pope's chair felt sort of foolish, and the ones who had been skeptical felt their suspicions confirmed. Matt wanted to get the discussion onto the question of justification by faith, and asked everyone to open their Bibles to Paul's Letter to the Romans.

For her part, Ellie felt a little miffed that her literary find should be dismissed in such an off-hand manner–even if she had to grant that perhaps the author was stretching in his interpretation of speaking *ex cathedra*. But she knew there was plenty more in the book and her chance to score a few points would come soon enough. Meanwhile, she certainly agreed with Pastor Matt that the Catholic Church was "open to attack." She smiled to herself, knowing that it could be attacked in several ways.

✠ ✠ ✠

Alan sipped orange juice from a small plastic cup, as Jessie fingered through a stack of forms, taking a count of the day's donations. "We may break last year's record," she said, then looked over at Alan. "Have some more juice, if you like. Finish up whatever's in the pitcher."

"This ought to do me," he answered.

"Feeling okay?"

"I'm fine. I used to give blood fairly often when I was in the Air Force."

Alan had timed the choir rehearsal to end precisely at quarter to nine, so anyone who wanted to could go down to the community room in the school and give blood. He, very considerately, let everyone else go ahead, not wanting to keep them out too late after rehearsal. His own plastic pouch filled with blood was the last pint into the ice chest, which Brian, the young orderly assisting Jessie, dutifully took back to the hospital. Now, everything was cleaned up for the day, all the donors and Red Cross volunteers had gone, and he was alone with the attractive nurse.

He watched her sitting, organizing her forms. It had obviously been a long day. Her hair was beginning to come loose from the pins that held it gathered under her cap, and a few stands hung wispily around her face. Alan studied Jessie's eyes, and he realized that they were her most striking feature, even more so than the slim figure or the chestnut hair. The deep blue irises looked out from under lids that seemed to droop, ever so subtly, at the sides, creating different expressions that suggested strong and conflicting feelings. When she smiled, her eyes took on a look that was irresistibly sexy. When her mouth turned down, her eyes seemed to be looking at all the pain in the world.

Well, a nurse does see pain. And how different she was from Sheila. Oh, Sheila had the sexy part, that was true enough. But avoiding pain–or anything that smacked of even seriousness–had been a religion to her. Life was a smorgasbord of pleasures for Sheila. And actually it was that breezy carelessness which Alan had found so refreshing, in the beginning.

Sheila was fun. And why shouldn't she be? Sheila *looked* for fun–searched for it with a passion that was truly single minded. Marrying a musician would be fun. Hanging around clubs, being with colorful, fun people. Even being an Air Force wife seemed like a fun idea. Travel. Living overseas. It was all great. Until it all got unbelievably boring. Alan's military police duty was so unpredictable, often with multiple shifts back to back. That interfered with his ability to pick up playing jobs. And when there were no gigs, money was tight. Loneliness and budgeting weren't fun.

But that was the Air Force.

Still, there *were* all those blue suits. And once, when Alan returned from a three-day prisoner transfer, he found one draped over his bed post. Its owner he found draped over Sheila.

Jessie poured the rest of the orange juice into the sink in the kitchen of the community room, which had once been the school cafeteria. Alan had followed her in, carrying his plastic cup. He tossed it into a trash can, and watched her standing in front of the sink, rinsing out the pitcher. "Say..." He cleared his throat. "Would you like to get a little something to eat? Carl's Doughnut Shoppe is still open. Or there's Minnie's. Minnie can have something whipped up for us. She loves it when people are well fed."

Jessie stood with her eyes looking down into the sink. "That might be nice," she answered, carefully not looking up, and feeling a sudden flutter of nervousness.

Alan was nervous too. "Well, whichever you prefer," he said awkwardly. "There aren't too many options this time of night."

"Oh...maybe a doughnut." Jessie was rinsing the pitcher thoroughly. It was already quite clean. Finally, she set it upside down to dry on the rack next to the sink, then took a breath and turned to Alan. "Shall we go?"

She smiled. Alan saw those sexy eyes. He thought of Sheila. Then he forgot about Sheila. "I don't have my car," he said. "I live across the square, and it's parked at my apartment. But Carl's is only a couple of blocks down the street. We can walk. It's not too cool out."

"We can take my car," Jessie said. "It's in the lot."

"If you like."

Jessie gathered up her cape and purse, and they went outside. She took out her keys and locked the door of the building. Alan noticed that her hands were small but strong. Nurses' hands. They got into her car and pulled out of the parking lot past a battered sport truck which was parked across the street. There were two dark figures in the shadows of the cab, which neither Alan nor Jessie noticed.

Second Interlude

In 1933, the year by which the Great Depression had gripped the valley with full force, the parishioners of St. Mary's decided to open a school. It seemed an impossible notion when Father Eamon Flaherty, the pastor at the time, first put forth the proposal in his homily one Sunday. But it had considerable appeal in a remote parish where the Catholic children had always had to attend public schools. Father Flaherty was a man of vision who saw more than just a means of fortifying the young in their faith. He realized that the mood of the community was as depressed as its economy. A major undertaking like a school would be a challenge to St. Mary's and a boon to the whole county.

Father Flaherty's original idea was to provide elementary-through-high school instruction all under one roof, even including *kindergarten*, a preparatory educational concept then coming into vogue among educators in the region. But the pastor saw early on that such an inclusive facility would not be practical. An elementary school, on the other hand, could be accomplished, to be staffed by nuns from an order that had its motherhouse in the state capital and provided teachers for schools throughout the diocese.

The plan galvanized the Catholics in town, who dug deeply into scant family reserves. The city fathers also lent encouragement to the project, seeing the employment potential and the boost to community hopes. Within two years, the bishop was sprinkling holy water on a building not quite finished in every detail but complete enough to open for the 1935-36 school year. The mayor and even the superintendent of the public school district were on hand for the blessing and ceremonial ribbon cutting, demonstrating community support for an effort that had raised spirits and put bread on tables throughout the valley.

Father Flaherty was made a monsignor and received a letter of commendation from President Roosevelt, noting how the priest's "faith, vision and tireless effort were a perfect embodiment of the New Deal spirit." The letter was framed and hung in the entryway beside Father's portrait. An editorial in the newspaper celebrated the unique contributions which the members of St. Mary's had made in the life of the community for nearly a century.

It was the high-water mark of Catholic-Protestant relations in the valley.

Chapter 7

There was a faint pounding on the door of the C-130 transport. But who could be doing the pounding? The huge plane was 30,000 feet off the ground. Alan knew they were in the air somewhere over the ocean. He could see water below, through the floor. He looked at Jessie. *Do you hear that noise?* he asked. *Someone wants to come in*, she said, and held out her nurse's cap to him. He reached for the cap and heard the pounding again. *Someone wants to come in*, Jessie said again. *Someone wants to come in*, said Sheila.

Someone wanted to come in. There was someone at the door downstairs. Alan sat up in bed and blinked. He looked at the illuminated numbers on his clock radio. It was a little after midnight. He had only been asleep a short while. Who could that be at this hour? He put on a robe, and went down the two flights of stairs barefoot. Through the glass door he could see a man lit dimly from behind by the street light. The face was too dark to make out, but there was the shape of a pipe jutting from the side of his mouth. Alan turned the knob on the lock, and pushed the glass door open. It was Popeye.

"Elroy. What are you doing here? What's the matter?"

"Alan Kemp," said the old man. "Alan Kemp. Something has happened at the school."

Alan's brain was fuzzy. He hadn't even realized that Popeye knew where he lived. But then, Popeye knew all kinds of things. "*What's* happened?" he asked.

"Something has happened at the school," Popeye went on, visibly agitated. "I didn't know what to do, so I thought about it for awhile. I thought about what happened, and I remembered that you asked me to tell you about things that happened at the school, and something has happened at the school. Tonight. Something has happened at the school tonight."

Alan took Popeye by the sleeve and pulled him inside. "Okay. Come on in. Let's go up to my apartment."

"Some people were at the school. Two people."

"*Who* was at the school?" Alan asked, starting up the stairs.

"Two people. Two *men* were at the school," said Popeye, following along.

"What were the men doing?"

"The men did something to the statue–the statue in the back of the school. They did something to the statue. They were there doing something to the statue, and then they ran away. And they got into a truck, and they drove away. And I thought about what you said, so I came to tell you."

There was a small grotto behind the school with a stone bench, a bird bath, and a statue of the Virgin. It was surrounded by tall, evergreen bushes with a low, iron gate at one end, and it had been a spot where the nuns used to seek solitude and a few minutes of respite from their teaching.

"What did the two men do to the statue, Elroy?"

"I don't know, Alan Kemp. But they were laughing when they ran away. I think they did something bad to the statue, so I came to tell you."

"That's very good of you, Elroy." They had reached Alan's apartment. "Certainly wouldn't have wanted this to wait until morning."

Popeye explored the flat as Alan got dressed. The old man was captivated by all the musical instruments and electronic gear. Then they went out to the street, across the square and down the hill to the back of the school. Alan opened the low gate, and they went into the grotto.

"What the–" The moon was shining brightly, and Alan could see that the figure of Mary had been covered with a large bag. It was a clear, plastic trash bag, and it was held tightly closed around the statue's round pedestal by a big elastic band.

Popeye stood looking at the covered statue. "Is this a bad thing, Alan Kemp?" he asked in a very confused tone of voice.

"It's a *weird* thing," said Alan.

"Sometimes people put bags over top of things to protect them when it's raining," Popeye said. "But it isn't raining. Why would someone want to protect the statue when it isn't raining?"

Alan leaned close to the statue and peered through the plastic. At the feet of the figure he could see about a half dozen small foil packets. "Yeah, well...I think this is supposed to be a protective thing, all right," he said. "But rain has nothing to do with it."

✠ ✠ ✠

"Chief Zubeck? I didn't expect them to call you." Alan was waiting outside the low iron gate when Zubeck and Volmer arrived. The chief was wearing a pair of Dockers with a knit shirt tucked unevenly into the waistband. He had quite obviously been called from his home. Volmer was better dressed and looked like he had been on duty.

"You asked that this be done discreetly," said Zubeck, looking just a touch annoyed. "I'm the one in charge of discretion."

"Yeah, well...thanks, Chief. I do appreciate that. Not flashing the lights or anything."

"So what's this all about?

Alan felt embarrassed. "I, ah... Look, Chief...this isn't really all that big a deal. And I never–I mean I'm sorry if they got you out of bed or anything. But after what happened...with the baby and all...well..."

"Get to the point, Kemp."

Alan led the two policemen inside the grotto, where Popeye was sitting on the stone bench.

"Well hello, Elroy," said Volmer. "What are you doing here?"

"Two men did something *weird* to the statue," Popeye replied, pointing at Saint Mary.

"What the hell–" Zubeck exclaimed.

"Take a look through the bag," said Alan.

The chief removed a small flashlight from his pocket, and shined it through the plastic. "Condoms?"

"The whole thing's supposed to be one big condom," said Alan. "Look at the way the elastic holds it closed around the pedestal."

"So what do you think this is all about?"

"Somebody making another statement?"

"Just looks like a stupid prank to me," said Zubeck, "though a particularly offensive one."

Volmer glanced at his boss' face. Zubeck's expression struck him as very mixed. Was there the merest hint of shock? The sergeant had watched this hardened, big-city cop deal with a wide variety of crime, vice and degradation and take it all in stride. Could the chief be somehow personally offended at this idiotic bit of mischief? That would be highly uncharacteristic.

Zubeck turned to Popeye. "What did you say about two men?"

"Two men did something weird to the statue. Alan Kemp said this is a *weird* thing."

"It's a little more than that," said Zubeck. "Did you see these men put the bag over the statue?"

Popeye looked at Zubeck and smiled. "You are Chief of Police Stanley Zubeck," he said smartly.

"Yeah, that's right, Elroy. Did you *see* the two men do this?"

"No, Chief of Police Stanley Zubeck."

"Just call me 'Chief,' Elroy."

The old man smiled more broadly. He felt proud that this official person wanted him to use what seemed to Popeye such an informality. "No, *Chief*," he said. "I didn't see the two men put the bag over the statue. But I saw them in here, and I saw them laughing and running away–Chief. And I saw them get into a truck, and I saw the two men drive away in the truck."

Zubeck was trying his best to be patient with the old man. He squatted down next to Popeye. Volmer was taking notes.

"Did you recognize the two men, Elroy?" Zubeck asked. "You know a lot of people in town. Did you know the two men?"

"No...*Chief*. I couldn't see the faces of the two men. It was dark. It was too dark to see their faces."

"Did you see what kind of truck they were driving, Elroy?" Zubeck asked.

"It was a small truck," said Popeye.

"You mean a pickup truck?"

"It was a small pickup truck, *Chief*."

"Do you know what color it was?"

Popeye thought for a moment. "It was... I think the truck was...blue...or black." Popeye was trying hard to remember. He looked at Zubeck with a pained expression. "It was...dark," he said sadly, disappointed with himself for not being able to provide the requested detail.

Zubeck put his hand on the old man's shoulder. "That's okay, Elroy. You're doing just fine. You're really being a big help."

Popeye smiled again.

"Elroy has some other information, Chief," Alan said. "Elroy, tell Chief Zubeck about the lady."

"What lady?" Zubeck asked.

Popeye thought for a moment, not quite making Alan's connection. Then he remembered. "Oh. Yes. I saw a lady go inside the school building in the middle of the night, and she was carrying a bag."

Zubeck looked up at Alan, then back at Popeye. "Do you know who the lady was, Elroy?"

"No, *Chief*."

"That's all he knows," Alan said. "I tried to pin him down about when this might have happened. All he could tell me was that he was walking around recently, late at night, and he saw a woman carry something into the school."

Zubeck stood up and rubbed his chin thoughtfully. "Well, Elroy doesn't miss a trick. And I know he walks around town through the night. If he says he saw a woman, you can bet there *was* one. Isn't that right, Elroy?"

"Right, Chief." The old man was beaming.

The chief turned his attention back to the statue. He stood quietly for a moment, just looking at it and shaking his head. "So what do you think it means, Kemp?" he said at last. "Criticizing the pope's stand on birth control?" He looked closely at the bag. "Jock, note down that this is an institutional trash can liner, the kind you see mostly in offices."

"We got those at the station," Volmer observed, "only smaller. It's the kind the cleaning service puts in our waste baskets. I got one next to my desk. They put an elastic band around it, to hold it in place, just like that one."

"They're common enough," said Zubeck. "You see them in commercial buildings, hospitals..."

"Schools?" Alan asked.

"I suppose."

Alan was onto a thought, but he hesitated to express it. "Chief," he said, "if it's not divulging anything that could compromise a case... I was wondering if you've made any progress on...the baby."

"So you think this trick has something to do with that."

"There may be no direct connection," said Alan, "but you know how one incident can prompt another. Even if it was only pranksters. The church was recently in the news. People get ideas."

"Look Kemp, I know about your background with the military police and the Air Force Inspector General's Office. I had you checked out."

Alan wasn't really surprised. He had gotten the feeling that Zubeck was thorough.

"So I'll tell you. We've got nothing that suggests anything clear. No suspects, no motive, no...*modus operandi*, as they say in the movies. Nothing that looks like anything. If the woman Elroy saw was really the dumper, then that's the biggest news yet. So any thoughts you might have, I'd appreciate knowing about them."

Alan hesitated again, then: "Let's take a walk, Chief."

Zubeck looked at Popeye, then at Volmer, and gestured toward the statue. "Take it apart, Jocko. And you might as well bag it all." He followed Alan out to the street.

"You're right about Elroy," Alan said. "He doesn't miss anything. And you never know what he says to people."

"So what's on your mind?"

Alan looked at Zubeck and wondered if the police chief would think he was *out* of his mind. "This is a really wild idea, Chief..."

"Wild ideas are better than no ideas," Zubeck prompted him.

"Okay." Alan figured *What the hell*. "Look...there's a political thing going on right now. You know this school reform bill that's up before the state legislature? Well..." He looked at the chief, whose expression was professionally noncommittal.

"Go on," Zubeck said.

"There's a rumor around town–among the teachers in the public schools–that the Church is planning to reopen Holy Innocents. A few of the people in the district think it's a grab for state funds if the voucher plan passes. I've talked to some teachers, and feelings are apparently running pretty strong. Now, as far as I know, the diocese has no plans for this place at all. But Father Karl's background does include running a prestigious Catholic school, and the people in the district know his reputation. So..."

"Father Karl's background includes a lot of interesting twists," said Zubeck.

"You know about his breakdown?"

"Among other things."

"Well, as I said, Chief, it's a wild idea."

"And like I told *you*, Kemp, wild ideas are better than no ideas." The policeman turned and looked back into the grotto, where he could see that Volmer had removed the bag from the Virgin. He turned back toward Alan. "Tell me, Kemp. You're obviously nosing around with this. Is it just curiosity, or are you working for somebody?"

Alan's eyes dropped to the ground. "The truth is," he said, somewhat reluctantly, "I've been asked by the bishop's office to see what I can pick up."

"Well, I'd appreciate it if you could let me know about anything you *pick up*," Zubeck said in a tone that struck Alan as intentionally hard. "Let's work together on this—for everybody's good."

"Along those lines, Chief," said Alan, not letting himself be intimidated, "*I'd* appreciate it if you could keep *this* little prank under your hat. There's a lot of pressure on Father Karl right now."

Zubeck's expression softened. He looked up the hill toward the rectory. "Father Karl. Yeah, okay Kemp. But you'd better have a talk with Elroy. God knows what he might blab around town. As far as I'm concerned, unless Father Karl's a light sleeper and he's looking out his window right now, there's no need for him to know about this."

Volmer and Popeye came out of the grotto. Jock had all the materials from the statue inside a large plastic zipper bag. Zubeck held out his hand to Popeye. "Thanks again, Elroy," Zubeck said. "You were a big help."

Popeye seemed to be thinking about something. He looked blankly at the police chief. Then there was the flash of a thought. "It was a Toyota," the old man said. "It was a Toyota truck. The two men drove away in a black Toyota truck."

"Did they, indeed," said the chief.

Volmer made a note in his pad.

"Well thank you once more, Elroy," Zubeck said. "You've been a *very* big help."

Popeye was beaming again.

Chapter 8

Sister Elaine sat on the floor with her legs crossed and her hands resting on her knees, palms turned upward, the tips of her thumb and forefinger touching on each hand. Her eyes were closed, and she felt the warmth of the morning sun on her face, as the light streamed in through the window. She drew in long, slow breaths, then let the air out just as slowly. Morning meditation was her "battery charger." And today's was especially needed, since she'd been up late last night writing a paper for a graduate program she was struggling through.

Elaine was working toward a doctorate in pastoral ministry offered on an extension basis by a prominent divinity school. Her paper explored the use of the enneagram in premarital counselling. She found enneagram theory fascinating, with its arcane geometry and its nine-point analysis of personality types, and she considered it a real spiritual breakthrough. The experimenting she'd done with it was limited and very low key, of course. Nothing so progressive as the enneagram, nothing so untraditional, maybe even so constructive, could possibly pass muster with Father Karl. But perhaps, if all went right–if she could firm up a dissertation plan, get a decent director, and clear some time for actual research–just maybe she could finish in two or three years. And then she would be in a position to move on. Then, finally, she could do the kind of work she felt called to do.

She had always been a scholar. She'd gotten excellent grades all through school, despite scant encouragement from her parents, whose only vision for her was as a wife and producer of many grandchildren: a model Catholic woman, by their definition. What a shock when she became a model of a very different kind of Catholic woman. Elaine had been strongly influenced by one of her high school teachers, Sister Rita, a bright young nun who had made her novitiate just as the sixties were revolutionizing Religious life. Rita had witnessed the gutting of the convents, as thousands of sisters deserted their orders in the post-Vatican ferment. While many of her contemporaries questioned the point of a sisterhood without habits, cloisters and the comforting regularity of convent life, Rita was inspired by the idea of strong, faith-filled women transforming the world. No pious, introspective life for her. This was the moment for a new, feminist-charged sisterhood. Her enthusiasm infected Elaine, whose bookish image masked the energy and rebelliousness her parents had worked hard to suppress.

So many new ideas were whirling about. So many opportunities for a young woman who could meld her personal faith with the spiritual, cultural and political currents of the time. A new charism was emerging, and Elaine felt it was truly, authentically hers. The Lord had called her to walk new paths. She believed it, and Father Edward had sensed it as well. Who could know where those paths might lead? Though, with Father Karl blocking so many of her explorations, right now, her destination seemed all the more distant.

Meditation time was over. Elaine opened her eyes and made the sign of the cross. "In the name of the Creator, the Redeemer and the Sanctifier." It was a formulation she employed only in her private prayers.

She was dressed and out of her apartment in short order–without breakfast. She rarely ate on rising, but instead preferred a mid-morning snack, usually a granola bar with a cup of herbal tea, around ten o'clock. As she was unlocking the door to her Ford Escort, she noticed Jessie emerge from the apartment building.

"Good morning, Jess," she called. "Last day of the drive today."

Jessie seemed preoccupied and didn't hear her at first, then she looked up. "Oh... Hi, Elaine. Ah...yes. Today's our last day of collections. Things are going well."

"You heading for St. Mary's now?"

"Yes. I've got my supplies in the car."

"I'll see you over there."

The two drove out of the apartment complex, Elaine following behind. Jessie was a tad faster and got through the one intersection with a stoplight between the apartments and the church before the light turned. Elaine got caught on red. Some of the blood-drive volunteers were carrying supplies into the school when Elaine arrived in the parking lot. Jessie herself had a large carton which she carried unsteadily.

Elaine hurried around her car to be of assistance. "Can I help, Jess?"

"I've got it, Elaine. Thanks. But could you get my keys out of the door?"

Elaine took Jessie's key ring from the lock on the school door, followed her into the community room, and set the ring on the sign-in table. "So how's the drive doing this year?"

"Excellent," said Jessie, hustling off to supervise the day's set-up. "We'll probably top last year."

Elaine looked around. The large room was cluttered with chairs, folding cots and blood-collecting equipment. And the walls were decorated with Red Cross posters bearing messages of encouragement to uneasy donors, specifying the collection procedures and–in the age of concern about fluid-borne diseases–offering reassurances that you can't get AIDS from giving blood. Over the years, drive week had become a regular fixture on St. Mary's calendar of activities, rather like its own little liturgical season. The Knights of Columbus made promotion of it an annual project. The pastor would be sure to give it a plug during Masses in the weeks leading up. And the congregation generally got into the spirit of the effort.

Elaine went to her office. She took out a stack of questionnaires which had been completed by participants in the RCIA program as part of the week's activities. She'd started reading through them, when Jessie appeared at the door.

"Got a minute?" the nurse asked.

"Sure," said Elaine. "Need anything?"

"Not for the blood drive," said Jessie, taking the chair opposite Elaine's desk. She perched herself stiffly on the edge of the seat, and glanced around the small room, apparently uneasy about something. "Elaine... What do you think of...Alan?"

"Alan Kemp?"

"Yeah." Her eyes fell to her lap, and there was a tightness about her mouth.

"He's a nice enough person, I suppose," said the nun. "Talented musician." She looked at Jessie, who was fidgeting with her fingers and clearly self-conscious. "Are you...*interested?*"

"Well...we went for coffee and a doughnut last night. After I closed up here. We were out...maybe an hour. And it was nice. We just chatted. Nothing special. He asked me if I'd like to come to the roadhouse to hear his band..."

There was a silence. Elaine read uncertainty on Jessie's face. "That sounds fine," she said, "if you want to go."

"Oh...sure..."

"Jessie, is there anything..."

Jessie bit her lower lip. It was a nervous habit that came out sometimes. "I'm...not very good with men, Elaine," she said awkwardly.

Elaine laughed. "You're talking to the wrong person about that," she said. "Nuns are hardly in a position to give advice about dealing with the opposite sex."

Jessie suddenly seemed upset. Her eyes darted about the room, and she looked like she might cry. Elaine got up and went to her around the desk. "Jessie, what's the matter?"

The nurse composed herself quickly. "I'm all right," she said. "A little nervous. It's nothing, Elaine. Like I said, I'm not very good–I mean I've never been *at ease* with men. That's all. It's foolishness." She stood up.

"It's not foolish, Jess. You can talk to me, if you–"

"No. Really. I'm fine. Alan's a nice guy. It isn't him." She took a handkerchief from her uniform pocket and dabbed her eyes.

Elaine had done enough counselling to know that Jessie was bothered about something. "Any time you want to share your feelings, Jess..." Wouldn't it be interesting to do an enneagram on *her*.

"Thanks, Elaine. I'd better get ready to open. People will be coming soon, to donate." Jessie turned and started out of the office, but found herself facing another person in the doorway. "Oh!"

"Excuse me," said the woman. Then she recognized who had almost bumped into her. "Oh, Jessie. Hi. You're just the person I was coming to see."

"Tamar. I'm sorry. I nearly ran you down."

Elaine was surprised to see her friend from the counselling center. "Tam. You know Jessie?"

"Of course. I was aware that Jessie was holding her drive here this week. I thought I'd stop off on my way to work and give some blood." She looked at the nurse and saw that her eyes were red. "Are you okay?" she asked solicitously.

Jessie's face flushed. "Oh yes. I'm fine. Just some silliness, talking with Elaine." She hurried past Tamar in the doorway. "I'd better get to work. Come on downstairs whenever you like, Tam, and I'll take your donation." She was at the end of the hallway.

Tamar looked at Elaine quizzically, and pointed toward Jessie disappearing into the stairwell.

Elaine narrowed her eyes and gave a quick shake of the head. "Just a little upset," she whispered.

Tamar came into the office. "I've seen that look a million times. Five'll get you ten, there's a man behind it."

"Well...yes." Elaine gave a slight giggle that was almost girlish. "Nothing really serious, though. Not yet, anyway. But this is certainly an unexpected surprise–seeing *you* on holy ground."

Tamar gave Elaine's tiny office a critical scan. "This is where they keep you?" She shook her head. "Pretty grim. I suppose the cell door's unlocked for exercise period."

"I'll admit it's not palatial. But it suits me."

"No, Elaine. The rectory up on the hill would suit you."

The nun smiled. "I'm not holding my breath till that happens."

"Well, they could at least give you one of the old classrooms for an office. They're empty, and you could certainly use more space."

Elaine noticed Tamar's outfit: cream-colored suit, impeccably tailored. Tamar had superb taste–the perfect image of the modern, professional woman. A Religious really shouldn't be affected by such worldly things, but when she was with Tamar, Elaine often felt rather dowdy in the simple jumpers which were, for her, the equivalent of a nun's habit.

Tamar was still looking around, and she gave a small shudder. "I have to admit, Elaine. Being in this building gives me the creeps. Too many memories of my days in Catholic school."

Elaine sat back behind her desk. "You went to Catholic school?"

"Oh yes. St. Athanasius. I remember it well. Plaid uniform, saddle shoes–the whole bit–and, if you'll forgive me, dear Sister, some of the most neurotic nuns you ever met."

Elaine didn't bite.

"I went all the way through eighth grade. Then I bailed out to public high school. There was only this Catholic girls' academy, which my sister attended. And I didn't want any part of *that*. My sister was a good little girl who enjoyed the regimentation. I wanted my freedom. And I wanted boys."

"It seems to me," said Elaine, "that boys are a lot easier to get than freedom."

Tamar sat down on the chair opposite Elaine's desk, crossing her legs. Elaine noticed her tinted hose and sling-back pumps.

"You're so right. And as soon as boys are in the picture, freedom goes out the window anyway."

"Didn't you attend a Catholic college?" Elaine asked.

"I did. One of those institutions that went through a lot of changes after Vatican II. Believe me, it wasn't really all that Catholic, by then." Tamar offered a breezy, non-committal smile. "They gave me a great scholarship. I couldn't complain."

The nun studied her friend for a moment. Such a strange contradiction, this bright, capable, attractive woman. She seemed to have it all so much...*together*...yet she was pulled in so many directions at once.

"Tam...do you ever...in the slightest way...*miss* the Church?" Elaine asked quietly.

Tamar's expression hardened all of a sudden. "No," she said emphatically, her eyes flashing across the desk. Then she turned her head abruptly to one side. "I don't wish to be offensive, Elaine. Please don't be disturbed by my sour outlook. You're a dear heart, and I wouldn't, for the world, question your beliefs or criticize your commitment. But I saw my mother crushed by the Church. Crushed with *guilt*." Her arms were crossed tightly, defensively in front of her chest. "She was nearly bleeding to death after three miscarriages. Her uterus was practically falling out of her. And our kindly old parish priest told her it would be a sin to have a hysterectomy or to get her tubes tied."

Tamar rose and walked to the window that looked onto the street. She stood staring out for more than half a minute, saying nothing. Elaine sat silently.

Finally, Tamar continued. "She had the operation anyway, and left the Church. She was a Catholic to the end of her life, but she never went to Mass again. On the morning she died, I called in a priest, a young one from a parish on the other side of town. He anointed her, and she died smiling."

Tamar turned around and faced the desk. There was deep feeling in her eyes. The hurt radiating from her was palpable across the small room, and Elaine felt herself taken aback by her friend's pained expression.

"When I think of the comfort my mother might have received from the Church all those years," said Tamar, "with her parents' deaths, and my father's, and everything else she went through." Tamar turned away and gazed out the window once more. Her shoulders stiffened, and she gave another small shudder. "I'll never forgive the Church, Elaine."

✠ ✠ ✠

A shipping carton bearing the chancery mailing label sat on the floor beside Father Karl's large, roll-top desk. The priest knew what it contained: a thousand mail forms, each perforated into three parts and pre-addressed so that, when separated and filled out by St. Mary's parishioners, the cards could be posted directly to the state's two U.S. senators and the representative serving this district.

The forms were part of a nationwide campaign to blitz Congress with the objections of Catholic citizens to the federal government's encouragement of abortion. They were to be distributed at Masses in every Catholic Church this weekend. And at last week's vicariate meeting, the bishop had called upon his priests to push the program as strongly as possible in their homilies.

Afterward, His Excellency had taken Father Karl aside, noting the bad timing of the program, given the unfortunate incident at St. Mary's. He would certainly understand, he said, if Father Karl felt in any way uneasy about raising the subject of abortion right now. Distribution of St. Mary's forms could be delayed, if Father chose, or done in a more understated way.

Father Karl did, in fact, find the whole thing somewhat distasteful. Much as he despised abortion, he never felt comfortable when the Church involved itself directly in the political process. He saw such efforts as squandering precious moral capital, reducing the Church to little more than a lobbying group. It brought back unpleasant images of the sixties–radical priests and nuns marching in the streets protesting the Vietnam War. He had found that sight shocking then, and he recalled it with no great fondness now. God's Church was not a *faction*. It was not a *party* or a *bloc*. If it was *militant* on this earthly plain, its cause was the saving of souls. It took its stand in the human heart.

But Father Karl was realistic. He knew that the enemy didn't fight fairly. Little by little, through political pressure and shrewd legal maneuvering, the Church's influence was being circumscribed, its voice confined to an ever smaller sphere. The prevailing attitude was that uplifting ethical messages from the clergy were fine, as long as they didn't prick too sharply at society's changing view of sexual mores. In fact, ecclesiastic endorsement of social programs was actually sought after. Nothing like a sympathetic bishop or two to confer moral legitimacy on some new government initiative. But that was pretty much that, when it came to how much involvement in policy making the Church would be permitted.

Non-political as he was, Father Karl could see the tragic consequences of removing Christian influence from public life. So if asking his parishioners to fill out postcards would help, if this was what the Catholic leadership thought was needed, then he would be a good soldier. Father Karl would do his duty. But he wouldn't *like* it.

The priest took a small utility knife from the center drawer of his desk, pushed out the retractable blade, and slit the top of the shipping carton, then reached inside for one of the three-part forms. The message to the members of Congress was simple and direct: the signer objected to the use of tax money for abortion and opposed any legislation to authorize such funding. The wording was terse, polite and respectful, and the implied threat to the member's reelection prospects was clear. Good, traditional politics.

Father Karl picked up the heavy carton and carried it with difficulty out into the small yard between the rectory and the church. Alan was crossing the street from the courthouse square, when he noticed the old priest struggling under the weight of the box.

"Father," he called out. "Let me help you with that." He caught up with Father Karl and took the carton from him.

"Oh, thank you, Alan," said the priest. "I was taking it to the sacristy."

"Heavy, isn't it?"

"Indeed. Here. Let me get the door." He unlocked the side door into the church and held it open, as Alan carried the box inside. They made their way across the dark interior, up the steps of the sanctuary and into the sacristy, where Alan set the carton on a small table.

"Much appreciated, Alan. Thank you."

"No problem, Father."

"By the way, Alan."

Alan stopped in the sacristy doorway. "Yes, Father."

"Have you selected the music for this week?"

"Pretty much. Is there something special you'd like?"

"I, uh... I have been asked by the bishop to deliver a special message. About...abortion."

Alan immediately thought of the dead baby.

"This is a difficult time for...the parish," Father Karl went on. "But I suppose the issue has to be addressed. That box contains postcards which will be given out to the congregation. Everyone will sign them, and then the cards will be sent to Washington. I'm planning some special remarks to emphasize the importance of this...project. I thought perhaps you might have an appropriate song. Something you could sing after I've finished my message. While the cards are being distributed."

Alan had heard numerous songs about abortion. They were all heartfelt pleas from unborn infants, or expressions of joy from children who had been allowed to live, or celebrations of life from mothers who had decided to face their fears and give birth. They were all atrocious, and Alan hated bad music.

"I'm not sure I know anything that would quite cover a thing like this," he said uneasily. "I mean...abortion songs...well–"

"Abortion songs?" Father Karl held up his hands. "No no no. That's definitely not what I had in mind. No abortion songs. Something about courage. Something about carrying on in the face of adversity. Turning to God for strength. Faith, Alan, faith. Lord help us–no abortion songs."

Alan was relieved. "Fine, Father," he said. "I'll come up with something suitable." Just then, Alan had a thought. "Ah, Father... I've wondered... Well, I'm sure you're aware of this proposal about vouchers. Providing tax money for students in private schools? I'd be interested to know your opinion on the issue."

As unlikely as it was that Holy Innocents would ever be reopened, Alan figured he'd take an opportunity to do a little probing. Just in case.

Father Karl looked at him. "Vouchers? Yes." He shook his head. "Dreadful idea. I have experience in Catholic education, you know. And I can tell you that the more dependent a private school becomes on public funds, the more it becomes like a public school. It's a great temptation, all that money. A great temptation. And unfortunately, the Church succumbs to such temptations."

The priest rubbed the side of his face thoughtfully. "I realize that church schools are subsidized by government in different parts of the world. In fact, it's a long-standing tradition in some countries. And perhaps, where there are well-established principles of separation, then it can work. Everyone understands which areas of concern fall within the civil sphere and which fall within the purview of the Church. But in this country there are too many strings attached to that money, Alan. Government mandates, restrictions, targets. It doesn't take long before a school starts to lose its character–its *soul*–the very qualities that set it apart, that made people want to send their children there in the first place. Dreadful idea, vouchers."

Alan found Father Karl's view intriguing. "It's funny you should see it that way, Father," he said. "I've always understood we have separation of church and state in America."

The priest smiled sadly. "We used to, Alan. And it was a great blessing to the Church. It was, in fact, what made Christianity thrive in this country in ways it has thrived nowhere else. But those days are gone."

He shook his head slowly, and his expression turned to stone. Alan realized he had tapped into a subject that weighed heavily on this old Catholic school master.

"The great lie of our time, Alan, is that the Church wants to run the country and dictate morality to everyone. That's the primary complaint about our stance against abortion. But the truth is it's the *government* that wants to run the *Church*. That's why we must keep away from those vouchers, Alan."

✠ ✠ ✠

Kyle Warner was finished with his evening news roundup, and Margaret Mary Benning was on the air in studio two with her nightly "Back Yard Trading Post." Kyle gathered up his news sheets, as she read the description of a John Deere garden tractor being offered, complete with snow plow blade and utility trailer cart, three years old, seven hundred dollars or best offer. Not a bad price, Kyle thought, and toyed with the idea of making a bid. The phone rang and he picked it up.

"WNT news line."

"How come nobody in this town reports any God-damned news?" The voice was oddly accented.

"Can I help you?" Kyle asked.

"Nobody tells the God-damned truth."

"I'm afraid I don't understand. Are you calling in a news tip?"

"If you had any God-damned reporters who weren't afraid of offending the God-damned Catholics, I wouldn't have to call in a news tip."

Kyle reached for a pad and pencil. "What are you referring to, sir? Has something happened?"

"Yes, something has happened, and I want to know why you haven't reported it? I want to know why it wasn't in the paper either?" The accent was not only odd but inconsistent. Kyle wondered if the caller was trying to disguise his voice.

"Well, what's happened? Give me some information, and I'll look into it."

"The campaign has begun. The good Christians in this town are letting the pope know we won't stand for the Anti-Christ in our midst."

"How are they doing that?"

"Ask the God-damned police."

"Look, if you'll give me some idea of what happened–"

"We will stand for no more papist abominations!" the voice thundered

dramatically. Kyle had to hold the phone away from his ear. *"No more papist abominations!"* And the caller hung up.

Kyle set down the phone and rubbed his forehead. What was all *that*? Papist abominations? Was this for real? That accent. It must have been a gag. But with the dead baby incident still fresh in everyone's minds, it was an especially *sick* gag. It was kids, Kyle thought. It had to be. Even so, this was hardly what the town needed right now. Stir the sectarian pot. Great.

He picked up the phone and dialed. A woman answered. "Hi, Charlotte," Kyle said. "This is Kyle Warner. I'm probably interrupting dinner. Sorry for that. Could I speak to Marty, please?"

"Certainly, Kyle. Just a moment."

Margaret Mary was reading an announcement about a male beagle available for stud: tri-colored, AKC-registered, pick of the litter in lieu of fee. Kyle turned down the volume on the studio monitor when Marty Casten came on the line.

"Hello, Kyle. Do I have a problem?" The high school principal liked to keep ahead of trouble. Since he knew that Kyle was so good at staying on top of things around the county, he had a standing request that he be alerted if one of his charges should be led into mischief by youthful exuberance. In return, he made sure WNT got the jump on the *Daily Herald* whenever anything was going to happen in the school district. Even in a small town, competition between the media was a fact of life.

"I just got a very strange call, Marty. I think it might have been one of your kids." Kyle recounted the message.

Marty was puzzled. "The police haven't contacted me," he said. "And I just looked through the paper before dinner. I didn't see anything about Catholics having trouble in town. Certainly nothing about St. Mary's."

"Maybe the whole thing's just a crank call," Kyle said. "Radio stations get them. But let me know if you hear anything around the school."

"I will, Kyle." He gave a little snorting laugh on the other end of the phone. "Actually, I almost called you the other week, when they found the baby. I was afraid that one of my goons might have been behind it. But then I figured it wasn't likely. Not that they aren't out knocking up their dimwitted girlfriends every other weekend. They probably know how to perform abortions themselves. Algebra's a mystery, but believe me, sex education they've got down pat. The thing is, they aren't aware enough to know that the Catholic Church is against abortion, so it couldn't have been one of mine. This isn't the protest generation."

"I guess you're right, Marty."

"Well, thanks for calling, Kyle. I appreciate it."

Kyle sat staring at the phone for a few minutes. Should he check with the police? His newsman's disposition told him he shouldn't let a lead go unpursued. But if this was just a crank call, why risk setting something in motion that could possibly cause a lot of unnecessary hurt in the community? He touched the receiver, not quite gripping it. Then he picked it up and called Pastor Matt.

Chapter 9

Alan didn't have an office, he had a two-door, brown metal cabinet in a classroom that also contained an old, upright piano, long past the possibility of staying in tune. It was all he needed, really–someplace to store the song books and choral arrangements used throughout the year. He commandeered Rosemarie's office whenever there was business to be transacted or official phone calls to be made.

Today, he had waited for her mid-morning break to use the phone. He had even sprung for a box of bran-raisin muffins–a favorite of everyone on the pastoral staff–if she would walk down to the co-op organic grocery to get them. Alan wanted to bring Deacon Collinson up to date, and since he tended to pinch pennies (his earnings being somewhat less than princely), he figured he'd avoid the toll call to the chancery office by using the church's phone. Well, it *was* sort of official business, after all–though now that he thought about it, the muffins would probably set him back more than a call. In any event, it would have been cheaper if he'd been able to reach Collie yesterday, the morning of Popeye's discovery. He had placed a call while Rosemarie was at the post office, but the chancery receptionist had said that Deacon Collinson was out of town on business for the bishop.

Collie came on the line, and Alan gave him a quick report of the incident in the grotto.

"Father Karl still doesn't know about it?" Collie asked.

"I've seen him a couple of times since then, and he doesn't seem to be aware."

"You think Chief Zubeck will be able to keep it quiet?"

"There's been nothing in the news. But then it's not exactly an assassination attempt on the pope. How much interest could there be?"

"You weren't raised Catholic, Alan. You may not appreciate how deeply offended some people could be at a thing like this. The idea of associating the Holy Mother with condoms–that's a volatile combination of symbols. Granted this is probably a teenage prank. But we're talking about a small town where sectarian feelings can run high. We don't want the Knights of Columbus storming the First Baptist church."

Alan wanted to see how Collie would react to the idea that someone from the public schools might be behind the baby-dumping incident. Ever since he had voiced his thought to Chief Zubeck, it had come to seem less and less likely. And after talking with Father Karl, Alan was convinced that Holy Innocents wasn't going to be reopened, at least not under the current pastor. Still, at this point, it was the closest thing he had to a theory, and as Zubeck had said, a wild idea was better than no idea. To Alan's surprise, Collie didn't find it as absurd as it might have seemed.

"I've been working on the voucher issue with the governor's office," said the bishop's assistant. "I've had a chance to observe these union people hustling the legislature, and you wouldn't believe the depth of animosity some of them show toward the Church. This isn't necessarily good old *Joe Pedagog* up the block, who teaches in the neighborhood elementary and coaches Little League. These people are the *vanguard*, Alan, the 'establishment' component of the 'New Age.' They may not be into crystals and pyramids, but very clear lines have been drawn regarding anything that has to do with traditional Christianity. '*Come zee revolution*,' the Church will have to *know its place*. And believe me, that influence reaches all the way down. The big movers and shakers have their compatriots in the local schools. Even in towns like yours, the lines are long."

"I guess I'm pretty naive about the schools these days," Alan said.

"Schools have changed since we were in them," said the deacon. "Today it's all money and politics."

"Maybe so. But I can't help feeling a little nuts making the leap from vouchers to dead babies."

"Nothing is impossible."

"But Collie, the obvious explanation seems like the best one: a protest against the Church's stand on abortion."

"Maybe. Maybe not."

"Feelings run pretty hot on the abortion issue," said Alan, "although, to tell you the truth, I've never really understood why people who are for abortion make such a big deal out of it. I mean I'm as sympathetic as anybody toward girls who get pregnant out of wedlock, especially when there's rape or incest involved. And of course, the question of birth defects is a very tough one. Hell, I can even buy the argument that women should have control over their own bodies. But it seems like pro-choice people are obsessed. It's *everything* to them. Whenever somebody's put up for the Supreme Court, they get grilled on the question. Every politician has to declare himself on one side or the other. Why is abortion so all-important?"

The deacon was reflective for a moment. "You raise an interesting question," he said at last. "It's one the Church has to grapple with on many levels. I believe it has to do with the modern concept of equality."

"How do you mean?"

"From a certain point of view, abortion is...the *sine qua non* of women's equality."

"I'm afraid my Latin isn't what it should be, Collie."

"*Sine qua non*: 'without which nothing.' The indispensable element which, if you take it away, everything else collapses. You see, women have achieved equality–more or less–in just about every aspect of life. They do jobs which used to be done by men exclusively. They're entitled by law to the same pay men receive when they perform the same kind of work. But no matter how equal the law makes them, women live with one profound reality in their lives which men don't face. They get pregnant. That takes them out of the labor market, often for many years. Certainly, it handicaps them in their ability to compete with men in any number of ways. Now I, personally, don't believe that carrying, bearing and raising children makes women less equal. To me, women possess a unique, God-given capability. It's a blessing. But then, I'm looking at it as a man. Those who hold to a certain notion of equality see abortion as the great *leveler*. Restrict abortion, and women will never be completely equal with men."

"And that's why it's considered so essential."

"Well, that's my take on it."

Something had been nagging Alan in the back of his brain since his midnight conversation with Chief Zubeck. It was the remark that Father Karl's background included a lot of *interesting twists*. "Collie," he said, "is there anything else about Father Karl–something personal, perhaps–that might help me in my poking around?"

There was the slightest pause before Collie responded: "What makes you ask?"

Rosemarie was out in the hallway. She was talking to someone. There was a man's voice as well.

"Damn! I'm not alone anymore, Collie. I'll have to check in with you next week."

"Look, Alan," the deacon said, "do me a favor, will you? The bishop would like to know how Father Karl holds up through his homily this weekend. There's a special project on abortion."

"Yes, I know about the postcards."

"Maybe you could figure out a way to record his talk?"

"I'll see what I can do."

"Appreciate it, Alan."

"See you, Collie." He hung up the phone as Rosemarie walked into the office, followed by Kyle Warner and a little boy.

"They were out of muffins," Rosemarie said, "so I got some of their whole wheat, honey-glazed doughnuts. Alan, you know Kyle, don't you?"

"Sure." Alan stood up and offered his hand to Kyle, waving with the other one to the boy. "Hi, Kevin."

The child, a little towhead not quite four, waved a half-eaten doughnut in response.

"Your band played for our remote," said Kyle, "when we broadcast live from River Park last summer."

"That's right." Why was the radio man here at this particular time? "What can we do for you?" Alan took the doughnut Rosemarie was holding out to him. "Care for one of these, Kyle? They're very good."

"Oh, I've had them. They *are* excellent. But no, thank you. My wife has me on this diet. And there's no sneaking anything past her."

"Whole wheat," said Rosemarie.

Kyle held up his hand. "They got the fiber in. Now if they could just get the calories out. Thanks anyway." He smiled at the boy, the major portion of whose face was covered with sticky crumbs. "What's his job around here?"

"Oh, this is my helper, Kevin," said Rosemarie. She took a tissue from the box on her desk and wiped the little face. "My daughter's youngest. He comes to the office two mornings a week while his mother takes classes at the college, and he helps me keep things tidy. Don't you, Kevin."

Kevin nodded his head. "I clean up da tash."

"Well, that's very helpful," said Kyle.

"*Trash*, Dear," said Rosemarie.

"Yeah. Tash." He went off to play with some farm toys in the opposite corner of the room.

Kyle chuckled. "Why I stopped by–" he said, "well, I was wondering how things are going around here? It's almost two weeks now, since the baby was found. I believe it was you who found him, isn't that so, Alan?"

"Well, Pat Foley, actually. But I was the one who first noticed the smell in the bathroom."

Rosemarie glanced at Kevin. She wasn't sure about such disturbing subject matter within range of little ears. But he seemed to be oblivious to everything except his toys. There were several quite sophisticated miniatures–the indulgences of a proud and generous grandfather–including a large semi marked "Tractor Supply Company," plus a quite detailed model of an antique International Harvester.

"I didn't try to do an interview with anybody at the time," Kyle said. "It all seemed so shocking, and Chief Zubeck gave me the facts I needed for my report."

"I appreciate your consideration," Alan said. "Everyone around here was pretty upset."

"I don't believe in sensationalizing things. But I've wondered how it's been going since. Has everything settled down?"

Alan had set his doughnut on a paper napkin, and was getting some coffee from Rosemarie's coffeemaker. "Would you like a cup?" he asked Kyle. "Rosemarie makes it half decaf."

"Oh, half leaded-half unleaded," Kyle said. "*That* I'll take. Just black, thanks."

Alan handed him the cup, then poured one for Rosemarie and one for himself.

"So anyway," Kyle continued, "nothing has happened around here since the incident, has it?"

Alan's grip tightened slightly on the handle of the coffee pot.

"We've just finished our blood drive," Rosemarie said perkily. "I understand we hold the record in the county for the amount of blood collected."

"Oh yes. We promoted the drive on the air. But I haven't gotten any figures on the results." Kyle took out a pad and pen. "What's the name of the young lady who was running it?"

"Jessica MacNair," said Alan.

"You can reach her at the hospital," Rosemary added. "Jessie will give you the number of pints collected. We were well over last year's total, and St. Mary's was top *then*."

Kyle wrote down Jessie's name. "Thanks for that information. I was thinking, though–I mean, I was wondering if anything has happened related to the baby incident. I take it there've been no new developments."

Alan was looking deeply into his coffee cup, stirring in a spoonful of sugar. "Have the police made any progress in their investigation?"

"Doesn't appear so," said Kyle.

"Well, everything's been quiet here," said Rosemarie. "And thank the Lord for that. We didn't know what to expect, after that dreadful business. The poor child."

"Well, I'm glad to hear it." Kyle was watching Alan, whose eyes were still examining his coffee. "I love this town," said the reporter. And it may seem funny for a newsman to say, but I prefer not having too many shocking things to report. Leave that stuff for the big cities."

Alan picked up his doughnut abruptly. "Thanks for getting these, Rosie," he said. "Nice seeing you, Kyle. I'd better get back to work." He headed out of Rosemarie's office and down the hall.

"Oh Alan," Rosemarie called after, "I've got your change."

Alan didn't come back for it. Rosemarie shrugged and set the coins on her desk. Kyle sipped his coffee. The newsman had a feeling. Just a sort of feeling.

✠ ✠ ✠

"I think the call was real," Kyle said out the van window. "Something has happened at St. Mary's–I'd bet on it–although I suspect not everybody over there knows."

Pastor Matt stood in the Bible Fellowship parking lot, a stack of books under one arm and the other hand on the roof of the WNT news van. "Are you going to ask the police?"

"It could be a legitimate story."

"Well, that's up to you, Kyle," Matt said thoughtfully. "You have to follow the ethical precepts of your profession. I know you care about the community. I'm sure you'll give this prayerful reflection and do what's right."

"Well, I can't do anything now," Kyle said, starting up his engine. "I have to go back to the station and get ready for my noon broadcast, and I've got something to cover at the hospital this afternoon."

The two men shook hands through the window, then Kyle drove off. Matt watched after, as the van disappeared down the road. The face of Father Karl came into his mind.

✠ ✠ ✠

Merve Conway didn't like the smell of this. Not one bit. He did his best to keep the hospital as far away from politics as possible. Sure, he knew how to massage the city council or the building inspector or the health department when necessary. The speed with which plans for the new wing were moving toward approval was proof of his skill at government relations. But that was just business. When it came to anything that had an ideological cast–anything that could possibly enmesh his institution in needless controversy–the hospital administrator was silent as a sphinx and twice as immovable. So how the hell did he let himself get sucked into this?

It was Tamar, of course. Lovely, charming Tamar, the director of the Interfaith Counselling Center. Merve had been quite taken with Tamar–impressed with her competence in bringing the Center back from the brink of financial chaos, and equally impressed with her feminine assets. He had suggested her for membership on the hospital board, the wisdom of which he was now beginning to question.

Tamar had come to him and asked if the Women's Rights Action Coalition might use the hospital's education room for a press conference. Since the story of the dead baby had been picked up on the wire, newspaper editorial pages around the state were being peppered with letters to the editor accusing WRAC of somehow being behind the dreadful affair. Tamar had been contacted by WRAC about the possibility of staging a media event in town to give the leader of the state chapter a chance to deny the accusations right where the incident had taken place.

Tamar was as reluctant as Merve Conway to get involved, having her own concerns about avoiding controversy. She certainly couldn't do anything that would link the Interfaith Counselling Center to an organization as politically charged as the Women's Rights Action Coalition. But she had received timely and much-needed encouragement from some members of the group after her marriage had collapsed. On top of that, the state chapter had provided helpful contacts in several of her cases. So Tamar couldn't really say no. She pondered how life is filled with irony. What goes around comes around.

Her tactic was to pass the ball to Merve. And what could he do? She *was* a board member, after all, and a very persuasive one. He sought cover behind the rationale that a hospital must serve its community, and perhaps this effort at public information would help to dispel some of the suspicions which had accumulated since the sad incident of the baby. To aid in the *healing* process. It was flimsy, but it would have to suffice.

Standing by a vending machine in the far corner, Merve took some comfort in the fact that the only media representatives in attendance were Kyle Warner from WNT, Claire Shelby from the *Daily Herald* (along with fat Charlie Dutton, the *Herald's* photographer), and a guy from the wire service whom Merve didn't know. The women from WRAC hardly shared that comfort. They hadn't realized that the metro papers didn't maintain stringers here, and even the controversial status of their organization couldn't induce the media in the capital or the state's major urban centers to send staff all the way out to the valley. Such a commitment of resources simply wasn't justified in any but the most extreme breaking-news situations. The city papers and the broadcast stations would make do with a press release or whatever came over the wire. What a disappointment.

State Director Lorraine Turnage surveyed the crowd–if, indeed, it could be called that–taking in the sparse media contingent and the small knot of curiosity seekers, mostly hospital staff. She shook her head dejectedly and whispered something to her assistant. Obviously, this had been a tactical error. They should have held the conference at the press club up in the capital. Now it would probably be necessary to prepare some kind of followup and walk the story around to all the media outlets. Certainly they would have to do more than just send out their own letters to the editor.

Tamar sat in the far corner of the room, which was used mainly for health education programs such as CPR training and Lamaze childbirth classes. She was trying to be as inconspicuous as she could be, which wasn't all that easy, given the poor attendance. She had her eye on the exit and a plan to make a quick departure, in case any of the news people should head in her direction in search of a comment on the WRAC statement.

Lorraine Turnage had waited as long as practical for more press to show. She was now resigned to the fact that this was the best she could expect. Kyle had placed a microphone on the table at the front, and Lorraine sat down behind it. Fat Charlie Dutton blasted off a shot, which took her unexpectedly. She looked in the direction of the flash and gave Dutton a friendly but purposeful expression. He centered her distinctive face in his viewfinder and snapped a couple more frames. Lorraine wasn't a beautiful woman, but she was very well put together. In her mid-forties, her face was strongly proportioned and serious. She used minimal makeup, but used it well. And her short hairstyle, streaked with grey, was businesslike and seemed perfectly complemented by a sharply tailored, pale gray suit and dark silk blouse.

"Good afternoon," Lorraine said. "Thank you for giving our organization the opportunity to address what has become an awkward and divisive issue." She was reading from a prepared statement. Tamar had asked her to skip any specific expressions of gratitude to the hospital or the Interfaith Counselling Center.

"Let me first say that the Women's Rights Action Coalition appreciates the distress which has been felt by the members of your local Catholic parish–St. Mary's, I believe–over the unfortunate incident of the fetus. Whatever was intended by placing this object in the church, the gesture was wholly inappropriate and certainly would have been disturbing to anyone, regardless of their views on choice and women's rights."

Kyle noted that Lorraine had said the "object" was placed in the church. Was she unaware that it had been left in the school? Of course, she had also described the object as a "fetus." Most people here in town felt comfortable calling it "the baby."

"In the past weeks," Lorraine continued, "there have been several allegations about the possibility that the Women's Rights Action Coalition was involved in this incident. I wish to state, *categorically*, that WRAC has absolutely no connection with this incident, that none of our chapters or members were involved, and that we, as an organization, deplore such a tasteless and insensitive act, even if it was intended as a defense of the constitutional right to abortion."

Tasteless and insensitive, thought Kyle. He would have described the incident in somewhat stronger terms than *tasteless and insensitive*. But he was laboring to set aside his own views on abortion. Much as he tried, Kyle had never quite cultivated the detachment for which journalists strive–or like to believe they strive–as a professional ideal. His opinions wouldn't show in the report he was planning to do on the WRAC statement. He would be careful about that. But right now, he was feeling what he was feeling.

Claire Shelby, on the other hand, was feeling a certain sympathy for the position in which Lorraine Turnage found herself, having to fend off all the accusations which had descended on WRAC–many quite vitriolic. The *Daily Herald* reporter was no active champion of abortion rights, and she too strove for the neutrality her profession prized. But she was a woman, and moreover a woman with ambitions to succeed in a competitive field that had a tradition of being especially hard on its feminine practitioners. Women had made a place for themselves in the nation's news rooms. Some had risen to positions of considerable power. But the stresses unique to the female half of humanity–the conflicts between family and career–made abortion an option which women like Claire were not prepared to rule out. For all its abrasive tactics, WRAC, an organization that fought hard for women's opportunities, was worthy of a respectful hearing.

Lorraine went on: "We want the person or persons responsible to know that we too are vigorous and single minded in defending abortion rights. The principle of choice is well established, and the courts of this country have been consistent in defining and supporting it, even in the face of well-organized efforts to undermine this ample structure of law and precedent. And make no mistake, those efforts are intense, they are well funded, and they are increasing. We too stand on the side of right. We too stand on the side of women. And we appreciate the feelings of frustration and powerlessness which might prompt someone to lash out in such a visible and impassioned way as the incident which took place here. But this is clearly the wrong way. We will not convince people of the rightness of our cause by assaulting their sensibilities. Tastelessness and insensitivity–"

Tastelessness and insensitivity again, thought Kyle.

"–will not win out against a powerful opposition intent on stripping women of their most basic and fundamental rights: the right to control their own bodies, the right to determine their own destinies, the right to live their own lives. If there are any individuals or groups planning other demonstrations along these lines, we urge them in the strongest possible terms to abandon those plans. Thank you very much."

That was the end of Lorraine's prepared statement. "I will be happy to take your questions," she said.

Claire hopped right in. "Ms. Turnage, do you discern any pattern in the criticism which WRAC has received in the past couple of weeks? Do you believe the attacks have been coordinated?"

Lorraine placed the statement on the table and folded her hands over it. "We have no direct evidence that there is any such effort," she said maintaining a thoughtful expression for the benefit of Dutton's camera, "but certainly the tone–and much of the language used–could suggest some...shall we say...*communication* between different sources. This would certainly not be the first time an organized campaign was made to look like a spontaneous public outcry. Of course, many of the expressions which have been used are pretty standard rhetoric among the anti-abortion rights faction. What troubles me is the viciousness of these charges. In the press materials you've received you'll find copies of some of the letters-to-the-editor which have run in newspapers around the state. I believe you'll agree that they're quite extreme."

The wire service correspondent, whose name was Chad Thurlow, looked up from the notes he was taking. "Lorraine, do you have any thoughts on who might have left the fetus at St. Mary's?"

"We have absolutely no information about that, Chad."

Thurlow worked out of the capital bureau. He and Lorraine came into contact with each other frequently.

"Could you speculate for us?"

"I'd prefer not to. And by the way, I must thank you for coming down from the capital, Chad. I appreciate your recognition of a newsworthy event." It never hurt to stroke a reporter's ego.

Thurlow touched the end of his pencil to his forehead in response. "I cover a lot of the out-state events," he said, looking professional.

"Ms. Turnage," Kyle said, "would you say that such use of a dead child's remains would suggest the working of a disturbed mind?"

Lorraine felt the edge on Kyle's question. She'd dealt with the press long enough to recognize hostility when she heard it, even when it was couched in the most polite of terms. She was not going to be pushed into a semantic corner by the phrase "dead child's remains."

"I think," she said, choosing her words tactically, "that we should be careful in trying to evaluate motives and impulses. What might seem like irrational acts can sometimes look entirely rational–even *appropriate*–to someone whose rights are being threatened. Never forget that there has been a concerted and prolonged effort to chip away at the constitutional right to abortion in every manner. The controversy that's been manufactured over this so-called 'partial-birth' procedure is only one example. Abortion rights are being assaulted on all fronts. In Congress, in the courts, on the streets. This is the reality women face today. We shouldn't be surprised to see people react in dramatic ways when their freedoms are in jeopardy."

Kyle started to speak again, but then decided not to. Lorraine was coming from a perspective–a world view, really–which was very different from his own. He told himself that, as a journalist, it wasn't his place to be argumentative.

For her part, Lorraine wanted to give this small-town reporter something to think about. "You know, it's easy for some people to be condemnatory about abortion," Lorraine continued, trying not to sound defensive, "especially if they have never had to deal with the consequences of an unwanted pregnancy. But we're talking about something that can ruin a woman's life. When you've actually had to face the problem–when it's been your daughter or your friend–your views on abortion can change."

Claire wanted to take full advantage of this opportunity to delve into an issue of genuine national scope–rare on her local news beat–and asked how Lorraine thought the much-discussed "morning-after pill" would affect the abortion debate. That set the conversation off in a new direction. Some of the onlookers began to lose interest and started chatting quietly among themselves.

Tamar glanced around and observed that several more hospital people had come in while Lorraine was talking to the press. One of them was Jessie. She had taken a seat just behind the news folks and was one of the few people in the room still paying attention to Lorraine's remarks. Tamar noticed that Merve Conway was still looking uncomfortable–perhaps even more so with the increased attendance, though there still weren't very many people present. She felt bad about pressuring him into this, but there was nothing she could have done.

The discussion had pretty much run its course, Lorraine bringing the proceedings to a close with a reprise of her point about how abortion rights continued to be under attack. Tamar was pleased that the reporters packed up and left without seeking comments from anyone in the audience, though Kyle had stopped briefly to ask Jessie for the final count on the blood collection. Tamar walked over to where the press people had been seated, as Lorraine came around the table to thank her for her help.

"I wish the turnout had been better," Tamar said.

"Don't worry about it." Lorraine was being philosophical. "I'm grateful for your help, Tam. I should have known we'd do better up in the city. Goes to show you what the press considers important. We'll just have to do a little more legwork. But at least we showed everyone we weren't afraid to come down here and tell our story right where the trouble started."

"People in town have been quite upset," said Tamar. "I hope hearing your side of things in the local media helps to calm the waters."

"It may do some good." Lorraine checked her watch. "Oh my, look at the time. We've got to get back. She held out her hand to Tamar. "Thank you again, Tam." And she smiled warmly. "You know, with all the fuss it's caused, I must admit that little bit of tissue has helped to keep the focus on abortion rights. Staying in the news is our ongoing challenge. The public has a very short attention span."

"I suppose so," said Tamar.

Lorraine and her assistants departed, and Tamar went to say a few soothing words to Merve Conway. When he was gone, she noticed that Jessie was still in the room. She was standing alone by the front table, wearing an expression Tamar couldn't read.

"What did you think, Jess?"

Jessie shook her head. "I think I found that woman very offensive," she said. "Her and her 'little bit of tissue.'"

✠ ✠ ✠

Jessie reached for the door handle, as Alan tried to hold both his guitar case and gig bag in one hand. "Here, let me get that," she said, smiling at his hobbled attempt at gallantry. She had noted that Alan opened doors for her and did other gentlemanly things when they had gone for coffee and doughnuts. It was kind of nice.

"Oh. Thanks," he said. "I am a little encumbered."

They found themselves in the hustle and bustle of Minnie's kitchen. A tall, black chef—one of Aunt Min's many relations—nodded at Alan. "Hello there, country boy," he called.

"Hello, Antoine," Alan replied.

"And who is this lovely lady?"

"Jessie, this is Chef Antoine. Antoine, this is Jessie."

"I would clasp your delicate fingers and brush them with a gentle kiss," Antoine said in his courtly manner. "But as too many hands in the pot spoil the soup, no hands on the stirring spoon burns the jambalaya."

Jessie laughed. "How do you do?"

"Charmed, I'm sure."

The kitchen help were scurrying up and down the aisles of the cluttered room, carrying cases of food, filling large pots with the pungent ingredients for Minnie's special cajun soups and sauces. Waitresses were folding napkins, filling salt and pepper shakers, and putting packets of sugar and artificial sweetener into their holders. Alan exchanged greetings with several people, as he and Jessie made their way through the busy kitchen and out past the bar into the main room.

Jack Compton was sitting on the edge of the stage adjusting the reed on his saxophone. Art Spiecer's daughter, Nicole, was standing off in a corner running over "The Sweetest Thing," without accompaniment. She would close the second set. Her father would drive her home afterward, during the break.

Alan set his guitar case down next to a table by the side of the stage, just off the dance floor. Jessie looked around the room, taking in all the activity–the typical preliminaries of a Friday night at Minnie's Roadhouse. There were a few early arrivals at the bar–among whom was Carlton Fitch, once more in Satan's grasp–and a middle-aged couple, who had turned in off the highway and looked very travel-weary, being seated at a table in the back by Lorna, a pretty black girl who handled the register Thursday, Friday and Saturday nights.

Alan opened his guitar case and took out a pristine, '62 Gibson Les Paul. "What a beautiful guitar," said Jessie. She had only seen Alan playing his Martin D-28 acoustic in church.

"This is my baby," he said, with that singular look of pride a musician gets when showing off a favorite instrument. "I usually bring my old Guild out here. But I figured tonight was...special." He closed the case and turned it up on edge. There was a small opening under the stage, and Alan pushed the case inside with his foot. Then he pulled a chair out from the table, put his foot up, and placed the guitar on his knee. He ran up and down a couple of scales, fast and flashy, showing off. He couldn't help himself.

"You're a very good guitarist," said Jessie, sitting down at the table. "And I always enjoy your singing at mass."

"Why, thank you," he answered, not quite blasé enough.

Jessie was smiling. Alan looked at her and was struck again by her attractiveness. She was out of uniform tonight, of course, wearing a soft, casual dress, and he noticed how full-breasted she was. Her long, chestnut hair was hanging loosely around her shoulders, and it shimmered where a stray shaft of light from a fresnel spotlight that wasn't focused quite on the stage nicked the back of her head.

In the middle of his observations, a familiar voice came from behind. "Hello, Alan." It was Aunt Min. "And who do we have with us tonight?"

Alan turned around. "Oh, hi, Min. Do you know Jessie, from church?"

"Why I don't know that I do," said the stout black woman, extending her hand. "You go to St. Mary's?"

Jessie rose and shook Aunt Min's hand. "Yes I do."

"Maybe you've seen her in uniform," Alan said. "Jessie is a nurse."

"Now, I have seen a pretty nurse at Mass, come to think of it," said Aunt Min. "But this is your first time out here at my place, isn't it, Honey?"

"Yes, it is. Alan invited me to come hear his band."

"And I'm certainly glad he did. What'd you say this lovely young lady's name is, Alan?"

Alan realized that formal introductions were in order and he hadn't actually made any. "Oh, yes...I'm sorry. Minerva Johnson, this is Jessica MacNair."

"We have to keep on top of these boys about the social graces," Aunt Min joked. "But you just call me Min or Minnie or Aunt Min–whatever you like, Honey."

Art Spiecer called to Alan. He wanted to talk about the intro to Nicole's song. Alan excused himself and went up on the stage, leaving Aunt Min inquiring about Jessie's experience with Cajun food. Jessie had to admit she wasn't all that familiar with southern cooking, but that she expected Cajun recipes could be rather spicey. Aunt Min suggested the blackened red fish with rice and beans as a basic introduction to the genre. She promised to have Antoine go easy on the spices, then hurried off to check on preparations in the kitchen, calling back that she'd return to check on Jessie a little later. Jessie thanked her for her kindness.

Alan saw that Jessie was alone at the table. He gestured to one of the waitresses to go over and ask if she'd like a drink. The girl nodded "Okay." Then he smiled at Jessie, mouthed "Order what you want," and reached for the cord draped over his amplifier. He plugged in the Les Paul and turned on the amp. There was a soft crashing sound, as the equipment sprang to life. The other musicians were on stage now, starting to tune up.

Alan had adjusted the choral effect on his amp, when he turned around and noticed Jessie chatting pleasantly with Aunt Min's nephew. Alan chuckled to himself. Good old Howie, doing his host thing. That lad was never shy about introducing himself to pretty women. Just then, Rick Renshaw was on the kick drum for the warm-up on "Achy Breaky Heart."

✠ ✠ ✠

All the way home, Jessie seemed vaguely uncomfortable. She was chattering brightly about how good Alan's band had been and how she had never expected to like Cajun food so much but it was really delicious. Actually, she was chattering too brightly, and Alan realized it. Not that he was all that serene himself, his social life having been as spare as it was since Sheila. He didn't feel on very firm footing out with a woman, especially one as desirable as Jessie. What were her expectations? What were his own? He knew he was feeling the power of her presence, and there was no question it was having its effect on him. Was there any chance this evening might end in something physical? Should he even hope for that? He *was* supposed to be a good Catholic now.

Alan glanced over at Jessie and noticed that her hand was gripping the handle of the car door with such force that the skin around her knuckles was white. *Guess there's no need to worry about any moral conflicts tonight*, he thought. She had seemed to be having a good time, but now she was off by herself somewhere. She clearly wasn't with him.

Maybe she *hadn't* had a good time. Maybe the whole evening had been awful for her and she just wanted it to end as quickly as possible. Alan's insecurities were in higher gear than the car.

The old Tercel bounced over a speed bump at the entrance to the parking lot at Jessie's apartment complex. "I hate those things," he said, searching for something pointless and sociable to say. "You always know they're there, but you never slow down in time."

No response from Jessie.

Alan pulled up in front of her building and turned off the engine. He recognized the car in the next parking spot as Sister Elaine's and recalled that he'd been vaguely aware she lived in this complex. "Well..." he said hesitantly, "I hope you liked Minnie's–and the band."

Jessie looked at him. Her mouth turned up into a smile, but her eyes had their sad expression.

"Oh. It was a wonderful time, Alan," she said with something less than enthusiasm. "Thank you so much."

Alan got out of the car and walked around to open Jessie's door. He admired the shape of her leg as she stepped out, and he felt the effect of her presence again.

They walked up the path and into the hallway of the building. Jessie reached into her purse, taking out her keys, as they approached the door of her apartment.

She turned to Alan and looked up at him. For the briefest instant, her expression seemed to soften. Alan acted on an impulse and took her in his arms to kiss her goodnight.

She stiffened suddenly, pushing him back. "Please."

Alan regretted his impulse instantly. "Jessie–"

She turned away, burying her face against the door jamb.

"Jess, I'm sorry. I didn't–"

"It's all right, Alan," she said, then turned back toward him. "I'm just a no-kissing-on-the-first-date kind of girl." She tried to smile, but it was an obvious effort for her.

Alan felt like the idiot which, at this moment, he was thoroughly convinced he was.

"Thank you for taking me to Minnie's tonight," Jessie said. "It *was* fun. Really."

Alan started to say something, but there was nothing. He turned to leave.

"Alan."

He stopped and looked back around. Jessie was standing in the middle of the hallway, twisting a lock of her chestnut hair in her fingers beside her cheek.

"I'm afraid I'm...not really very good...when it comes to...this dating thing," she said. "I never have been." She paused, sighed deeply, then continued. "You're really very nice, Alan. And... Well...you don't have to call me again...if you don't want to."

Alan felt a small ache in his chest as he saw her just sort of hovering there, looking confused and desolate.

Jessie tried to smile again. "But I'd like it very much...if you would."

He smiled back, sadly. "I'll call," he said.

Chapter 10

"The Gospel of the Lord," intoned Father Karl.

"Praise to you, Lord Jesus Christ," the congregation responded. There was rustling in the pews, the sounds of children jabbering, a baby crying in the back of the church, as everyone was seated after the Gospel reading. Alan placed the Martin D-28 on his guitar stand, then sat in the small armchair off to the side by the spinet. There was a straight-back, wooden chair and a kneeler right behind the cantor's lectern. That's where Alan sat during the Old Testament reading and the Epistle, whenever he played up at the front of the church. But during the homily, he always removed himself to the side.

Father Karl closed his lectionary and stood in the pulpit, silently, gathering his energy. He was determined he would not allow himself to be shaken by the demonstration on the lawn of the courthouse across the street. Word of the postcard campaign had apparently gotten out, and some pro-choice organizations had planned to picket at the cathedral up in the capital as a show against the bishops' project. But when the story about Lorraine Turnage's press conference hit the Saturday papers, a women's-rights group associated with a Unitarian-Universalist Fellowship over in the next county decided that it might be a good idea to stage their own demonstration at St. Mary's.

Father Karl had been startled to look out an upstairs front window of the rectory that morning and see a group of women holding large, crudely-lettered signs. Not that it was much of a demonstration. There were only about a dozen people present. Still, it was all very unnerving. As the picketers marched around in a circle, shouting their women's-right-to-choose slogans across the street at the parishioners coming to Mass, Karl Muller felt a knot in his stomach and a strong sense of confirmation about his views on Church involvement in politics.

But his course was set. He would not be deterred. A deep breath helped him to focus, and he straightened his lean, angular body in the pulpit.

Alan, seated on the far side of the altar, reached down beside his chair. He pushed the *Record* and *Play* buttons together on a small cassette unit. A thin cord ran across the floor to a microphone lying against the monitor speaker under the cantor's lectern.

"There is much to contemplate in today's readings," the priest began. "I urge you to take out your Bibles during the coming week and revisit these passages." Father's eyes were turned downward to the sculpted-metal cover of the lectionary. Would they take out their Bibles? Did they ever? Simple country folk. Salt of the earth. How many of them thought about scripture as anything more than what you had to sit through to get communion and go home?

"Today, however," Father Karl continued, "I wish to speak with you...about something else." He looked at the congregation, picking out a few faces here and there. "This is a difficult time to address this subject. But in a way...it's very appropriate." How many of these people cared about hearing what he might have to tell them, whatever it happened to be? "I'm speaking, of course, about...abortion."

There was a stirring in the pews. The baby-dumping incident was still a topic of gossip and conjecture among the members of St. Mary's, and local news coverage of the Women's Rights Action Coalition press conference had reinvigorated discussion. Sister Elaine, who was the lector for this mass and was seated in the first row, directly in front of the pulpit, felt herself cringe slightly when Father said the word "abortion." She hoped her reaction hadn't been too noticeable.

"We have recently had a very shocking and sad occurrence," he said. "I, myself, am very distressed about it." How many others were distressed? For most of them, was it anything more than a matter of bizarre interest? "So, you can imagine my feelings when the bishop informed me and my brother priests about an effort being undertaken throughout the American Church."

Father Karl paused, contemplating his obligation to the bishop, then forged ahead with resolve. "This is a campaign to express to Congress the objections of

American Catholics about the ongoing encouragement of abortion by agencies of our government...in particular, to speak out most strongly against the barbaric practice of that type of late-term abortion known as *partial-birth*, which I'm sure you've all read about in the press."

There was the slightest ripple of a reaction through the room.

"This is not a petition drive. It is not an attempt to influence any specific piece of legislation. The Church is not a political organization, of course. And, God knows, no one wants to provide any more ammunition to those who would try to silence the Church by challenging its tax-exempt status for lobbying. The Church's enemies need no help in developing their strategies of attack." He thought about the demonstrators on the courthouse lawn across the street.

"Quite honestly," Father Karl admitted, "abortion was the last subject I wanted to even think about, much less prepare a homily on." Did anyone appreciate his conflict? Could anybody understand how difficult such a thing is to address? "But as I reflected upon that poor child, whose life was taken so cruelly–whose tiny body was disposed of in such a cold and cynical way–it occurred to me that here was the perfect illustration of this evil which has taken hold of our time."

Who truly grasped the evil? How many of these good Catholics had had abortions themselves or had taken part in arrangements for others? For girlfriends? For daughters? Even Alan had a personal brush with abortion in his past, though he had been spared having to confront the question head on. It was early in his marriage. A young woman in his Air Force unit, who had become friendly with Alan and Sheila, came to them in tears. She was pregnant, she said, and there was no hope of marrying the father of her child. This was in the days before service women in maternity uniforms had become a common sight on military bases, and she feared her Air Force career would be ruined. Would Alan and Sheila help her to get an abortion?

Sheila was most sympathetic, but Alan found himself torn–much to his surprise. Having children was something the two of them had spoken of only in a future tense, a far future tense. Neither was Catholic, so birth control wasn't an issue. But here was a young woman they both liked who was in desperate trouble. "We'll stand behind you, whatever you choose," Alan had told her, though there was an odd feeling nagging at him, a feeling he didn't really understand.

In the end, the woman couldn't do it. She applied for an early discharge and had the baby.

Just as he never understood the conflict he'd felt over helping someone plan for an abortion, Alan didn't understand why he felt so relieved when it didn't come to be. But he knew he was grateful that this particular cup had passed from him.

Alan looked around the room, scanning faces, gauging feelings. The congregation seemed more interested than usual. But then, the dead baby incident was so fresh. And, there was something about the way Father Karl was speaking. His phrasing. His presence. The intentness in his eyes. The posture in which he was holding himself. He was engaged, and that was different. In the months he had been at St. Mary's, the old priest had seemed so tired, so detached. His messages had reflected sound doctrine. But they were flat. Conventional. Priestly. Now, he was speaking with a purposefulness which Alan had never seen in him before.

"We don't know who did this horrid thing, right here in our own community, or what its object might have been," Father said. "We don't know where the baby was obtained or if, indeed, it was the very child of the person who left it. In this day, when the most atrocious acts have become commonplace, nothing is too outrageous or remote to consider."

Remote as it was, the idea sent a chill through most of the people in the room. But to at least one person, Father Karl's suggestion was as outrageous as a hard slap. *How dare he speculate on such a thing?* thought Sister Elaine, just to make his cheap little point about our 'decadent' modern age. What was he after, *dramatic effect*? She remembered the scripture passage: "Even if a mother could forget the child in her womb..." The passage was intended to illustrate the depth of God's love–that even if a mother *could* disregard the child she carried, God would never disregard us. The very impossibility of a mother forgetting her child makes the point. If–God forbid–the mother of that dead baby *did* have some part in leaving it, if the absurd were possible, then what overwhelming forces could have brought a woman to such an end? These were things this priest couldn't begin to imagine.

"But there is one thing we know," Father Karl continued. "Abortion does not exist in a vacuum. Taking that child's life was no isolated sin. It was merely the worst in a *sequence* of sins that began even before that life was created." He paused. "And when did the sequence begin?" The question was rhetorical. "How can we know? Did it begin with a poor moral formation, an aimless upbringing, an impious family life? Or in believing the deceptive promise that love is to be found in the uncommitted and transitory pleasures of the flesh?"

Whose poor moral formation? thought Elaine. *Whose aimless upbringing or impious family life? The woman's? Who believed the deceptive promise, and who held it out? What of the man who impregnated her? Surely, there was a man involved in the creation of that life.*

"Whatever the background to this sequence of sins," Father Karl said, "it happened because it was *able* to happen. Not just because we have come to a point where someone could *conceive* of taking a child's life or disposing of its body so disrespectfully–that's not new. The ability to conceive all manner of wrongdoing is part of our fallen nature." Another pause, and then suddenly: "*No.* We have come to a point where, in the mind of someone, this seemed *right*."

Alan noticed heads nodding in assent to Father's point.

"This was, after all, an intentional thing. Someone troubled themselves to *transport* the body of that poor child. To *find a way* into the school building. To *place* the baby where its discovery would be most ironic."

Father Karl was rising to a level of emotion that took everyone by surprise. The congregation was riveted. Even the occasional chirping of the baby in the back of the room didn't provide much distraction.

"Was this a *protest*?" the priest continued. "Was this someone's comment on the Church and its 'inflexible' resistance to 'freedom of choice?' We don't know this either. But if it *was*, then it's of no consequence." Once again, the demonstrators came to his mind. "I assure you, the Church will not be deflected from its mission. The Church is not *intimidated*."

People seated toward the front jumped as Father Karl hit the pulpit with his fist. The baby in the back started to cry.

"The salient point is this: If someone *did* choose such a revolting means of making a statement–*whatever* statement was intended–they concluded that this act was justified. Desecrating a human body in such a manner was not only conceivable but *acceptable*. And this is where we have come."

More heads were nodding in agreement. Someone actually spoke the word "Yes!" aloud. Alan looked around to see who had responded in such a spontaneous and un-Catholic way.

"I believe that the unrestricted practice of abortion itself has helped to bring us here. We have become *accustomed* to this wanton destruction. It is part of a larger pattern of exploitation and violence and degradation–in our homes, on our streets, around the world. And it is very much a part of the *cause*." Father Karl was sweeping the crowd with his eyes now. "Abortion does not exist in a *vacuum*. It is the result of sin and suffering. And the real tragedy is that it creates more sin and suffering. Abortion exists among all the expressions of human selfishness and self-deception. It exists among all the secret failings we harbor...in...our...*hearts*."

No one dared look away as the priest peered into their guilty consciences, into their unresolved feelings and uninformed opinions, into all the presumptions they worked so hard to avoid questioning. Alan was beginning to realize why the bishop held Father Karl in such high regard. There was *power* in this old man. Perhaps this was the source of his reputation as an educator.

"And in case anyone should think I hold women alone responsible, let me assure you that the mantle of blame rests as heavily on the shoulders of *men*."

Elaine's eyebrows raised slightly.

"Women do not become pregnant by themselves," Father Karl went on. "But they all too frequently face the prospect of bearing and raising and caring for and feeding and loving their children, without the help of the men who were so eagerly present at the beginning."

"Well well..." thought Elaine.

Father Karl paused, and for a moment, the expression on the old priest's face looked to Alan as one of conflict. His mouth was open, and he seemed to be deciding whether he wanted to continue. Finally he went on.

"But I have been speaking in generalities," Father Karl said. "It's not enough...to think about abortion as an abstract problem of society. Let me bring it down to a more specific level. I have had...a *personal*...experience with abortion."

People in the congregation leaned slightly forward in their seats.

"I can tell you, first-hand, of its destructiveness. There was...a woman...in my previous parish–a very sad and disturbed woman–who became pregnant. I'm sure she was desperate. And in her desperation, she believed that she had no hope...no alternative. She had lived a very...difficult...life. A life in which she had known much abuse and very little love. She came to me to share her pain and fear. I counselled her as best I could. I encouraged her to seek help from an order of sisters whose special ministry is giving help to women in trouble. I assured her that they would aid her in her pregnancy and assist in placing her child for adoption, if that was what she chose after the baby came. I even contacted the sisters and made an appointment for the woman to speak with them. But she made a different...choice."

Father Karl was speaking in a much softer tone now, a much slower pace. There was a subtle quaver in his voice and, Alan noted, a glistening in his eyes.

"Of course, you realize the woman had an abortion. I understand it was a relatively simple procedure...as those things go. But the trauma of that experience somehow set a spark to all the accumulated suffering of her life, all the volatile emotions trapped inside her. And it was too much."

The priest stood holding onto the pulpit. There was a commotion in the back of the church. Someone had apparently gotten up to leave. Alan had his eyes on Father Karl and didn't see who it was. The priest continued to stand silently, then finally spoke again.

"After some–after *considerable*–distress, for herself and...for me...I was called out of bed one night when it was discovered that the woman had taken her own life."

There was an audible reaction.

"I cannot say that abortion killed this woman. That would be a gross oversimplification. Rather, she was driven by hopelessness, by a lifetime of pain and despair which somehow we–the Church–had been unable to set right." Father Karl had the look of someone who was very far away in his thoughts. "I blame myself...in a sense." He drifted in that place for a time. "But I know in my heart it was the abortion that precipitated her final tragedy. And in the end, *two* lives were lost."

The church was silent, except for some whimpering from the baby in the back. That innocent, mournful sound echoed through the room like a call from all the children whose voices would never be heard. Many people had a lumpy feeling in their throats.

Father Karl recovered his composure and spoke again in the engaged way he had been addressing the congregation earlier. "So I can tell you that abortion is not an answer. Abortion is not a solution. It cannot undo a mistake or salvage a life. It cannot restore the youth of a pregnant teenager. It cannot fulfill dreams crushed by an impetuous moment or an unwanted child. It can only...*destroy*."

He raised a hand to signal the ushers, who came down the aisles from the rear of the room, passing out the three-part mail forms. "It may be," he said, "that there is little we can do to stop abortion–beyond loving our children, standing beside young women in trouble...and of course, prayer. Indeed, the tide has been against us for more than two decades now. But if it's possible to keep abortion from becoming even *more* available–if there is something we can do to at least *contain* this evil, to restrict its most vicious forms like this partial-birth horror–then we are under a clear obligation to try. The cards you are receiving..." And he went on to explain the mechanics of how the forms should be filled out and how they would be sent to the state's two senators as well as the congressman for this district.

Alan got up, took the guitar from its stand, and put his head and arm through the strap. As he stepped up to the lectern, he noticed Sister Elaine seated in the front pew. She was crying. He watched her for a brief moment, then began his song.

✠ ✠ ✠

The sound of Astor Piazzolla squeezing out a sensual melody on the bandoneón wafted gently across the room from Randy Burke's formidable stereo system, the components of which pretty much filled one wall of his apartment. Randy strove to stay ahead of the popular curve in his musical tastes. He subscribed to several cutting-edge music magazines out of New York and San Francisco, and kept on top of the arts news groups on the World Wide Web. If there was a musical trend building, he always tried to have several representative CDs in his extensive collection.

Of course, even with such sophisticated communication resources at hand, one could only be so current, living in an out-of-the-way place like the valley. There was a certain lag time between his awareness of new groups or musical genres and the availability of tangible product through the mail-order record clubs to which Randy subscribed. But he did his best.

Randy's latest musical passion was Tango Nuevo—or new tango—a sophisticated update of traditional tango which had swept out of Buenos Aires to become a major buzz on the global music scene. He was drawn to the hypnotic, whining sound of the accordion-like bandoneón, the signature instrument of the new tango motif. And he had been mildly titillated by an article he'd read which likened the spirit of Tango Nuevo to that of an Argentine whorehouse. New tango was well represented on his CD rack.

At Randy's urging, Tamar was scanning the notes on the insert from the Piazzolla album that was playing. Randy had mentioned the whorehouse reference several times with playful repetitiveness. Tamar liked the music. She was used to Randy.

"We should start the reading, everyone," Randy called, hands fluttering above his head. "Do come now. Come, come."

He whisked about the room, which was decorated in shades of mauve and pale greens and dominated by numerous large, potted ferns, some placed about on the floor, some hanging from the ceiling. The atmosphere was very Northern California, the apartment's occupant having taken his design cue from a coffee shop he had once visited on the bay in Sausalito. Randy himself was decked out in a blousy gaucho shirt and baggy trousers that reflected the background music, and which he fancied made him look something like Rudolph Valentino.

"I'd like to wait for my friend," said Tamar. "She should be along any minute now."

"One shouldn't have friends, Tammy-poo. They're habitually late. They spoil every party."

"The philosopher, as always," Tamar said, placing the Piazzolla insert in its plastic cover by the CD player. "I've been telling her about your little Sunday afternoon gatherings. She loves poetry and hasn't been to a reading in years. Do give her a chance to get here."

"Tempis fugit. Tempis fugit." Randy started rounding up other guests.

Tamar drifted over to the window and gazed down onto the street. A car slowed and pulled up to the curb. It was Sister Elaine's Escort.

"My friend is here," Tamar called to Randy.

"Be still, my frolicking heart!" he called back, skittering off to pull some people out of the kitchen.

Tamar rolled her eyes.

Elaine parked the car, got out, and looked around to check the address of the duplex. She glanced up and spotted Tamar waving from the window to catch her attention. Tamar met her at the top of Randy's stairway.

"Sorry I'm late," said Elaine, not looking directly at her friend. "I got held up after Mass."

At Tamar's indication, Elaine took off her sweater and handed it to her friend, who hung it on a rack by the door. She surveyed the room, noting the abundance of ferns as well as the attire of some of the guests, which divided mainly between Hollywood gaudy and beatnik revival.

Tamar led her around, introducing her as "my friend, Elaine Ryden." She knew Elaine tended to drop the religious appellation in most social settings. There were some of Randy's students along with several people who were active in local arts circles, plus a couple of lean, artistic-looking young fellows with closely cropped hair and earrings, friends of Randy's from out of town, whom Tamar didn't know.

Elaine was acquainted with one of the guests, a woman named Bootsie Moran, who was president of the Town-'n'-Country Players, the community theater group. Bootsie had once consulted Elaine, seeking authentic details of life in a convent, when she was preparing to direct a production of *Agnes of God*. Elaine hadn't been all that helpful to Bootsie, since the atmosphere in her order's motherhouse was a good deal less structured than that of the more traditional convent depicted in the play.

Elaine met everyone in turn, including Randy, who zipped by at one point with a fleeting handshake and a cursory *How'd-cha-do*. Elaine was friendly, but–it seemed to Tamar–somehow less than her usual warm, enthusiastic self. Tamar wondered if she was having second thoughts about coming to this poetry reading. Not a nun-like thing to do? Perhaps Tamar shouldn't have asked her. She knew Elaine had a sophisticated outlook and was accustomed to dealing with a wide variety of personality types. Still, one could never predict Randy's antics, and there were those lavender mannerisms he enjoyed exaggerating so intentionally.

"Are you okay, Elaine?"

The nun averted her eyes. "I'm all right, Tam," she said. "Something at church this morning."

"I heard about the demonstration across the street," said Tamar. "That was probably a little upsetting."

"Oh, that was nothing," Elaine said. "It's just– Well, Father Karl's homily, to tell you the truth. Just something I have to think about." She gazed off distractedly for a moment, then came back to her friend. "It's not important."

The first series of readings was given by a young girl, a striking sixteen-year-old named Sonja Duranyi, one of Randy's students. Bootsie whispered to Elaine that Sonja was a *marvelous* young actress who had played several small parts for Town-'n'-Country and looked like a real comer. Sonja read from a chapbook by an East Coast poet named Al Ferber. The poems were dryly humorous and a bit salty, recounting the observations of an urban Everyman character called Gus.

"Isn't she *marvelous*!" Bootsie enthused. "The child is *marvelous*. Just *marvelous*."

"She is very good," Elaine said quietly.

"*Marvelous*. Don't you think, Tamar? Isn't she *marvelous*?"

"Marvelous." Tamar tried to suppress her smile at Bootsie's gushing effusiveness. And she kept an eye on Elaine, who still seemed far away.

Other guests read bits of their own writing, which varied greatly in subject matter and even more in quality. Some were rather off color. One was close to lewd, and Tamar really began questioning whether she should have invited Elaine–though the nun didn't show any special shock. In fact, Elaine was rather amused by Randy, who took visible delight in each questionable passage. The naughtier the better, it seemed.

Another student, a boy named Terry Conner, offered a somber piece about blind forces engaged in pointless, unceasing combat. The poem contained what seemed to be vague high-church allusions. It all struck Elaine as youthfully cynical and extremely derivative, owing much to Matthew Arnold and his ignorant armies clashing by night on Dover Beach.

But Randy was quick with encouraging praise as befit his role as a teacher. "Stunning, Terry. Just stunning. Powerful imagery. Your work just gets better and better."

The host himself read a passage from Carlos Fuentes. Tamar suspected some effort at continuity with the day's musical theme. Well anyway, it was all Latin American. But geographically at least, the work of this Mexican writer was a long way from Buenos Aires. Had Fuentes ever written in Argentina? Randy didn't say. She whispered to Elaine that Randy should have consulted a map. Elaine speculated that perhaps there was a connection with Latin American Liberation Theology. Tamar shrugged.

There were several other readings, punctuated by applause and interspersed with erudite discussions of poetic form, imagery, allegory and literary influence. Elaine could see that Randy enjoyed sharing his special insights, which were generally quite perceptive. He did know a lot about poetry. The students were especially impressed. They hung on his every word, and appeared to compete for his approval of their own observations. He must have been a very good teacher.

Finally, the host asked Tamar if she had anything to contribute.

"I'm afraid I'm no poetess, Randy dear."

"You must have *something*," he said. "We're all friends here. Surely you can bare your tormented soul to us." He covered his eyes playfully. "Or anything else you might wish to bare."

There was chuckling around the room.

"Oh! Did I say that?"

More laughter.

"You told me one shouldn't have friends," Tamar said pointedly with one eye cocked.

"Then we're all fellow artists. Have it your own way. But do share, my love. *Share*."

Tamar looked at Elaine, whom she could see was showing the typical response to Randy's oddly amusing antics. This colorful English teacher had his routine down pat, and when he was in the full throes of *being Randy*, he somehow projected a weird magnetism. One couldn't help finding him interesting. It was what drew young people to him so readily.

"All right,"Tamar said, standing up in front of the group. "If you insist. I shall share with you a few immortal lines learned at the knee of my paternal grandfather, who always favored the classics." And she smiled slyly...

"A bunch of the boys were whooping it up
in the Malamute saloon;
The kid that handles the music-box
was hitting a jag-time tune;
Back of the bar, in a solo game,
sat Dangerous Dan McGrew;
And watching his luck was his light-o'-love,
*the lady that's known as Lou..."**

"Oh, gag me, *gag* me, Tammy-poo. *Please*!" Randy said, gesturing dramatically, hands to his throat. "You can do better than *that*. Toiling down in the social muck and mire, as you do, where life is lived on the raw edge of degredation." He addressed the others with an exaggerated stage whisper. "Runs that counselling center, you know. Cleaning up the debris of shattered young lives, the messy residue of misspent youthful passion." He pointed at Tamar, wiggling his extended finger teasingly. "Surely, Tam-Tam, all of that should give you a much keener poetic sensibility. Not to mention sharper material."

Randy put his hands on his hips, tossed his head, and cleared his throat portentously. "Perhaps something like this," he said...

"My grandmother sells prophylactics
After puncturing their heads with a pin

* "The Shooting of Dan McGrew" by Robert W. Service

But that's just the start of her tactics
My God! how the money rolls in."

There was considerable laughter throughout the room, much of it in spite of shaking heads and skeptical expressions. The predictably unpredictable Randy was at it again.

"Randy, you're just too *too*," said Bootsie Moran.

Tamar saw that Elaine's expression had changed. She sat down next to her friend. "I'm sorry, Elaine," she whispered. "Randy's out of control."

"That's all right, Tam. He's just a bit full of himself."

Randy had noted Tamar's concerned whispering.

"Oh, my dear, I trust we haven't offended your sweet friend," he said.

"I've enjoyed the readings," said Elaine, being kind. "And I've enjoyed the humorous banter. You've just touched on a subject I don't think can really be treated humorously. That's all."

Randy clutched his hands to his chest, grabbing at the gaucho shirt. "Ah, but if we cannot laugh, then we must surely weep."

Elaine sat looking at him with a soft, sad smile. "Sometimes tears are the appropriate response," she said.

Tamar was upset. Randy's antics had struck at the very point on which her relationship with her friend was most sensitive. Abortion. *Damn* abortion! "Would you like to leave, Elaine?" she asked.

"Oh, *don't* go, Sister," said Bootsie. "Please don't let Randy scare you off. He's just being his usual irreverent self."

Randy turned to Bootsie. "Sister?" he said.

"Yes. Elaine's a nun. She's from St. Mary's."

"A *nun*?" He jumped back, feigning an elaborate expression of shock. "Well, please do excuse me then. It was *never* my intention to affront a representative of Holy Mother Church."

"I think that's quite enough, Randy," said Tamar sharply.

"Not that I pay all that much attention to Holy Mother Church." He winked broadly at his audience. "After all, how does one take seriously a religion whose priests have such *dreadful* taste in dresses? Those horrible frocks. Much too *showy.*"

"That really *is* enough, Randy." Tamar rose slowly, with a distinct look of threat about her.

Randy ignored it, pressing on after Elaine. "By the way, Sister" he said, his smile turned mocking. "Any more mysterious deliveries lately?"

Most of the guests had reached their limit.

"Randy!"

"Hey, Randy, that's too much now."

"Tacky. Very tacky."

Elaine continued studying Randy, saying nothing. The star-like enneagram symbol floated through her mind. *What an oddly conflicted person*, she thought. Up to this point Randy had only appeared silly–obviously bright and certainly talented, but silly. She hadn't been bothered by all the fluttering about. In fact, deep in her feminist heart, Elaine had a warm spot for men who were willing to let their softer, womanly side be revealed. She had even sensed some commonality of interests with Randy. His choice to read from Carlos Fuentes had intrigued her.

But such a sudden flood of vehemence. Where had it come from? Did being a nun make her his enemy? Why? What was this apparent hatred of the Church? What was Randy's story?

She looked around the room, which had fallen into a hush, everyone's eyes on the quiet nun and the wicked host. This was hardly the setting in which Randy might be touched. He had created a charged moment, and his ego was at stake.

Elaine stood up and turned to Tamar. The two women exchanged a look. Elaine could see that her friend was furious, and she wanted to offer her a word about the virtue of charity. Forgiving seventy times seven. But what derision would that bring forth from Randy in his present state? Her mind fixed on another biblical passage: about shaking the dust off one's sandals. Elaine touched Tamar lightly on the arm, then took her sweater from the rack and walked calmly out of the apartment.

Tamar stood seething, her eyes tightly closed.

✠ ✠ ✠

Still as moving as it had been that morning. Alan sat listening to the tape of Father Karl's homily as he ate his dinner. He marvelled at the energy and emotion the old man put into his presentation. It was like a different priest was speaking. Where had *that* priest been these months Father Karl was at St. Mary's? Alan planned to take the tape to the post office in the morning and get it off to Collie in the first mail. But he decided he'd make a copy of it before letting it go. This was a keeper. He could dub from the cassette over to his reel-to-reel. The equipment was at the other end of his flat.

Alan finished eating and put his dishes in the sink, where there was already a substantial pile. It was definitely a bachelor's kitchen. *Sunday night*, he thought. *Better wash them for the week. Later.*

The cassette had reached its end, and he hit the rewind button. As the tape whirred back, he went to the phone and dialed a number that was already deeply etched in his mind. He had tried calling Jessie several times through the afternoon, but had gotten only her answering machine. After the odd ending of things Friday night, he didn't want to leave a message she might not return. The phone rang four times, then to Alan's surprise Jessie's voice came on the line.

"Hello?"

"Jess, this is Alan."

"Oh. Hi, Alan.

"Hi. How are you? I looked for you in church this morning."

"Yeah..." There was a pause. "I wasn't feeling well."

"Oh. Are you okay now? I tried to call you several times."

"I've been doing a lot of sleeping. I turned off the ringer."

"Well, I hope you get back on your feet. I thought you might like to do something this week."

"Alan. Like I said the other night–"

"I told you I'd call."

There was another pause. "Thank you, Alan."

"How about tomorrow night? I usually have rehearsal with the band on Mondays. But Rick Renshaw, our drummer, can't make it, so we put it off till Wednesday."

"I think I have to work tomorrow night. Let me check my book." Alan heard the flipping of pages. "Yes, Alan. I'm afraid I've got an appointment."

"You call it."

"How about Tuesday?"

"Fine."

"Alan..." Jessie hesitated, then spoke in a halting voice that struck Alan as girlishly shy. "I did have...a nice time Friday. Minnie's was fun. And since you...took me to dinner *there*...what if I make you...a dinner at...my place?"

Alan's heart leapt. "That would be...great...Jess."

"Fine. About seven, then." Another pause. "Alan. What I said the other night–"

"Jess...there's no pressure. Honestly. I just...like you. And I'm...lonely."

"So am I, Alan."

"See you Tuesday."

"See you Tuesday."

Chapter 10

On weekday mornings, business at Carl's Doughnut Shoppe followed a predictable pattern. The initial wave of customers consisted mainly of truckers and the first mill shift on the way to work. Then came the white-collar crowd from the downtown offices, picking up treats for coffee break later in the morning. Around nine, the letter carriers would pull up in their little white Jeeps to fortify themselves with Carl's rich coffee for their morning routes.

The "breakfast club," a group of elderly gents, mainly old mill hands and retired county workers, would start trickling in around nine-thirty. They would hang out until about eleven, discussing topics that mostly reflected the seasons. The deer herd was their primary focus in the fall. Ice fishing predominated in winter. And speculation about why the local farmers were so late getting crops into or out of the fields carried them through the growing months.

But the backbone of Carl's morning trade was the police. This was the county seat, so there were both city officers and sheriff's deputies. There was also a small State Police barracks out on the highway, and the troopers completed a steady parade of uniformed customers that kept the coffee and doughnuts moving briskly.

Kyle Warner sat in the end booth, scanning the morning paper from the capital, which he'd just gotten out of the vending machine in front. He looked up each time a police officer came in, hoping to catch one in particular. There was an analysis piece on the state page assessing the prospects of the school reform legislation. It quoted a spokeswoman for State Senator Ben Dillard to the effect that the senator was having reservations about certain aspects of the voucher plan and was hoping that the governor could offer stronger assurances that public school districts would not face undue financial hardship if private schools were able to draw on state funds.

A small item in the lower left corner caught Kyle's eye. It noted the anti-abortion postcard campaign which had been launched this past weekend in the Catholic churches. The bishop was hopeful of good support in all the parishes of the diocese. Kyle made a mental note to call Rosemarie later in the morning to arrange an interview with Father Karl. Between the press conference Friday and Sunday's demonstration on the courthouse lawn–meager as it was–the issue of abortion had taken on a distinctly local angle.

Two uniformed city policemen came in and sat at the counter. A moment later, they were joined by a man in street clothes. That was who Kyle was waiting for: Jock Volmer.

Kyle folded his newspaper and picked it up along with his coffee cup. He walked over to the counter and sat down next to Volmer. "Morning, Jock," he said.

"Kyle. How are you?"

"Fine, Jock. Haven't seen you in awhile. Been busy?"

"The usual," said the policeman. "How are things on the radio?"

"Oh, we still give it to the folks the way they like it. Down home and personal."

Kyle signaled the counter girl for a refill. She brought the pot over and poured coffee into his cup. "Got a fresh batch of custard-filled coming out in a minute, gentlemen."

"Sounds good," said Volmer. "A tall cup to go with it."

"I can't handle custard, Hannah," said Kyle. "Maybe just one of those little ones with no glaze." Kyle took a sip from his freshly filled cup. "Jock, I've been wondering if there's anything new on the dead baby at St. Mary's."

Volmer was watching Hannah fill an oversize foam cup with coffee. "Naw. We've got nothing on that," he said. "And to tell the truth, I don't think it's gonna go anywhere."

"No ideas?"

"It was just a sicko, that's all. Maybe somebody who doesn't like Catholics, but mainly just a sicko." He took a sip of coffee. "Chief's been upset about it, though."

"Has he?"

"Yeah. He's not a church-going fellow, as far as I can tell. Course, he is Catholic. I guess if you're raised that way, you take it personally when all these things happen at a church."

All these things?

"Then too, I guess it's like he says, he did see a lot of weird stuff in Baltimore," Volmer continued. "Chief's an alright guy, and he cares about this town. He hates to see these kinds of things happening here."

These kinds of things?

Volmer sipped at his coffee again. "I can certainly understand it. Some things just strike you kind of personally."

Hannah brought the doughnuts. "Here you go, gentlemen," she said. "Custard for you, and plain for you."

"Thanks, Sweetheart." Volmer winked at her.

"Thank you, Hannah," said Kyle. He took a bite out of the doughnut, thinking about how he could pump Volmer without being obvious. But his scheming was suddenly interrupted.

"Detective Sergeant Jock Volmer."

Both Kyle and the policeman turned around.

"Elroy," said Volmer. "Well, how're you doing, Elroy?"

"I am very fine, Detective Sergeant Jock Volmer." Elroy recognized Kyle. "And you are Kyle Warner in the WNT newsroom. Except that you are not *in* the WNT newsroom." The old man laughed at his own joke.

"You're right, Elroy," said Kyle. "Very clever of you. When are you going to stop around the station to visit me? You haven't come by in a while now."

"I've been very busy, Kyle Warner."

"Have you?"

"Yes. I'm on patrol. Keeping my eyes open. Helping the police. Aren't I, Detective Sergeant Jock Volmer?"

"You sure are, Elroy," Volmer said with a mouthful of custard-filled doughnut. "You're a big help."

"I *am* a big help. And Police Chief Stanley Zubeck lets me call him '*Chief*.'"

The two uniformed officers got up to leave, carrying their foam coffee cups with them. Volmer waved after them.

"That's pretty special, calling him 'Chief,'" Kyle said. "What do you do that warrants such a special thing?"

The old man sat down at the counter on the opposite side of Kyle from Volmer. He leaned in close. "I *see* things," he said in a hoarse whisper. "I see all kinds of things. I walk around at night, and I see all kinds of things that the police want to know about."

Volmer was absorbed in licking custard and powdered sugar from his fingers. Then he took some money from his pocket, and put it on the counter. Kyle noticed that he seemed about to leave, and was concerned that he might lose his chance to query him further.

"I saw what happened to the statue," Elroy whispered to Kyle.

"What statue?"

"The statue of Mary, the Holy Mother of God. I saw what happened to it."

"Well, I'll see you, Kyle." Volmer was standing up.

"What?" Kyle looked around. "Oh. Right, Jock. Take care, now." He turned back to Elroy as Volmer left. "Do you mean the statue behind Holy Innocents School? What happened to the statue, Elroy?"

"Something *weird* happened to the statue."

"Like what?"

"Someone put a bag over the statue. Two men put a bag over the statue, in the middle of the night. I saw them laughing, and I saw them run away from the statue, and they got into a black Toyota truck. And then they drove away. But I didn't know who they were. And I went to tell Alan Kemp, and he called Police Chief Stanley Zubeck. *Chief*." He emphasized the familiarity. "And *Chief* came with Detective Sergeant Jock Volmer. And they took the bag away."

"When did all this happen, Elroy?"

The old man thought for a minute. "It happened a *little* time ago."

"There was just a bag? No one painted the statue or broke it?"

"No. It was just a bag. *Chief* said it was an institutional trash can liner–the kind you see in offices." That remarkable memory for detail. "And there were some little packages under the bag, at the feet of Mary, the Holy Mother of God. *Chief* said they were...*condoms*. And Alan Kemp said that the whole thing was supposed to be one big condom." He looked at Kyle with a confused expression. "Alan Kemp said it was a *weird* thing, but I didn't really understand what he meant."

Kyle put his hand on the old man's shoulder. "Don't worry about it, Elroy. You did a good thing going to get Mr. Kemp and helping the police the way you did. Tell me, has anything else weird happened at the school or at the church since then?"

"No, Kyle Warner. Nothing weird has happened at the school or at the church since then. *I* am watching. *I* am on patrol."

"I'm sure you are," said Kyle. He called to Hannah and treated Elroy to a cup of hot chocolate and a custard-filled doughnut.

✠ ✠ ✠

Tamar knocked on the door jamb. "I wanted to catch you before you went out," she said, looking troubled.

Elaine glanced up from the small student desk that occupied one corner of the counselling room. She smiled at her friend. "I'm glad you did. I have something for you."

"I'm sorry about Randy, Elaine." She sat down on the molded plastic chair next to the desk. Her hands were clasped in front of her, the elegantly manicured fingernails of her two index fingers tapping together. "He's such a wild card. I should have known he couldn't be trusted. I'm really sorry."

The nun smiled at Tamar's anxious expression. "It's all right, Tam, really. I did enjoy the poetry readings. It was nice to be in a kind of intellectual atmosphere again, even if it was a bit on the pretentious side. And Randy wasn't so shocking. I could see he tries to be outrageous. But he's really just a clown. Too bad. He's a very intelligent person. But there's obviously some deep need there. Do you know what makes him like that?"

"He just seems to crave the spotlight."

"But where does that hatred of the Church come from?"

Tamar was thoughtful for a moment. "Randy said once that he had been raised Catholic. He and I both fell away." Her eyes turned down. "We have that in common. But I think...with him...it was a matter of being sort of *bludgeoned* with the Church. I'm sure he was always pretty odd–the black sheep of the family. And it's not hard to tell in what way he was odd. I believe the Church was held over his head. He was told he had to straighten up and be a proper Catholic young man or he would burn in hell. He must have felt a lot of rejection. From his family and probably from the Church, too. Or maybe he just blames the Church for his family. I don't know for sure."

Elaine sat with her hands in her lap. "Christ tried so hard to teach us love."

"I don't think Randy's really a bad person, though," said Tamar. "He cares about his students, I know that. He's brought several of them here to the center for help with various problems."

Elaine looked sideways at Tamar. "With pregnancies?"

There was a silence.

"Yes," Tamar said. "Some were pregnancies."

The silence was repeated, both women feeling uncomfortable again.

But Elaine had an objective, and she wasn't going to be deflected from it by their ongoing awkwardness. She turned around and picked up a packet of papers bound into a thesis cover lying on the small desk. "Well anyway, here's my proposal for changes in the center's pregnancy counselling," she said. "I've written things up pretty thoroughly. And I've already made some contacts, so I know that everything I'm suggesting can be done. Catholic Social Services can help with adoption arrangements, and they're eager to take referrals. They'll make their people available for counselling. Calls on the girls' families. Anything we want."

"We've worked with them before," Tamar said, taking the proposal from Elaine, "as well as pretty much all the other agencies in the state." She was grateful for the shift in tone, which was now blessedly businesslike. "It's just that we...really don't see much interest in adoption. I have to say that most of the girls we deal with–here in this county, anyway–they either want to keep their babies or they want a...quicker solution." She flipped through the pages of the proposal, not looking at Elaine.

"That's what I'm concerned about," the nun said, "that quicker solution."

"You'd be surprised, Elaine. A lot want to keep their babies. There's a kind of romance about being a single mother that's really taken hold, and it isn't only the black girls in big cities–the ones you see on all those television news reports about out-of-wedlock births. There are a lot of little, white farm girls raising children right here in this valley."

"I know," said Elaine. "It's a tragedy. But there are answers. *Better* answers. That's what I want the girls to realize."

"It might be a harder sell than you'd think. These girls want to be loved, and they want someone *to* love–either the babies themselves or the children's fathers. In many cases, the babies are the only links they have to the men who got them pregnant. If the fathers are young, the babies can provide some leverage, though not all that much. It works even less well when the fathers are older, which is often the case. The older men are usually gone in a flash. Unless they're in the family. And you don't want to know how much of *that* goes on around here."

Elaine winced slightly.

"You'll see," Tamar continued. "It isn't easy to push adoption. The days of hiding the family shame by spiriting the girl off to stay with Aunt Sally for the duration–those days are long gone."

"Well, I certainly don't want to shame anybody, but we simply have to try harder." Elaine was determined. "We have to be more...*pro-active*...with adoptions. I've got a couple of Sister friends who can come down to speak with any girls you refer, Catholic or non-Catholic. There really are a lot of resources in the Church." She held up a hand to forestall any adverse comments. "I know you're not a fan, Tam. But there is much the Church can do. Especially certain of our orders."

Tamar smiled. She wasn't going to get into any of that with Elaine now. She owed her better. But there was one thing pricking at her curiosity.

"Elaine," she said. "I know you're a very devoted person, and you're faithful to the teaching of the Church."

The nun smiled. "Father Karl might not agree with you," she said.

The two women laughed.

"Well...you're a whole lot more faithful than I am," Tamar said. "No mistake about that. But... Well, forgive me if I'm prying. But then...prying is kind of my business, isn't it. You've seemed so determined about this proposal...I've wondered if it's something...personal."

Elaine looked away and was carried off by a thought for some seconds. Finally she turned back to Tamar. "Yes Tam, it is. You see...I was adopted. And I can tell you that being an adopted child is no cakewalk, either. I had some problems growing up. Quite a few conflicts with my parents. A lot of mixed feelings about my biological mother and questions about why she did what she did. Why couldn't she love me? Why couldn't I have had a real mother and father? But I came to appreciate my adoptive parents and what motivated them. And I must say I regret all the hell I gave them."

"Sister!" Tamar said in a mock-scolding voice.

Elaine laughed. "Oh, this little nun gave her folks a few gray hairs, I have to admit that, Tam." She drifted back into her thoughts again. "So for me," she said after a time, "it's more than what the Church teaches. In the end–even with all the heartache–I've come to the conclusion that being adopted beats the alternative."

There was a knock on the door jamb.

"Yes?"

One of the young volunteers from the college who helped out at the counselling center stuck her head in. "It's your ten o'clock, Mrs. Kittredge."

"Thanks, Jenna." Tamar stood up. "I'll look this over thoroughly," she said to Elaine, holding up the proposal. "And I promise to be open minded. There might be some things I'll have to take to the board, of course."

"I understand," said Elaine. She glanced at her watch. I've got to get out to the nursing home."

The two women walked into the reception area. There was a delicate girl with a bright shock of orange-red hair. Couldn't have been more than fourteen, if that. Another local tragedy in the making? Elaine knew enough not to ask. "I'm grateful for the chance to do *something*, Tam. You follow whatever procedure is appropriate."

"I'll let you know," said Tamar. She reached out and touched her friend's hand. "And...thank you, Elaine."

✠ ✠ ✠

The little jerk was surrounded by students again. How the hell did he do it? Marty shook his head as he watched Randy Burke bantering with a group of girls in the cafeteria. He could probably have any one of those little babydolls he wanted, Marty thought, although he'd probably be more interested in the boys. And if Marty could ever prove that he *had*–well, wouldn't *that* just make the principal's day.

"I don't know a *thing* you're talking about," Marty heard Randy say in his most melodramatic voice.

"That's not what Terry Conner told me," said a hot little number with a freak hairdo and a skirt that promised more than it concealed.

"Now I *aaaask* you, is Terry Conner to be believed over *moi?* I, who bring truth and light into your dull and benighted little lives?" He flashed a sly smile and rolled his eyes.

"Oh, Mr. Burke..." And there was girlish laughter.

Oh, Mr. Burke, thought Marty with a sneer as he made his pass through the lunchtime zoo and out into the hallway.

The smell of French vanilla reached his nostrils from the coffeemaker when Marty walked into his office. Ah, peace. He closed the door behind himself and walked over to his desk. There was a pink message slip lying on the blotter. He picked it up and saw that there had been a call from Kyle Warner while he'd been down with Grover Hutchins.

Grover. What a pain in the ass. Never stopped complaining, and you never knew when he'd have the damned union in over some grievance or other. Didn't he remember that Marty had been one of the strongest voices for bringing the union into the district? And it was damned well needed, salaries being what they were in small-town schools back then. Teachers were expected to have a *vocation* in those days. Like priests. They were supposed to teach for the love of it. Well, there *was* love in it–for Marty, anyhow. It *was* a vocation, in some ways. But it was a vocation that didn't do much to feed a family. So Marty had fought the good fight. And did Grover remember *that?* Did Grover appreciate *that?* Forget it. Marty was *management* now. *Management*. Ungrateful son of a bitch.

Kyle wanted Marty to call after the noon news. The principal glanced at his watch. Kyle was still on the air. He went over to the coffeemaker and poured some French vanilla into his mug. There was a soft knocking sound behind him. Marty went to the door and opened it.

"Hello, Holly. What can I do for you?"

Mr. Casten, can I...speak with you for a minute?" Holly Steward was a throwback–a perky little junior with short, blonde hair, one of the few who didn't dress like a tart, got consistently good grades, and treated her teachers with respect. She reminded Marty of how girls were when he first started teaching, and he loved her. Holly held a vinyl, three-ring binder and a pile of books clutched tightly against her chest, and she looked upset.

"Of course, Holly. Come in. Is there anything wrong?" He closed the office door behind her.

"Mr. Casten..." She didn't know how to begin. "Mr. Casten, you know I'm Catholic."

"Yes."

"Well...there's a rumor going around about something that happened over at the old Holy Innocents School." She paused, obviously nervous.

"Go on, Holly," Marty urged. "What's the rumor?"

"Mr. Casten, I don't want to get anybody into trouble, but what happened was *wrong*."

"What have you heard, Holly?"

"Mr. Casten, somebody has desecrated the statue of Our Lady. And I think it was some kids here at school."

Marty still had the pink message slip in his hand. He looked down at it and thought of Kyle.

"I don't know who it was, Mr. Casten, but I heard something about the statue and some–" She stopped abruptly.

"Some *what*, Holly? What did you hear happened to the statue?"

She was embarrassed to say the word, which surprised her. Even in this anything-goes age, it wasn't an easy thing for a good Catholic girl to speak about–and with the *principal*, for goodness sake. She took a deep breath, letting her outrage overcome her embarrassment. "Condoms, Mr. Casten. Somebody stuck condoms on the statue of Our Lady."

"Where did you hear this, Holly?"

"Oh, Mr. Casten. I don't want anybody to get–"

"It's just a rumor, right?"

"Yes."

"You don't know who did it, right?"

"Yes. I mean no." She was starting to cry.

"This is obviously a very offensive thing to you, Holly. It's disrespectful. And I can see you're upset about it. Tell me where you heard the rumor, and I'll look into it. I promise no one will ever know you came to see me."

Another deep breath. "Terry Conner was talking to some of the other boys, and I overheard."

Marty looked at his office door, which was in the general direction of the cafeteria.

✠ ✠ ✠

"WNT news line."

"Kyle, this is Marty. I think I know what you're going to tell me, and I just found out about it myself."

"The statue?

"You got it."

"Think it's some of your kids?"

"It's some of my kids, all right. But not just."

"What do you mean?"

"Listen, Kyle, I might have a *real* story for you. There's this candy-ass English teacher over here who I think put some of the boys up to this. If you'll be patient and help me out, I may be able to do a little house cleaning."

"Marty, I'm always interested in a story. But this could be a sensitive thing. The police are already involved–"

"Are they?"

"And this is the kind of thing that could really stir up feelings, Marty. Especially after they found that dead baby at St. Mary's. I don't want to see this community torn apart along religious lines."

"Nobody wants that, Kyle. But this is a guy who could cause real trouble in his own way. He's too damned chummy with the kids. He doesn't know where to draw the line, and he's got a real slimy side. Now, you know I'm no choirboy, Kyle. But I've seen his kind before, and sooner or later, something bad goes down and somebody gets hurt. And it's usually some teenaged bimbo with more in her blouse than in her head. Then you've got a scandal that smears everybody in the district. I won't let that happen, Kyle."

"Just don't do anything rash, Marty."

"Not to worry, my friend. I'm gonna play this little jerk like a trout. He's not gonna get away. But tell me, what details did you get from the cops? I don't have too many specifics other than it involved condoms."

"Well, I didn't exactly hear this from the police. But my source was on the scene–with Stan Zubeck, in fact–and I'm sure what he told me is accurate." Kyle related the details Elroy had provided.

"Good. Very good," Marty said as he took notes. "Two boys. I think I may know who one of them was, and it's somebody *you* might know."

"Who's that?"

"A junior named Terry Conner. He's got an older brother–half-Chinese kid who graduated a couple of years ago–and a sister who's a senior this year. Their mother is on our kitchen staff, and I understand she's some kind of mover and shaker at your church."

"I know them," said Kyle.

Marty considered the implications of that connection. "I guess that gives this a little extra edge for you, doesn't it?"

"Yes, it does."

"Well, we can keep the kids' names out of it. It's just juvenile mischief, as far as they're concerned. It's the teacher I want."

"Marty," said Kyle, "you don't know if this English teacher of yours has any particular beef against the Catholic Church, do you? Maybe he's an ex-Catholic or some such?"

"Yeah, he's Catholic all right–at least he used to be. But frankly, I can't see him thinking much about religion, one way or the other, these days. And you know this is coming from somebody who hasn't seen the inside of a church in a long time, except for the occasional funeral. I'm no holy roller and I'm no hypocrite, Kyle. But at least I'm respectful. That jerk doesn't have much respect for anything."

The question was on Kyle's mind. He hesitated to give voice to it, but then decided there was no way to avoid asking. "Do you think, Marty... Is there any possibility...that your English teacher could have been mixed up...in the deadbaby incident?"

The principal was silent on the other end of the line. "Well now..." he said after a moment. "I hadn't considered that. I'd like to kick his ass out of here, but that's... I mean I'd almost hate to think..."

"You'd better proceed very cautiously with this, Marty," said Kyle. "*very* cautiously."

Third Interlude

In the 1970s, it was becoming apparent that public education had entered a period of decline. Student achievement, as measured by college entrance exams and other standardized tests, had peaked in the previous decade. The movement for civil rights affected education as well, not just in terms of integrating schools, but by redefining the rights of students in ways that tended to undermine individual discipline and institutional order. At the same time, the process of transmitting knowledge was increasingly burdened by two legacies of the sixties: drugs and an ideological outlook that saw all knowledge as culturally biased, all fields of study as inherently political.

As a result, throughout the country parents were seeking alternatives to public education, and many families found church-related schools the logical choice. With enrollments swelling, Catholic education should have experienced a "golden age." But Catholic schools were being acted upon by some particular stresses of their own.

With the decline of vocations after the Second Vatican Council, the numbers of priests, nuns and brothers available to teach in Catholic schools were drastically reduced. Operating costs ballooned, as the ratio of Religious to lay teachers shifted radically. Catholic schools found themselves having to meet the higher salaries and more comprehensive benefits demanded by independent-minded lay teachers and their increasingly aggressive unions.

Meanwhile, more students–including ever-larger numbers of non-Catholics–were attending Catholic schools at tuition rates which traditionally had been subsidized heavily by parishes. Efforts to bring those fees to realistic levels caused hardship to families already squeezed by dramatic inflation.

Holy Innocents felt these conflicts as keenly as any other parish school. By the early 1980s, St. Mary's parish council had to agonize over some difficult questions with then-pastor, Father Michael Gerard. Numerous fund-raising devices were employed–from dances, car washes and raffles, up to grant proposals made to charitable foundations in the region. Tuition took three large leaps in four years, eliciting screams from all over the valley. Parents were recruited for volunteer service in vain attempts to control out-of-pocket costs. In the end, Father Mike had to face the storm. The school was closed.

Not everyone was disappointed. It had been known to the school board and the administrators of the local district that children who attended Holy Innocents were consistently swamping their public school counterparts in performance on standardized achievement tests. A Gifted and Talented program was established to provide supplementary enrichment, primarily for the youngsters transferring in from the Catholic school. The former Holy Innocents parents were pleased.

The Gifted and Talented program was cancelled two years later.

Chapter 12

Rosemarie had never seen Father Karl in such good humor. On Sunday, people had lingered after Mass and later even stopped by the rectory to tell the old priest how deeply they had been touched by his preaching. Today there had been several phone calls. After nearly half a year at St. Mary's, Father had finally connected with his congregation. And their words of appreciation seemed to bring him out of himself. All morning, he had fairly danced around the church compound. He had come down to speak with Rosemarie in her office three times, rather than just buzzing her on the intercom from the rectory, as was his usual practice.

Even Sister Elaine had to grant that Father seemed a changed man. When she'd seen him that morning, she was surprised to find herself speaking to her pastor with an ease she hadn't felt since Father Edward. Well, Father Karl *wasn't* Father Edward, to be sure. But things were looking up.

The phone rang, and Rosemarie answered, "St. Mary's Parish Center."

"Rosemarie? This is Kyle Warner."

"Oh hello, Kyle. What can I do for you?"

"I saw a piece in the capital paper this morning about the anti-abortion postcard campaign. I assume St. Mary's took part in it."

"Oh yes. We distributed the cards at both Masses yesterday, and Father Karl gave a wonderful homily. It was very moving."

"Really. What did he say?"

"He told a story about a woman he had known who had an abortion and was so distraught that she committed suicide."

"Sounds very intense."

"It was so sincere and heartfelt. You could tell the incident had really affected him. It was the best homily he's given since he's been here."

"Do you think Father Karl would be willing to do an interview with me about the campaign?"

"Well now, I think he might. People have been congratulating him, and he's just all pumped up right now. It's really kind of charming. But you know, Kyle, if you're planning to do a report on the radio, you might want to include some of Father actually giving his homily."

"Do you tape his sermons?"

"Not usually. But I believe Alan Kemp may have done this one. I noticed him messing around with a little cassette recorder."

"Is Alan there, by any chance?"

"Not at the moment. But you might be able to reach him at his apartment. He lives across the square, on the top floor over Reilly's drug store." She gave him Alan's phone number. "Would you like me to make an appointment for you with Father?"

"Why don't you feel him out and see if he'd be interested?"

"I'll do that."

✠ ✠ ✠

"...abortion is not an answer. Abortion is not a solution. It cannot undo a mistake or salvage a life. It cannot restore the youth of a pregnant teenager. It cannot fulfill dreams crushed by an impetuous moment or an unwanted child. It can only...*destroy*."

Alan hit the *Stop* button and then *Rewind*. The two large tape reels began spinning rapidly backward. "After that, Father explained how the cards should be filled out and what the Church would do with them. Then I sang a song, and we went on with Mass."

"Rosemarie was right," said Kyle, sitting in one of Alan's canvas chairs. "It was a very moving little sermon. I wouldn't have suspected Father Karl of being such an inspiring preacher."

"We wouldn't have either, let me tell you."

"Can I use the tape?"

Alan was hesitant. "Look, Kyle...You know...Father has come through some...pretty rough times. I'm not sure how visible he wants to be just now. And I wouldn't want him to feel under any undue pressure."

"Let me assure you, Alan," Kyle said, "I have no intention of pressuring Father Karl or of letting him be hurt in any way. And I also don't want to do anything that could create conflict among the churches in town. This is my community. I've made my home here for a long time. This is where they're gonna put me in the ground. Still, this postcard campaign is a national story, and the fact that it's going on right here in the county gives it a legitimate local angle. I especially think that using excerpts from Father Karl's sermon would cast a rather complex issue in more personal terms. It could help people understand the Catholic Church's position on abortion, and it could help them understand something about Father Karl. That might do *everybody* some good."

The tape had rewound all the way, and the loose end slapped against the head cover as the reel slowed to a stop.

"I can understand any reservations you might have," Kyle continued. "Especially after the dead baby. Maybe I can gain some credibility here if I tell you that I know about the condom incident and I'm not going to do anything with it."

This was an unexpected turn. "Oh. Well...thank you, Kyle. I really...appreciate that." Alan glanced at the tape recorder, then back at Kyle. He rubbed his hands together apprehensively. "Let me ask you a favor, though. If Father agrees to the interview, please don't say anything about the statue."

"He doesn't know?"

"Nobody at the church does. And I don't want them to. I don't know how you found out about it, but it would be best all around if the story went no farther."

"I'm afraid it's too late for that, Alan. It was a couple of kids at the high school who pulled the prank, and Marty Casten, the principal over there, got wind of it."

"Damn!"

"I think he'll keep it all as low key as he can. But there may be a teacher involved, too–"

"A teacher?"

"It's possible that one of the teachers put the boys up to it. If that's the case, there will be some action taken."

"Do you know why he did it?" Alan asked urgently. "I've got a friend in the bishop's office, and ever since we found the baby, they've been worried that there might be anti-Catholic trouble brewing down here."

"Well, I can't say for sure. But the impression I got from Marty is that this teacher is just some kind of loose cannon–a kid that never grew up."

"Let's hope it *was* just a prank then, and not somebody with a serious axe to grind." Alan took the full reel off the tape deck and put it in its box. He handed it to Kyle. "Here. I've done some EQing, and it's got Dolby noise reduction. I cleaned it up as best I could, dubbing from my little cassette deck. Maybe the sooner we get the message out the better. I'd still appreciate your not saying anything about the statue to Father Karl. I'll try to find a way to tell him."

"Actually, I might be able to help you with that," said Kyle. "I hate to say it, but one of the boys involved goes to my church. Our pastor is very sensitive to these...inter-denominational problems. He knows how touchy they can be. In fact, he went over to see Father Karl after the baby was found. Perhaps it would be good to bring him in on this. It might assure Father Karl that there's nothing more behind the incident than a couple of teenagers and a screwed-up teacher."

"If there *is* nothing more," said Alan.

✠ ✠ ✠

The chief leaned back in his chair and made a face that showed he was intrigued by this new information.

"Raises some different possibilities, doesn't it?" said Volmer.

Zubeck flicked the corner of the fax paper with his finger. "Yes it does, Jocko. An individual living here in town with this kind of personal connection–quite likely some old animosities, given the circumstances. It could be that there's nothing political going on at all. Let's hope, anyway." He held up the sheet. "Maybe we've got it all right here."

"The statue thing, too?"

"That I'm not sure. The statue thing may be just what it looked like: kids. But this," he said, holding up the paper, "might be Elroy's dumper."

✠ ✠ ✠

Oh God, now what? Ellie Conner had just gotten home from work, the trailer was a mess, and here was Pastor Matt. She tucked a few loose strands of hair behind her ears. "Come in, Pastor. What a surprise."

Matt could see Ellie was flustered.

"Please excuse this place," she said. "It's an absolute disaster I know. Teenagers. You can't keep a thing straight with teenagers in the house."

"I understand entirely," Matt said good-naturedly. He spotted a stool at the small breakfast bar, and sat on it uneasily. "Ellie, I'm...sorry to come here unannounced like this, but there's something I have to speak with you about."

Ellie felt the beginnings of a knot in her stomach.

Matt looked around the trailer. It was a single-wide, and the interior was more than messy. It spoke of a family living at the margin–and of a whole series of bad decisions that were likely to keep them there. The shabby furnishings contrasted sharply with a new and expensive wide-screen television set that dominated one end of the tiny living room–fresh from the rent-to-own store and obviously more than Ellie could afford. Video games, the components of a stereo set and other electronic devices added to the clutter. Compact disc cases were tossed here and there, an eclectic mix of Christian artists and heavy metal. And everywhere–on shelves and tables, in piles–inspirational books, magazines and pamphlets.

"There's been some vandalism at the Catholic church," Matt said with sad eyes. "Well, the old school, actually, behind the church..."

Ellie felt the knot in her stomach get tighter.

"There was no serious damage. In fact, there doesn't appear to have been any *physical* damage at all. But what happened is the kind of thing that could cause a lot of hard feelings..."

She sighed deeply, closing her eyes. Of course she was aware of what happened. In fact, she'd known in advance that the boys were up to *something*, though she didn't know precisely what until after the fact. Hadn't she harangued her kids often enough about *papist abominations* and the need for good Christians to strike back at the Roman cult? She just hadn't known what the boys had in mind. Now, with the pastor in her home speaking of these things, her heart sank.

"You see, Ellie...what happened was– Well, there's no point beating around the bush. The fact is that it looks like Terry and probably one other boy–"

"It was Scott Brickley."

Matt looked at her. "You know?"

"Yes Pastor, I know all about it."

The minister was a little perplexed, but at the same time felt a keen sense of relief. He'd been uncomfortable about approaching Ellie on such a sticky matter ever since Kyle had called him earlier that afternoon. "Then there's no need to press the issue further," he said. "I know you've often expressed strong feelings about the Catholic Church. But I also know you'll do everything you can to avoid letting any harm come to the Body."

"I'm sorry, Pastor. I should have done something before. I'll see that this is...taken care of."

"I know you will, Ellie." He stood up and took her hands. "Why don't we pray?"

She bowed her head, as much to hide the flush rising in her face as to assume an attitude of reverence.

"Father God," Matt began. It was a prayer he had worked out in his head on the way over. "Keep us ever mindful of You, and give us a clear understanding of Your will for us. Sow in our hearts a true spirit of charity toward those who love You in ways which may be different from our own. Grant us discernment to know the right, and keep us unwavering in our commitment to lead others on the *path* of right. But in our efforts...never let us do *harm*. We ask these things in Jesus' name. Amen and amen."

"Amen," said Ellie, still looking down.

Matt departed with a few pleasantries that didn't even register on Ellie. She stood in the doorway, steeped in humiliation. As Matt's car drove away, a battered, black Toyota sport truck pulled up. Ellie's son, Terry, got out and came to the front door. She turned her back to him, her mouth set into a tight expression of anger.

"Hey Mom, what was Pastor Matt doing here?" Terry asked as he came inside the trailer. Suddenly a sharp pain stunned him. It took a second for him to realize that his mother had slapped him across the face. "What's that for?"

"For being stupid!"

"What're you talkin' about?" He touched his cheek gingerly.

"The statue. That's what I'm talking about."

"But you knew about the statue. You wanted us to make a statement. To teach the papes a lesson."

"I wanted you to do something *clever*. This wasn't clever. This was *dumb*."

"But you've known all about it."

"And I haven't felt good about it. Not with those...*condoms*. What the hell kind of a thing was that? It's disgraceful. You couldn't come up with something that wasn't–that didn't use something...*immoral?* And where did you get condoms, anyway?"

"You can get 'em everywhere. And anyway, the whole thing was Burke's idea. I told you that. You thought it was funny."

"Well I don't think it's funny anymore. And you stay away from that faggot, Randy Burke."

"Mom, he's my teacher."

"He's un-Christian, and he's immoral. God only knows how he lives his life. And he's influencing teenagers, Lord help us."

"I don't understand any of this, Mom. You're the one who's always talking about 'Catholic idolatry.' Well, we fixed their idol for them."

"Catholics *are* idol worshippers."

"Then what did *I* do that was wrong?"

Ellie sat down on the stool Pastor Matt had used, and leaned against the breakfast bar. She closed her eyes and rubbed her forehead. *I know what you did*, she thought to herself. *You listened to me.* But she didn't say it out loud.

✠ ✠ ✠

Sister Elaine was much later getting back than she had expected. But it was quite a drive in from the Hagerty farm, and Emma had needed a shoulder to cry on. The old woman knew she was about to become a widow, her children were spread far and wide around the country, and she was understandably frightened. You can't just say a few encouraging words and run. So it was nearly midnight, and all the tea Elaine had consumed at Emma's grandmotherly urging was having more of an effect on her bladder than on her alertness.

As she came around the curve before the Old Valley Road met the highway at an angle, she was jolted to attention when she spotted a small van emerging from an opening in a high hedge. Elaine slammed on the brakes and felt her car skid off to the right. The other driver spotted her as she slid onto the road shoulder and came to a stop with gravel flying. He pulled over to the side, got out, and ran back to see if she was hurt. Elaine was dazed and didn't realize she was being spoken to.

"Are you all right?"

The face of the young black man was familiar.

"You're Sister Elaine. Are you okay, Sister?"

"Yes... Yes, I'm fine. Oh. I know you. I know you from church."

"Howard Hansen, Ma'am. Minnie Johnson's nephew."

"Is everything all right?" a woman's voice called from the van.

"It's Sister Elaine. She's not hurt."

"Sister Elaine?"

Elaine saw a woman in a white dress come running from the van.

"Jessie?"

Howie opened the car door, and Elaine got out.

"What happened, Elaine?" Jessie said. "Are you sure you're okay?"

"Yes. I'm fine. I... I must have started drifting off or something. Thank God I saw you at the last minute."

"Do you want to go inside and see Dr. Fowler?" Jessie asked.

"I'm okay, really." She became aware of a funny sensation on her legs, and she pulled at the skirt of her jumper to examine it. There was a large stain. "Oh no. I think I wet myself. Isn't this just great."

"Think nothing of it, Ma'am," said Howie. "You had a shock."

"I've got to get *home*."

"Are you sure you can drive?" asked Jessie.

"Don't worry. I'll be just fine. You can bet I'm wide awake now."

She got back into her car, and Howie headed back to the van, but Jessie stood by the open door for a minute. "Elaine... I thought you might like to know that...I'm seeing Alan again."

Elaine was feeling utterly embarrassed as she sat on the damp seat, and frankly, she wasn't interested in Jessie's social life at this particular moment. But she could see that her friend was trying to express something. "Oh. That's good, Jessie," she said, mustering an appropriate level of nunlike concern. "Do you feel all right about it?"

"I think so. He's coming over to my place for dinner tomorrow night."

"That's great. You have fun. And try not to get too uptight about anything. Just enjoy the evening, and let things happen on their own."

"I'll try," said Jessie. "And...thanks."

Elaine watched the nurse walk back to the van, wondering about the strange ill ease that seemed to grip her whenever the subject of men came up. As Jessie opened the van door, the dome light inside illuminated the red hair of a young girl.

Chapter 13

Alan was getting impatient. He had wanted just to leave a message for Deacon Collinson to call him back, but the chancery receptionist put him on hold—and it was *his* dime. Finally, Collie came on the line.

"Alan, the tape arrived this morning, and I just listened to it. Sounds like Father Karl still has the spark."

"Yeah, it was pretty moving. But listen, Collie, I have some information for you. Word is getting around about the statue. A couple of teenage boys did it. But get this, it looks like one of the teachers over at the high school put them up to it."

"Do you know why?"

"Not really. But my source said this teacher is something of a wild child. He doesn't think there's anything more behind it than that."

"Where did you get this?"

"From a fellow named Kyle Warner. He's a news guy for the local radio station."

"Radio!"

"Don't worry. He said he's not going to use it on the air, and I believe him. I think he genuinely wants to avoid stirring up any church troubles. But...there is kind of a price to pay. I gave him my copy of Father Karl's tape. He's planning to interview Father about the postcard campaign. I think he'll handle it all right. And in any event, there's nothing I can do about it. Kyle's being a real good sport on the statue business."

"Nothing to be done," said Collie. "How's Father been since Sunday?"

"He's been *great*. I can't remember ever seeing him so warm and friendly. He seemed a little rattled by the demonstrators– Did you hear about the protest we had going on across the street?"

"Yes. Was he very upset by it?"

"I think at first. The start of Mass was kind of shaky. But once he got to the homily, he just took off. And he's been flying ever since. He even seems to be getting along with Sister Elaine, and that's something I never expected to see."

"Ah yes, your little organic nun. What is it, *The Holy Sisters of Mother Earth?*"

"Something like that."

"Well, the Lord moves in mysterious ways."

"Look, Collie, somebody has to tell Father about the statue before it's all over town. Now, Kyle had a suggestion. He attends an Evangelical church called Bible Fellowship. They're involved in pro-life, and the pastor went to see Father Karl about the baby, to tell him all the churches were behind St. Mary's, in case somebody was stirring up trouble. Kyle thinks maybe it would be good to have this minister on hand for support."

Collie considered it for a moment. "That might be a good idea. Hometown solidarity, that sort of thing."

"Yes."

"I think the bishop would agree. And you're right that we can't wait. If your radio guy has the story, there's no telling who else knows. It could be page one in tomorrow's paper, especially if it involves someone connected with the local school district. With this educational reform thing so hot in the legislature, anything involved with the schools is news. I'd say go ahead and set it up. Let me know what happens, and I'll inform the bishop."

"Okay." There was still a question on Alan's mind, one he hadn't been able to get answered when his last conversation with the deacon was cut short. "Collie, when I spoke with Chief Zubeck, he said something odd."

"What was that?"

"He seemed to *know* something about Father Karl. Something about his past. Could there be anything in Father's background that...might possibly be connected with the baby? I mean, maybe this thing wasn't a protest at all. Maybe it doesn't have anything to do with St. Mary's or the school or this town. Maybe it's personal. Maybe it's somebody with a grudge against Father Karl himself."

The line was silent for a time, then Collie spoke. "There is...a possibility," he said. "The woman Father mentioned in his homily, the one who killed herself... What he didn't say was that...after she got pregnant, she charged him with being the father of her baby. She claimed he was sexually attracted to her and that he...assaulted her during a counselling session. This was all at St. Ann's, right at the tail end of the controversy about closing the school. Father had counselled her. He urged her strongly not to have the abortion. Actually, I think he may have come on a little *too* strong. Kind of heavy handed. But he had been under enormous pressure over the school. Well, it was pretty clear that the woman was disturbed. When the police were called in, she kind of panicked and recanted her story. She admitted she'd made it all up. The bishop tried to get her into therapy, and he did what he could to keep a lid on things. There was never an arrest, so whatever official record might exist, nothing made the papers. I don't think the story traveled too far, fortunately, at least not more than some vague rumors in the parish. But coming on top of the school dispute, it shook Father pretty badly. When they found the woman dead, Karl snapped."

Alan sat quietly, taking it all in.

"I'm sorry I didn't share this with you before, Alan. I wanted to protect Father's privacy, and it didn't seem relevant. But you *could* be right that there's a connection."

"How?"

"A relative, perhaps. The woman did have a sister. In fact, it was the sister who claimed the body. I don't know where it was buried. Out of the diocese, I suppose. Not from St. Ann's, that I do know."

"A sister?"

"Yes."

"Collie... There's some indication now that it was a woman who left the baby in the school."

"How do you know this?"

"There's a possible witness: the old codger who saw the boys with the statue. Popeye–well, his name's really Elroy, but he looks like Popeye the Sailor Man to me. He's slightly retarded, but he makes it his business to know everything that goes on in town. He spotted a woman entering the school building in the middle of the night."

"The police know?"

"I told Zubeck, and he takes it seriously. I was hoping for some kind of confirmation before I mentioned it to you. But... It's a stretch, I admit, but if there's an angry sister..."

"Yes... It's possible."

"You don't know the sister's name, by any chance?"

"No, and at the moment I can't recall the woman's name, either. I think it was something simple–Jones or Smith or whatever–single syllable. I'll see what I can find out about her. One thing I do recall, though, is the date of the suicide. It was May first. May Day. I remember the bishop commenting how sad it was not only that someone would have had an abortion but that she would kill herself on the day when children had traditionally venerated the Blessed Mother. You wouldn't remember May crownings, Alan, but–"

"Collie," Alan interrupted. "May first is the day we found the dead baby."

There was another silence. "That's right," said the deacon finally. "I hadn't even realized that, Alan. It was the second anniversary of the suicide."

"But it would have been the first anniversary to occur since Father Karl came to St. Mary's," Alan said. "This could be the connection."

"You might be right."

✠ ✠ ✠

"Sit down, Mr. Conner."

Terry didn't know what to expect. First he was called out of gym to the principal's office. Now, here was not only Fart-face Casten, but his own mother, *and* Mrs. Garner, his guidance counselor, *and*–holy crap!–Schloesser, the superintendent of schools. What the hell did he *do*?

Ellie's face was absolutely without color. She sat, head down, wearing her kitchen uniform, by the credenza that held Marty's coffeemaker, at present empty of the aromatic liquid on which he depended for his midday solace. She didn't look at Terry when he came in.

"Terry, I'll make this short and sweet," Marty said. "We know about the statue."

That explained why Mom was here. But she wouldn't have squealed, would she? She'd been mad, sure. But she always said families have to stick together–and especially that parents have to stand by their kids. It was always *us against the world*. No. Casten must have found out some other way and called her in. Poor Mom.

"Now, the truth is, Terry, that this isn't a matter for school discipline. It happened after school hours and off school property. So there's nothing we can do to you–*officially*."

There was something decidedly un-reassuring about the word "officially."

"However–"

Terry swallowed hard.

"–this *could* be a matter for the police." Marty had been a teacher and principal long enough to have cultivated an outstanding *hard-guy* presence. He didn't call upon it often. The truth was he had become so disillusioned and detached that, most of the time, he just plain didn't give a damn. But it was still there, he still knew how to use it, and it was making Terry squirm.

"We live in a very small town. And in this kind of community, it's particularly important not to create divisions between people. One of the things that can divide a community most painfully is *religion*. People are very touchy about what they believe in, and they get their backs up real fast when they think somebody's making fun of those beliefs." Marty sat against the front edge of his desk and folded his arms, glaring at Terry the whole time.

"Now, you're not Catholic, so you may not fully understand why what you did is so offensive."

On the contrary, Terry realized that the statue of the Virgin was a potent Catholic symbol. His mother had made that eminently clear. It would certainly not do, however, to point that out at this moment.

"But the fact that you're associated with a church whose views are very different from Catholic beliefs makes this situation extremely sensitive." Marty got up and walked to the window, his back toward Terry. "So you can see, Terry, that calling in the police is the *last* thing we would want to do."

Oh?

"Our *first* concern, of course–" Marty's tone was softer now. "–has to be peace in our community." He turned around and looked at Terry. "I'm sure you agree that's what's most important, don't you Terry?"

"Uh...sure..."

"Of course," Marty said, with a smile that was slight but ever so sincere. "I know that you're really a good kid, Terry. And frankly, I find it hard to imagine that you actually wanted to cause any hurt. I mean, this is your hometown, too. I have to believe you care about it." He had cast his line and was setting the hook.

"But you know, Terry...there are people who may not have the best interests of our community at heart. Individuals who might think of mocking someone's beliefs just for a laugh. People like that might even influence others to do something disrespectful–plant the seed of an idea, and then hide behind their...position." Marty looked directly into Terry's eyes. "Did you discuss the statue with anybody like that, Terry? Or perhaps someone suggested the idea to you?"

The boy was sweating profusely. He looked at Marty, then looked at his mother who was glaring at him now. Did she tell Casten about Randy Burke? She had called him un-Christian and said she didn't like him influencing teenagers. On the other hand, maybe Casten found out from somebody else. And why wasn't Scott Brickley in here? Had Casten already spoken to him? Did Scott squeal? On the other hand, did it matter?

"Well, Mr. Casten...I did have some talks with...Mr. Burke."

Marty smiled and glanced at Dolph Schloesser, who nodded his head almost imperceptibly.

"I see, Terry," Marty said. He walked over to him and put his hand on Terry's shoulder. "I appreciate your sharing that with us. I really do. It's very unlikely that the police will have to be involved in this matter."

A sigh told of Terry's relief.

"That being the case," Marty continued, "I should think it wouldn't pose a problem for you to let us know who was with you that night."

Mom didn't tell them about Scott. And if she hadn't squealed on Scott, she certainly hadn't squealed on Terry. Good old Mom.

"You can see that no harm will come to either of you." Marty smiled once more.

Terry looked at Ellie. She was glaring again. "Yes, Mr. Casten," he said. "It was Scott Brickley."

"Scott Brickley." Marty still had his hand on Terry's shoulder. He gave it a gentle pat. "That's fine, Terry. That's fine. We'll probably be calling on you and Scott to give us a more detailed statement about what happened–in particular...how the whole thing...got started. Meanwhile, I think you can go back to class."

Terry stood up and glanced at Ellie again. Her eyes were closed.

"Thank you...for coming in, Terry," Marty said.

Terry was out the door as quickly as possible.

✠ ✠ ✠

The chief's phone rang, and he pressed the button to engage the speaker. "Yes?"

"It's a Mr. Kemp on two, " said Sherí, the police receptionist/dispatcher. "He said he's from St. Mary's Church."

Zubeck picked up the receiver. "Hello, Kemp."

"Good afternoon, Chief. I was talking with the chancery this morning, and I found out something that may be of interest."

"Yeah?"

"You mentioned something about Father Karl having...well, having a past, I suppose."

"What about it?"

"Are you aware that someone once accused him of sexual...misconduct?"

"Actually it was sexual assault, and the whole thing was bogus."

"Then you know."

"We do the best we can."

"I assume, then, you're aware that the woman who made the charge had had an abortion and then later committed suicide."

"Yes."

"Did you know she had a sister? I'm afraid I don't have an I.D. on her, but–"

"Look, Kemp, I'll save you the trouble. We have the sister's name. I'm not at liberty to divulge her identity, because it could bear on the case."

"I see."

"But we also know that she lives here in town."

Well well... "You're ahead of me, Chief. That I didn't know."

"Consider it a freebie, Kemp. You got anything else?"

Alan wondered if he should tell Zubeck about the two teenage boys and the teacher. He decided he'd let the school officials make that call, whatever they were up to. "Afraid not," he said. "But it looks like you guys are doing fine without me."

"Well, I appreciate the interest, in any event. Keep in touch if you hear anything more."

"I will, Chief. Thanks." Alan hung up the phone. *The sister lives in town*, he thought. Was she Catholic? Did she attend St. Mary's? The dead woman had been a parishioner of St. Ann's. But she hadn't been buried from St. Ann's. Was there the remotest possibility that she could be buried in St. Mary's cemetery? Alan had provided music for virtually every funeral held in the parish since he took the job at St. Mary's. But that was only a little over a year ago. Since Father Karl had been pastor for nearly six months and had spent more than a year prior to that in retreat out west, the suicide and the funeral would have taken place before Alan came. Someone at the church had to know if any parishioner's out-of-town relative had been buried from St. Mary's–someone who would have been here during Father Edward's time.

Alan headed down the stairs and across the courthouse square. When he walked into Sister Elaine's office, she was just hanging up the phone.

"Sister, do you have a minute?"

"I'm afraid I really don't, Alan," she said, gathering up her purse and jacket. Colin Hagerty just died, and I'm going out to the farm with Father Karl and Rosemarie."

"Oh, old Mr. Hagerty. I'm sorry to hear that. Is Rosie closing the office?"

"Yes. She and Emma are longtime friends. You might want to think about funeral music."

"I will. But, ah...just quickly, on the subject of funerals...can you recall any in the last couple of years where St. Mary's buried the sister of one of our members?

The deceased would have been someone from out of town."

Rosemarie called from down the hall. "Are you ready, Elaine? I've put the phones on the answering machine. Father says he'll meet us in the parking lot."

"Be right there," Elaine called. "What was that, Alan? Somebody's sister was buried?"

"Yeah. I don't know who she was. But it would have happened when Father Edward was here, back before I came."

"Well...not off the top of my head. Why do you ask?"

"Look, Sister...this is in confidence. But it's possible that the person who put the baby in the bathroom might be a parishioner."

"Of St. Mary's?!"

"Please. I have to rely on your discretion. But I've been looking into this matter for the bishop's office–"

"The bishop?"

"Yes. And there is reason to suspect that this incident might have been connected to something that happened when Father Karl was at St. Ann's."

"I can't *believe* it's anybody at St. Mary's."

"It's hard, I know. But give it some thought. And *please*, keep this to yourself."

"Elaine!" It was Rosemarie again.

"Coming!" She was in the doorway. "Somebody's sister, from out of town."

"That's right."

She headed down the hallway. Rosemarie was there with her grandson in tow. "Is Kevin coming?" Elaine asked.

"I'm afraid so," said Rosemarie. "My daughter is still in class. She can't pick him up until after two."

"I can watch him," said Alan, coming down the hall from Elaine's office.

"Oh, could you, Alan? That would be so helpful." Rosemarie knelt down to the boy. "Kevin, honey, you stay with Alan until Mummie comes. Okay? She won't be long, and Grandma has to run an important errand."

"I'll show you how to play the piano," said Alan.

"No," said the little boy sternly. "I have to clean up da tash."

"Okay. First the trash, then the piano. How's that? Deal?"

"Deal."

"Thank you, Alan," said Rosemarie.

"No trouble."

Rosemarie headed down the stairwell to the lower level. Elaine followed, pausing at the top of the stair to look back at Alan for a moment, then continued after.

"So where's this trash?" Alan asked. "We'd better get our work done."

"Over here."

The little boy marched purposefully to the door of an old classroom that served as a multi-function office/meeting hall. Father Karl used the room for parish council sessions around the old dining table from the rectory. Elaine also used the room, mostly for the Monday night gatherings of her RCIA adult catechumenate group. Inside on the table there was a paper grocery sack, rolled over at the top, and a transparent plastic bag, filled with Styrofoam coffee cups, disposable plates and other debris from the previous evening's RCIA session, and knotted closed.

Kevin climbed up on a chair and grabbed the paper sack, pulling it to the edge of the table and lowering it to the seat of the chair. Then he climbed carefully down, took the sack from the chair, and carted it off. Alan was amused to watch the child working with singular determination, carrying the cumbersome bundle–which made for a considerable load out in front of his little torso.

"Dis room is always *messy*," Kevin said with a child's seriousness. "Grandma says da arsy-acey group was raised in barns."

Alan laughed. "She does, huh?"

"Yes."

"And you clean up the room?"

"Yes. Dat's my job." He tottered off unsteadily down the hall.

"That's a pretty big bag," Alan said, following after and smiling at Kevin's intentness. "What do you do with all that trash?"

"I put it in da boys room."

Alan stopped in his tracks. "Where do you put it in the boys room, Kevin?"

The little boy turned around and looked at Alan with an expression that said, *Where do you think I put it, you stupid grownup?*

"In da tash can."

Alan knelt down in front of the child. "Kevin, do you always take the trash from the conference room into the boys room?"

"Yes."

"Every week?"

"Yes."

"And you always put it in the boys room trash can?"

"Yes."

"Do you fill the trash bags yourself?"

Kevin was puzzled.

"Do you clean all the trash off the table and put it in the bags?"

"Grandma does."

"Kevin...are there ever other bags with trash already in them?"

Kevin thought for a moment. "Sometimes dere's tash."

"Already in the bags?"

"Yes."

Alan looked at the meeting room door, then turned back to Kevin and tousled the little boy's hair. "You're a really hard worker, Kevin. You go finish putting the trash in the trash can, and then I'll teach you how to play the piano."

Kevin went off to complete his duties, and Alan stood up. He moved slowly back to the meeting room and read the name plate on the door: "Pastor's Conference Room."

✠ ✠ ✠

Matt had been out on a home visit: old George Sanderson, who had suffered a mild stroke and hadn't been to church in four weeks. When he got back to his office about 3:30, the church secretary, June, handed him a stack of messages. Matt flipped though them and determined that there was nothing that couldn't keep for awhile–which was just as well, because driving back, he had gotten some thoughts for this Sunday's sermon, and he wanted to rough them out before they slipped away. One of the notes was a message from Kyle Warner to the effect that the pastor should expect someone named Alan Kemp, from St. Mary's, to call about a meeting.

All of that would unfold in the Lord's good time, so Matt sat down at his desk and flipped on his computer. As the machine buzzed and beeped through its start-up sequence, Matt opened his Bible, turning to the psalms. Just then, the phone rang.

"Yes, June?"

"It's that Mr. Kemp that Kyle called about."

The Lord was faster than Matt had expected. "Oh, yes. Put him on." He heard the line connect. "Mr. Kemp, this is Matt Pell."

"Hello, Reverend. Thank you very much for speaking with me."

"No trouble at all. How can I help you."

"You are aware of the incident that occurred at St. Mary's involving the statue in the grotto behind the old school?"

"Yes I am, and I've spoken with the mother of one of the boys who were involved. She assured me that nothing like that will ever happen again."

"I appreciate that, Reverend. Now I wonder if I might ask a favor."

"Yes?"

"Father Karl, our pastor, is not aware of the incident. I dealt with the police when it happened, and I've been able to keep it all from him, so far. He was quite shaken up after we discovered the dead baby, and I thought it best not to bother him about the statue. It didn't seem likely that the two situations were related, and I thought I shouldn't give him more to worry about."

"That was probably wise, Mr. Kemp, especially since it would appear that you were right and there is no connection."

"The problem is that the facts of the vandalism are coming out now, and will likely be public knowledge very soon. I'm going to have to tell Father Karl before he finds out through the grapevine. Since at least one of the boys attends your church, Kyle suggested that perhaps you could be on hand to assure him that this was just a prank. Kyle said you've spoken with Father Karl before. And...to be honest, Reverend...Father Karl has come through some rather difficult emotional times–not just over the baby, but from things that happened...well, before he came to St. Mary's. A few words from you might go a long way–"

"I understand, Mr. Kemp. I... I would be happy to do what I can."

What was it about this priest, this whole chain of events? Somehow, Matt was being pulled into the trials of the local Catholic parish, ever since the body of that poor, dead baby had been found. The irony echoed through his brain. The Roman Church had always been a bone of contention between him and his father. He knew about the elder Pell's history with the Church, of course, and his father's deep revulsion toward all things "popish." How could he not know? It had been the lore of his childhood. It had come with his mother's milk.

But the old minister's bitterness was *so* extreme. Even as a child, it had made Matt uncomfortable. And when he grew up, went away to college, came into contact with a wide variety of people—even, God forbid, *Catholics*—he began to look on his father's burning, consuming hatred as a neurotic contradiction in a life that was, otherwise, quite holy. To Matt it was a deep shame. It was un-Christian.

"When would you like me to come over to St. Mary's?"

"Father Karl's mornings are usually pretty loose," Alan said. "He mostly takes care of paperwork in his office before he says noon Mass. Could you come tomorrow...about ten?"

Matt glanced at his desk calendar. "That would be fine."

"Why don't we meet in the school?"

"All right. I'll see you there."

"Thank you, Reverend. I'm grateful for your help."

"Ten o'clock tomorrow, Mr. Kemp."

✠ ✠ ✠

Rosemarie was upset. She and Emma had been friends since they were girls. Emma was several years older, and had been her babysitter. Rosemarie was a bridesmaid when Emma had married Colin. She and her family had spent many happy hours on the Hagerty farm. Now she sat quietly, as Elaine drove along the Old Valley Road, by the base of College Hill at the edge of town. Father Karl had ridden back with Tom Simpson, the funeral director, to discuss arrangements. Emma's sister-in-law, Florence, was staying with her at the farm until the kids came in, sometime tomorrow.

"They're such fine folks," Rosemarie said, not with any particular intent, but needing something to cushion the memories. "Colin was a good man."

"Yes. Very nice people," said Elaine. "Emma is a dear. We had a wonderful conversation last night."

"I remember we used to go to that army base they set up outside the capital during the Second World War. The USO held dances. We used to dance with the boys. Emma was engaged to Colin, but he was overseas in the Marine Corps. He wasn't at all happy about those dances. But Emma always used to say there was no way of knowing who he was dancing with."

They both laughed.

"So many memories," said Rosemarie. "Now Colin's gone. They've always been such fine folks."

"And very good parishioners," said Elaine.

They approached the curve where Elaine had almost run into the van the night before. As they passed the opening in the hedge, she glanced through at the large, stately house. There was a sign, but the lettering was very small, and she couldn't read it.

"Rosemarie, do you know what that place is?"

"Hmm? Oh, that's a doctor's office. Obstetricians. Dr. Fowler delivered my daughter's baby. I believe he has a partner–some fellow from India or Pakistan or someplace like that. Those foreigners are really taking over medicine in this country."

Obstetricians. What would Jessie have been doing coming out of an obstetrician's office late at night? Well, she was a nurse. In fact, she was in uniform last night. But she worked at the hospital, not in private practice. And there was somebody else in that van with her and Minnie Johnson's nephew. A patient from the hospital? A hospital patient would see the doctor in the hospital. Someone with an emergency, say, someone about to give birth? Well, someone like that might be on the way to the hospital. But from the doctor's office? Would a doctor call a nurse from the hospital to accompany someone to the hospital in a van? If it was such an emergency, wouldn't he call an ambulance?

Jessie.

She could see her in the white uniform.

Jessie.

Yes.

Now Elaine remembered. Jessie had come to her, about a year and a half before, to inquire about a funeral. Elaine had referred her to Father Edward, because the circumstances were rather unusual. She'd forgotten all about it–it had all been done so quietly. The Mass hadn't even been posted, and Elaine hadn't had much to do with the arrangements. The deceased had been from another part of the state. It was Jessie's sister. *That's* what Alan was talking about: someone's relative from out of town. But how could Jessie's sister's funeral have anything to do with the dead baby?

Elaine's fingers began to tighten on the steering wheel.

Obstetricians. Jessie was coming out of an obstetrician's office in the middle of the night. The dead baby was an aborted fetus. Do obstetricians perform abortions? Of course. Those are precisely the kind of doctor that performs abortions. Is Jessie *involved* with abortions? My God, *could* she be?

Elaine suddenly remembered the glimpse of red hair in the van. A young girl. The young girl who had been waiting to see Tamar at the counselling office? She had red hair. *Very* red hair.

A deep, cold, sour feeling gripped Elaine in the guts, and she began to feel like she was going to throw up.

Did Jessie put the dead baby in the trash can?

Rosemarie felt the car swerve slightly. She looked at Elaine and saw that her face was an image of sickness. "Elaine, what's the matter?"

Chapter 14

The flowers were shaking so badly in his hand, Alan was worried they'd lose their petals. He stood in the hallway in front of Jessie's door, took a deep breath, and tried to calm himself. What was going on here? He felt like a teenager on his first date. He had taken Jessie out before. But she was so fragile. There was some conflict raging inside her, and Alan had the distinct feeling that tonight would determine whether or not they were ever going to have a relationship.

He ran down a mental checklist with a concern for detail that was almost childish. Flowers. Bottle of wine–he didn't know what she was cooking, so he'd opted for a rosé. Hair combed. Teeth brushed. Deodorant. Everything properly buttoned and zipped. Was he wearing the right thing? Sport shirt. Casual slacks–well, they *were* pressed. Who knew how formally *she* would be dressed? Oh, it was only dinner at home, for crying out loud. She'd probably have slacks on herself. Maybe a skirt.

Alan took another deep breath, and put his hand up to knock on the door. The wine bottle was in it. He looked at the bottle for a moment, then tapped its base against the door. There was a pause. A long pause, it seemed to him. The door opened.

"Hi...Alan."

She looked wonderful. Casual–soft cotton blouse, slacks, heels–well, the casual look women work so hard to achieve. The illusion of casualness. And her hair was down. That magnificent, chestnut hair. Alan had hoped her hair would be down.

"Hi, Jess." He stood in the hallway, gazing at her.

"Come in."

Right. Come in, dummy. "I, uh... I brought these. Thought you might enjoy them."

"Thank you. They're lovely." She closed the door behind him and took the flowers. "That was very sweet."

Good start.

"Something smells great."

"Fettucini. I...hope you like Italian."

Alan noticed that Jessie seemed the slightest bit apprehensive. Uncertain about the dinner selection perhaps?

"I *love* Italian. Fettucini's perfect. I wasn't sure what kind of wine would be appropriate." He held out the bottle. "You suppose rosé goes with fettucini?"

"Rosé goes with anything, I guess." She took the wine–"I'll chill this a little."–and hurried out to the kitchen.

Alan looked around the combination living-dining room with great interest. Simple furnishings. A few small pictures and collector plates on the walls. Porcelain figurines. Tasteful. Feminine. A home created by a woman–the comforts of which he hadn't enjoyed for some time. He became aware of music playing softly on the stereo.

What he couldn't see was Jessie in the kitchen. She had put the wine bottle into the freezer, and was holding onto the refrigerator with both hands, trying to collect herself. *Don't get uptight*, she thought, just as Elaine had said. Enjoy the evening. *Let things happen on their own.*

"Can I do anything to help out there?"

"Oh–" The question startled her. "No thanks. I'm just checking on a few things. Dinner will be ready in a couple minutes." *Get hold of yourself, girl!* Actually, everything was already waiting on a warming tray. She drew in a long breath, then let it out slowly. It didn't help. Her hands were beginning to shake.

Alan wandered over to the stereo. He recognized what was playing: Reba McEntire. There were several brand new CDs with their wrappers still on. Patty Loveless. Kathy Mattea. Dixie Chicks. Alan smiled. Jessie had no way of knowing that his musical tastes extended well beyond the country tunes he played with the band at Minnie's. She was obviously trying to please him, and he was touched.

Jessie swallowed a small pill, and put the plastic container back into her purse. She had tried to wean herself from these things often enough. But they had helped in the past. They were the *only* thing that helped. Certainly, all that therapy hadn't been worth a damn. She still had those dreams. And she still broke out in cold sweats whenever she was alone with a man.

How was it she could function as a nurse? She could bathe naked male patients. Oh, she *hated* their stupid remarks, of course. Always something *sexual*. Sure, she realized that most of it was their own self-consciousness at being exposed in front of a woman. But–good God!–did it always have to be about *sex*? Did it always have to be some stupid comment about her body–especially her ample breasts–just because men were shy about their own bodies?

Still, she was a nurse. She was a professional. She even wore the traditional uniform as a badge of that status–as well as to afford some measure of protection. It was like a nun wearing a habit. The formal clothing said: *This woman has authority. Mind your manners.* And it worked–up to a point. At least it kept the sexual stuff on the level of talk. Usually, no one tried to touch. And that was good.

So she could deal with men in a professional context. But this was different. The personal side–it was *always* different. Alan in the next room. Sweet, shy Alan. She knew she was drawn to him. She knew she wanted love. She *needed* love. She was a woman. Doesn't a woman need to be loved? But what did *Alan* want? What was behind that shyness? Did he want love, or did he just want...?

The calming effect of the medication was beginning to wash over her. She didn't feel completely together, but she was better. She found a vase in the cabinet, filled it with water, and deposited the flowers. Then she unplugged the warming tray, made a spot for the vase, and carried everything out to the table. "Hungry?"

"Yes. As a matter of fact, I am. That looks pretty impressive."

"I'm afraid I'm not as much of a cook as I'd like to be." She took the vase from the tray and set it in the center of the table. A few of the elements had to be rearranged slightly. She should have anticipated Alan bringing flowers. It was something he would have done.

"Well, I'll give you my assessment in a little while."

"You'll undoubtedly be a perfect gentleman and tell me it's wonderful, no matter how it tastes."

"Food is something I never lie about."

Both of them knew they were nervous and indulging in dating chatter–stupid, charming, pointless, indispensable.

"Wait a minute," said Jessie. "I forgot the wine." She went into the kitchen, took the bottle out of the freezer, then grabbed a cork extractor from her odds-and-ends drawer. It gave her an opportunity to take another deep breath and encourage herself. Okay. She was handling it all right.

"Would you do the honors?" She came back to the table and handed the wine and the opener to Alan.

The man-opening-bottle ritual followed, Alan poured the wine, and they started into the salad which Jessie had tossed in a large crystal bowl sitting on a sideboard. More dating chatter, more nervousness, Alan's verdict on Jessie's *wonderful* dinner. Actually, she was quite a capable cook.

Jessie was reasonably in control through the main course. She even felt herself relaxing into the pleasure of Alan's company. And she did enjoy the sincerely exaggerated compliments on her dinner. But by the time they were half through the fruit compote and she realized that the meal portion of the evening was coming to an end, it occurred to her that they would soon be into the sitting-on-the-couch portion, and the nervousness started to return. *Get hold of yourself, girl!*

She stood up and began gathering dishes, trying to keep in motion to hide the trembling that was taking her over.

"Let me help with those," Alan offered.

"No!" said Jessie, a bit too abruptly, then caught herself. "No, that's all right, Alan. Why don't you go relax on the couch? This'll just take a minute."

Alan saw the over-reaction and sensed that Jessie's ill ease with men was showing itself again. He smiled, groping for some disarming remark. "Hey, I wash dishes at home–once a week, whether they need it or not."

Jessie appreciated the attempt. "Well, tonight you're a guest. Next time, you can wash, and I'll dry." She headed quickly out to the kitchen.

Next time, Alan noted. That seemed a good sign.

The plates were rattling as Jessie set them in the kitchen sink. *Next time*, she thought. *There won't be any next time, if I don't stop this.* She reached for her purse and took out the pill container. No. It was too soon. And she'd had wine. *You can't keep doing this to yourself. You're a nurse.* She put the pills back into her purse, and leaned against the refrigerator. More deep breaths.

What does he want? What does he want? I know what he wants. Well, all right. So he wants that. All men want that. But can he love me? Can he cherish me? Will he...hurt me? There was no way to know–until she knew–and she resolved to find out. She tried to compose herself, straightened her shoulders, and walked back to the table as calmly as she could. She picked up the wine bottle and glasses, took them over to the couch, and set them on the coffee table. "There's still a little rosé left."

"Well...I guess we can clean that up," said Alan.

Jessie sat on the couch next to Alan and smiled at him. It was another of those droopy-eyelid smiles that Alan couldn't interpret but which stirred such feelings inside of him. He looked at her–the eyes, the chestnut hair falling around her shoulders. He felt the effect of her more strongly than he ever had before. There was not the least question in his mind that he desired her. But this was not a woman to be toyed with. Jessie was complicated. He realized that. She needed...*something*. Alan hadn't the foggiest idea what it was, and he wanted to know.

"Jess..." he said, dividing the last of the wine between the two glasses. "I've been enjoying this evening."

Alan held out one of the glasses, suddenly realizing that he wasn't sure it was Jessie's. Uncontrollably, he had the kind of thought that always seemed to creep into his head at the most inopportune moment–like wondering if the dead baby in the boy's room had been a boy. He heard his thoughts say: *germs*. Then he glanced at Jessie's lips. He wondered if he dared hope that, before the night was over, such a concern wouldn't matter.

"I haven't spent an evening like this in a long time," he said. "And I want you to know, Jess...well, that it's been nice."

Jessie took a sip of wine. "I'm enjoying it too, Alan." She desperately wanted that to be so. But Alan noticed the wineglass shaking in her hand.

"You know..." Alan said, with a boyish smile, "I'm not real smooth in these situations, myself." He was trying to put her at her ease. Of course, it happened to be true. His aim might have been to calm Jessie, but the fact was that Alan had just about run out of small talk. They damned well had to get sincere pretty soon–not just for her sake, but for his.

Jessie closed her eyes, holding her wine glass in her lap between her trembling hands. "You're a very nice man, Alan," she said. "And I'm glad you called me again, after..."

"Jess. I like you. I like you a great deal. You're a beautiful, intelligent and charming woman." He paused for a moment, swallowing. "I like the feeling I get when I'm with you."

She still had her eyes closed. "I told you... I told you that I'm...not good with men."

"I know, Jess. And I told you I understand."

Jessie opened her eyes abruptly, looking across at Alan. *I understand*, he had said. *I understand.* But how could he understand?

Alan didn't catch the glance at first, but then he looked back and was taken by what seemed the most perplexed, questioning twist to Jessie's face. Then a faraway look that didn't seem to focus on him at all.

"There's no pressure, Jess. Really. There's no pressure."

Alan slid his hand across the cushion between them, and touched Jessie's hand at the base of the wineglass in her lap. He smiled at her, but he wasn't sure she saw it.

She didn't. But she felt his touch, and she looked down at his hand on hers. *There's no pressure*, he had said. *No pressure.* But he was touching her. How could there be no pressure, when he was touching her? She felt the merest shiver run through her body, and she shifted her legs slightly away, removing her hand from under his.

"I'd just like for us to spend time together," Alan continued, softly, reassuringly. "I'd like for us to get to know each other."

He hoped the words didn't sound contrived. He *certainly* hoped they didn't sound completely phoney–didn't sound like a *line*. Because he meant them. More than in a long time, he could feel the combination of loneliness and desire pulling at him, and he wanted very much to be close to Jessie. If that closeness ever became something more–something deep, something passionate–then wouldn't that be beautiful? Wouldn't that be some kind of fulfillment, after all his effort at leading the chaste Catholic life?

Alan had no illusions about love. Not now. Not after Sheila. He had to admit that, after Sheila, he was more than a little scared of love. But this wasn't Sheila. This was Jessie. And this was Alan. Pulled by loneliness and desire. This was worth a try.

"So please believe me, Jess–" Alan was still talking, but Jessie wasn't really hearing. "–there's no pressure. Honestly. I understand."

She looked at him, then. Eye-to-eye. Attentive again at the word "understand."

"No Alan, you don't understand."

Alan still couldn't read her face, and this expression was different from anything he had ever seen on her.

"I *know* men, Alan. I work with men, deal with them all the time. I know what they're thinking when they look at me. I know what they've *always* thought." She set the wine glass on the coffee table and put one hand on the back of the couch. "You're a nice man, Alan, but I know what you're thinking when you look at me. You feel desire for me, don't you, Alan?"

Alan didn't know quite what was happening, but he had wanted sincerity. "You're a desirable woman, Jess."

"You'd like to make love with me, wouldn't you Alan?"

What was this?

"I told you, Jess...you're...very desirable."

"Yes. That's what men always feel. Oh, I'm not conceited, Alan. It's simply the truth. You'd like to make love with me. It probably doesn't even have very much to do with me, when you come right down to it. It's simply what men want."

This line of conversation put Alan at a loss. Was Jessie joking? Teasing?

Mocking him?

"Hey, I assure you, I have standards," he said kiddingly.

"I'm sure you do," she said. "You probably don't think about making love with women who are too old–or too fat. But I'll bet there's a pretty wide variety of women you do think about. Isn't that right, Alan?"

Alan could see that a definite change had taken place in Jessie. She was no longer trembling, but he surely couldn't describe her as calm. She was drilling him with her eyes, and her mouth was set in a flat smile that made him feel extremely uncomfortable.

"I don't know what you want me to say, Jess. I look at women...and I feel a certain amount of...attraction. I think that's natural. Unavoidable, really."

"And what do you feel when you look at me, Alan? Be honest. What do you feel for me?"

"I told you, Jess. I've felt a great deal of desire for you."

"Is that all, Alan? Is it just desire? Or is it love? Could you love me, Alan?"

"Jess... We've only known each other–"

"Could you love *any* woman?"

"I've been in love."

"But desire is *first*, isn't it, Alan? It's always sex first. Admit it. First comes the physical, then the love."

"Well, there has to be *some* attraction, yes. If two people don't know each other, what is there beyond the physical?"

It was a quick rebuttal and an obvious enough point. But Alan knew this was a question with more to it than that. He'd often considered it himself, looking back over his life. He hadn't been involved with any women since Sheila. But there had been women *before* he married Sheila. In fact, there had been *Sheila* before he married Sheila. And yes, physical attraction always came before love. Too often, *everything* came before love. But wasn't that part of being human? Wasn't that a reflection of our *fallen nature*, as Father. Karl would put it? We might struggle against it. We might try for a higher level of moral purity, for greater commitment, for something more beautiful than simple animal craving. But the truth was that all our natural impulses pushed us toward the physical.

Real love was hard.

"I guess you're right, Jess," Alan said. "Physical attraction does come first."

"Of course it does. And that's what you're feeling now, isn't it?" Jessie's smile was derisive, almost sinister. "You're very attracted to me now, aren't you? You're attracted, and you're aroused. Isn't that true, Alan?"

Alan sensed himself backing away from her. At the moment, what he was feeling was something very different from arousal. It was an odd fearfulness which he couldn't explain. What was wrong here?

"You'd like to push me down on the couch and have me, wouldn't you, Alan? Right here. Right now. Admit it. That's what you'd like. Isn't that true, Alan?"

Alan started to stand. "Maybe I'd better go, Jess."

"Go?!" she said. "Maybe you'd better go?!" Jessie sprang to her feet, an expression on her face of utter fury and contempt. "You're just like all of them, aren't you? You can't have what you want, so you'd better go." She was spitting out the words through her teeth. "Don't you *ever* touch me again, you filthy pig! I'm not going to let you do this any more. I don't care who you are!"

What the hell was she talking about?

"I trust you, and you do *this*! Get away from me. You don't love me. You *hurt* us! You *always* hurt us! I can't stand it any more. We trust you, and you hurt us."

Us?

"Jessie, who are you talking–"

She was sobbing hysterically, her two clenched fists pressed tightly against her eyes. "Get away from me!" she screamed. "Joey, make him stop! No! No! *Don't hurt us*!"

"Jessie, I don't understand. Who are you talking to?" He tried to put his arms around her, but she pushed him away violently.

"Don't hurt us anymore! Please, don't hurt us anymore!"

"Jess, nobody's doing anything. It's me, Alan. Nobody's hurting you."

Over and over she kept screaming it: "*Please, don't hurt us anymore! No! No! Please don't hurt us*!"

Alan was confused, frightened. Jessie was clearly out of control, and he wanted to do something to help her. But what? He became aware of a hard pounding on the apartment door.

"Alan!"

He heard his name from out in the hallway.

"Alan!"

He went to the door and opened it.

"Elaine?"

The nun rushed in and ran across the room to Jessie, grabbed her by the shoulders, and started shaking her. "Jessie! Jessie, it's me, Elaine! It's all right, Jessie. It's Elaine."

Jessie stopped sobbing and looked at the woman shaking her. It took her a moment, but she finally recognized who it was. "Elaine," she said, dimly.

"Nobody's hurting you, Jessie. It's all right. Nobody's hurting you."

"Elaine..." Jessie fell into Elaine's arms. Alan rushed over, and the two of them helped Jessie to the couch and laid her down. Jessie wept with her face against the cushions–low, quiet weeping–but she wasn't hysterical anymore.

✠ ✠ ✠

Alan stood in front of the sink, washing the dishes by hand. There was an automatic dishwasher, but he needed the activity while Elaine was trying to help Jessie settle into sleep in the bedroom. He wiped the sponge round and round across the face of a dinner plate, absently, his mind far away.

Was there a pattern here? First Sheila had to sow her wild oats. Then–God knows–there were no women to offer any comfort after the divorce. Well, Barbie. But that hardly counted. Now he seemed to be driving Jessie to some kind of breakdown.

I've really got a gift, he thought.

No. He had to drop the self pity. There was obviously more to Jessie's anxiety about men than Alan had imagined. Much more. Jessie was in serious trouble. Thinking back, Alan should have realized something was wrong. That air of sadness. So pervasive. But she was so beautiful.

Elaine came into the kitchen. "Alan, I have to talk to you."

He was startled back to awareness, rinsed the plate, and put it into the dishwasher rack to air dry. "What's the matter with her, Elaine?" he said, turning to the nun and wiping his hands on a dish towel. "You do a lot of counselling. Is Jessie really sick?"

"Yes Alan, I think she is." Elaine sat down at the small dinette. "Jessie and I had a long talk. It was kind of...disjointed. But I think I understand a few things now." She gestured for Alan to take the other chair. "Jessie and her sister were sexually abused as children."

"Jessie has a sister?" Alan asked, sitting down.

"That's what I really have to talk to you about, Alan." Elaine's eyes fell into her lap, and she fidgeted with her fingers. "This is probably going to come as a shock. I know it did for me."

Alan turned directly to the nun across the small table, leaning forward on his elbows.

"Alan..." She looked up at him. "It was Jessie's sister who was buried from St. Mary's. I didn't remember it when you talked to me this afternoon. Actually, I hadn't been very involved in the arrangements when it happened. Jessie had wanted it all very low key. She dealt with Father Edward pretty much directly, and there was virtually no one at the funeral. But Jessie's sister was the out-of-town relative. Her name was Joanne Brown–which I couldn't even recall. I had to look that up in my old schedule book."

"What are you saying, Elaine?"

"There's more, Alan. Jessie has been working for some doctors who–" Elaine found it difficult to form the words. "Jessie assists with abortions, Alan. She works part-time for two obstetricians out on the Old Valley Road. They do abortions at night."

Alan sat, staring at the nun. Then took his head in his hands. Thinking. Not wanting to think. Thinking again. "Jessie left the dead baby at the school."

"Yes Alan, I believe she did." A memory of the sick feeling she had experienced in the car came back to Elaine. "But I don't know why she did it."

"I know why," said Alan. "I know why." He straightened up, and looked at her, nodding his head with resignation. "It was revenge."

Elaine's eyebrows came together, perplexed.

"It may not have even been conscious," Alan said, "if she's really disturbed. But it was revenge."

"Revenge for what? And against whom?"

"She was taking revenge on Father Karl for the death of her sister."

"Father Karl?"

"Elaine...Jessie's sister was the woman Father talked about in his homily on Sunday–the one who committed suicide after having an abortion."

"Oh, Lord... She blamed him?"

"Yes. And she didn't put the baby in the trash can. She put it in Father's conference room. Rosemarie's grandson took the bag to the trash can, thinking it was rubbish from the RCIA meeting. But it was meant for Father Karl."

"Alan, I've never been a fan of Father Karl, but why–"

"Jessie's sister had brought charges against him. She claimed he raped her, that the child was his."

"What?!"

"They investigated thoroughly, and he was cleared. The sister admitted she made it all up. But maybe Jessie wasn't sure. Maybe, when her sister died, it was more than she could handle. Maybe–if the two of them had been abused, like you say–maybe somehow...deep in her mind...Jessie saw Father Karl as the person who had abused them. Who knows? Who could possibly know what was going on inside her head? But I think something like that is what happened. It was revenge. Some kind of...irrational...tragic...revenge." Alan slumped back in the chair and let his head fall forward. "Dear, beautiful Jessie."

Elaine could see Alan's despair. "I'm so sorry, Alan," she said. "I know you've had feelings for her. And if it's any consolation, she has feelings for you."

"Thank you, Elaine." He sat quietly for several minutes, trying to sort out the whole confusing situation. "What I don't understand," he said at last, "is why Jessie would be involved with abortions. I mean...possibly in some emergency situation, in the hospital–you know, if a woman's life is in danger, complications in delivering a baby, something like that. Jessie is a nurse, after all. But doing abortions at night, in some doctors' office on the Old Valley Road?"

The nun suddenly looked as if she was going to cry. Her eyes were puffy, and she had difficulty speaking. "Alan... Jessie told me something that–" She choked up slightly. "Excuse me, Alan... It was so heartbreaking." She took a tissue from her pocket and dabbed her moist eyes. "Jessie said she felt *guilty*–guilty that she hadn't been there when her sister needed her." Elaine cleared her throat. "Joanne told Jessie she was planning to have an abortion, and Jessie objected. They had words about it afterward, too. When Joanne killed herself... Well, I guess everything...the sexual abuse, the years of feeling guilty over all that–you know, children who are abused frequently blame themselves."

"Maybe so," said Alan, " but actually doing abortions... It makes no sense."

"Alan... Jessie told me that she's a Christian and she knows abortion is murder..." Elaine's voice began breaking again. "But she said that when her sister needed someone to hold her hand, she wasn't there. Jessie said, 'I hope God can forgive me, but I didn't want other girls to be alone when they killed their babies.'"

Chapter 15

Sister Elaine looked tired. She had spent a very fitful night at Jessie's apartment, and hadn't done her morning meditation. In fact, it was all she could do to get Jessie off to work, then go back to her apartment to shower and change and come into the office. She even accepted Alan's offer of a cup of coffee, which was usually a no-no for Elaine–she described herself as a "caffeine-free zone"–and she took a doughnut, as well. At least the doughnut was a whole wheat honey glazed from the co-op organic grocery.

"I just don't know what to make of it, Alan. Jessie was absolutely fine this morning. She got up. We had some grapefruit juice. And she went off to the hospital. It was like nothing had happened last night."

"Did she say anything about me?"

"She said she had a wonderful time, and she was sorry to disappoint you, but she always has trouble with men. She said she would understand if you don't call her again."

"She didn't remember carrying on as if I were raping her?"

"I don't think she *does* remember. It's like all that hysteria has just been blocked out."

"Did she give any indication that she remembers...the baby?"

"None. Absolutely none. I'm beginning to wonder if this is some kind of multiple-personality situation."

"There has to be *something* extreme going on," said Alan, shaking his head. "How can you account for all of this, really? The human mind is so bizarre, when you think about it. A dead baby. What exactly was Jessie trying to accomplish?

Just showing Father Karl that she held him in contempt? Or that she wanted to see him dead?"

"To remind him of her sister's dead baby, obviously. But beyond that, who knows?"

The two of them sat gazing off into space for a moment. Then Alan stood up, shook his head again, and walked over to the window. He put his hands on the sill and looked outside. It was a lovely, clear morning. The sky was blue, and everything seemed in such bright contrast with the turmoil of the previous evening.

"Well, there's no point trying to second-guess this one," he said. "Like our friend, Chief Zubeck, observed, people do very odd things. I suppose this is something we'll never really understand."

"I can't help wondering, though," the nun said. "Why *now*? Father Karl's been at St. Mary's all these months. Why would Jessie suddenly–"

"May Day," said Alan, turning back around. "We found the baby on the *first* of May, which was the anniversary of her sister's suicide. The first anniversary since Father Karl arrived. I'm sure Jessie didn't bring the baby into the school building that morning. It wouldn't have smelled as bad as it did, for one thing. It was obviously sitting around for awhile. She had to have brought it in late Monday night, after your RCIA meeting. Little Kevin would have taken it from Father's conference room and put it in the trash the next day, when he was helping Rosie clean up. But knowing that May first was coming must have put a lot of pressure on Jessie. It was probably building in her for a long time."

"I'm way out of my depth here, Alan," Elaine said, and took another sip from her uncharacteristic cup of coffee. "I can't counsel Jessie in this. We've got to get her into some serious therapy. And I mean *real* serious and probably long-term. She might even need to be hospitalized."

"All of *that* may be out of our hands," said Alan. He leaned against the window sill. "The police are involved in this matter. Zubeck knows about Jessie and her sister. If they haven't put the whole story together by now, they soon will."

"My God, do you think they'll arrest her?"

"I don't know what the charge would be, but I imagine they'll do something." Alan's expression was grim. He reached for his own cup sitting on Elaine's desk.

A sip of warm coffee softened his features a little. "By the way, Elaine, there's a question I've been meaning to ask you. How did you happen to come beating on the door at just the crucial moment last night? You would have been about the last person I'd expect to see."

Elaine nodded. "The screaming," she said. "I recognized Jessie's voice. I live right down the hall from her apartment."

"I'd forgotten about that," Alan said.

"Jessie had told me she was going to cook you dinner last night, and I guess I kind of had one ear cocked, hoping to catch you when you came out. So when I heard Jessie scream..."

Alan smiled ironically. Elaine *was* a nun, wasn't she. "How did you know I wouldn't have been in there all night?"

"Alan, I was *trying* to hold a better opinion of you than that." Elaine suddenly looked extremely nun-like. "And I certainly had a better opinion of Jessie."

His smile turned from irony to wistfulness. "Well, as the evening went," he said, "there wasn't much chance of such a thing, was there? Looks like I stirred up some pretty bad memories for her."

"She must have been hurt so deeply," said Elaine.

Just then, they heard a man talking to Rosemarie out in the hallway.

"I believe Alan's in with Sister Elaine, Pastor," said Rosemarie.

Matt appeared in the doorway. "Mr. Kemp?"

Alan went to him, holding out his hand. "Reverend. Thank you so much for coming."

"Good morning, Matt," said Elaine.

"Good morning, Elaine. How are you? Haven't seen much of you since we worked on Right to Life."

"Reverend," said Alan, "there have been some additional developments since you and I spoke yesterday."

"Developments?"

"We now know how the dead baby got into the bathroom."

"Really..."

"Yes, and it didn't have anything to do with protesting the Church's anti-abortion stance–which is what I believe you were concerned about when you last talked with Father Karl."

"Yes, I was."

"Well, strangely enough...it turns out to have been a member of..." He lowered his eyes. "St. Mary's parish."

"My Lord! Who would have– *Why*?"

"It's someone who's..." Alan had difficulty speaking the words. "It's our opinion that the person is...quite badly...disturbed. Out of control, really. I don't think she even knows she did it." He looked away. "I hope to God she doesn't know..." His voice trailed off.

"She's someone who apparently needs a great deal of help," said Elaine. "We're going to be looking into what can be done. Meanwhile, Father Karl has to be told."

"Well, I'm here to help in any way I can."

The three of them went over all the details of the recent events. Elaine was surprised to hear about the statue incident. They considered ways of broaching matters to Father Karl. Finally, they gathered up their courage and headed for the rectory. When they got to the front porch, Alan knocked on the door. After a moment's pause, it opened, and Father Karl looked out at the trio with some surprise.

"Well, good morning," he said. "What...can I do for you folks?"

"Father," said Alan, "we have to speak with you...about some things that are rather...important."

There was a seriousness in Alan's voice, and on all their faces, which the old priest took for urgency.

"Please do come in," he said, holding the screen door open. "Nice to see you again, Reverend."

"You too, Father."

"Pastor Matt has been very gracious in coming over, Father," said Elaine. "He has some information which bears on one of the things we have to speak with you about."

"Reverend Pell has expressed his concern before," said Father Karl, "and I've appreciated it. I sincerely have."

Father Karl put his hand on Matt's shoulder, which took the young minister by surprise. The priest showed them all into his office. Matt and Elaine sat on the low settee, while Alan drew up a straight-back chair. Father sat with his back to the roll-top desk.

"Now then..." he said in a businesslike manner.

Alan took the initiative. "Father," he said, "something happened recently that–for a time–seemed to be a kind of follow-up to the baby incident."

He related the details of the statue desecration, of how Popeye had spotted the two boys and come to get him in the middle of the night, how Alan had contacted the police, and how he and Zubeck had agreed to keep the incident quiet. Pastor Matt expanded on the story, explaining how the high school principal had identified the boys involved–and how one of them was a regular at Bible Fellowship. He recounted his conversation with the boy's mother, noting the woman's strong anti-Catholic sentiments–feelings which he did not encourage among his congregants, he hastened to point out–and stressing her promise that nothing like this would ever happen again. Father Karl thanked him for his intervention and his spirit of collegial loyalty. It seemed to Elaine that the old priest was genuinely touched. She caught the two clergymen smiling at each other, and sensed an actual warmth between Father Karl and Pastor Matt.

Alan observed that same smile, and was struck by some interesting contrasts. The old, gray-haired Catholic priest and the handsome, young Protestant minister. The servant of universal tradition. The champion of individual grace. Two missionaries of Christ. So different and–Alan was surprised to think–so alike. It occurred to him that this was the closest thing to genuine ecumenism which he'd experienced since the Air Force.

But there was more information to convey, and this was the hard part. Again, it was Alan who led off.

"Father..." he said. "I know you've felt...a considerable amount of anxiety over the sad–the *horrible*–incident of...the baby." He watched Father's face for a reaction, but the old priest was impassive. "We've all worried that there might be more trouble brewing. I hope that what we have to tell you will relieve your mind."

Alan glanced at Elaine, whose eyes were diverted. "You see, Father...we now know who brought the baby into the school." Alan paused over the image of Jessie's sad, beautiful face which appeared in his mind at that moment.

"Go on," said the priest.

"This may be...shocking..." Alan said hesitantly.

"Alan," said Father Karl, "a priest sees quite a lot and comes to know many aspects of human life–some of which are shocking indeed. I've had my portion of shocks. With God's help, I've survived them."

"Of course." There was no point trying to ease into the bad news. Alan, Elaine and Matt exchanged glances and nods. Alan pressed on. "Father, the baby was left by a member of this parish. We believe it had nothing to do with any protest against the Church. It was, in fact, directed against you personally. A kind of vendetta. In all probability, the baby was obtained from an obstetrician's office here in town where abortions are performed. The person who left the baby is a nurse. Her name is–" Alan choked on the name, cleared his throat, then sat for a moment, collecting himself. Elaine reached over and touched his arm encouragingly.

"The woman's name," Alan continued, "is Jessica MacNair, and she is the sister of...Joanne Brown."

That brought a reaction from Father Karl, though not any kind the others would have expected. The old priest closed his eyes. "Of course," he said quietly.

Alan, Elaine and Matt all looked at each other.

"You're not surprised?" Elaine asked.

"It confirms a suspicion I had," said Father. "I have seen this nurse, and she was vaguely familiar to me." He looked directly at Alan. "I must assume that you are acquainted with the details of my unfortunate relationship with Joanne Brown, Alan. I will further assume that your interest in this matter is more than casual curiosity. In fact, since I'm aware of your law enforcement background, I wouldn't be the least bit surprised if you were invited to look into this matter by my good friend, the bishop."

"I don't recall ever discussing my background–"

Father held up a hand. "As I said, Alan, a priest knows many things." His mouth was turned up on one side into a wry smile. "In any event, I hadn't associated Miss MacNair with her late sister until she stood up suddenly in the middle of my homily on Sunday–"

Jessie *had* been in church, and it was she who had caused the commotion.

"–and I saw on her face an expression I'd seen once before: at the meeting on Mrs. Brown's charge against me. How can I describe it? Fear. Anger. Shame. Rage. Disbelief. A complex and terrifying expression."

It was just such an expression that was etched into Alan's mind. It was what he had seen on Jessie's face last night.

"There had been an outburst at the meeting. The woman was removed from the room," Father continued. "I was so shaken by that–that *frightful* look–I wasn't even aware of the person behind it. Someone told me later it had been Mrs. Brown's sister, and of course, I knew nothing about her. But as the facts of Mrs. Brown's life emerged, one could only assume that her sister had shared in her torment. I must admit that, at the time, I would hardly have been in a state of mind to be magnanimous toward someone who had shown me such violent hatred. That was my failing. But looking back, I guess Miss MacNair saw in me all the men who had hurt her sister–and possibly herself as well. Who would have thought she was a member of the very parish to which I would later be assigned?"

"There's another coincidence, Father," said Elaine. "Joanne Brown is buried in St. Mary's cemetery."

Father Karl laughed inwardly at this ironic turn, expelling some air through his nostrils. "Well, the circle's complete, isn't it?" He sat quietly for a moment. "But it makes sense, I suppose," he said, finally. "As I recall it all now, Mrs. Brown's sister was angry with the whole parish. She seemed to feel her sister had been betrayed, and she didn't want her buried at St. Ann's." He looked directly at Alan. "Does Miss MacNair assist with abortions?"

"Yes, she does."

"She admitted the whole thing to me, Father," Elaine added. "And I had seen her coming out of the doctors' office in the middle of the night. She was in uniform and riding in a van with a driver and a young girl. It seemed rather suspicious. I assume the girl was a patient."

“Right to Life has suspected for some time that there’s an abortion provider operating here in the county,” said Pastor Matt. “In a small town like this, it would make sense for the clinic to function surreptitiously. They might even do the work at night, to draw as little attention as possible.”

“I suppose that would be logical,” said Father Karl. He sat back in his chair, stretching his legs out in front of him. “I must admit that I feel a bit foolish jumping to the conclusion that all this was some kind of protest. If I had looked deeper, I might have realized it didn’t have anything to do with politics at all.”

“No one could have known that, Father,” said Matt. “And it might very well have been some kind of disgusting demonstration. There’s very little that’s considered out of bounds these days.”

Father Karl shook his head in sad agreement.

“In any event,” Matt went on, “it isn’t likely this would have happened if that clinic wasn’t functioning here in the valley–or, for that matter, if abortion wasn’t as common as it is. So, in a way, there was a political side.”

“As you suggested in your homily, Father,” said Elaine, “abortion doesn’t exist in a vacuum.”

“Sin and suffering,” Father Karl said. “Cause and effect. It all goes together, and you can’t always know which comes first. Life is indeed complicated.”

“If I might ask,” Matt said, turning to Elaine, “which doctor is it?”

Elaine thought for a minute. “I believe Rosemarie said his name was...Dr. Fowler. He delivered her daughter’s baby, and he has a partner.”

Everyone noticed Matt lurch suddenly in his seat. “Is his partner’s name Dr. Singh?”

“I don’t know,” said Elaine. “But Rosemarie did say he’s from India or someplace.”

Father Karl looked at the young minister searchingly. “Is there anything wrong, Reverend?”

Matt gave the same inward, ironic laugh the priest had. “It’s a small town,” he said. My wife and I have been consulting Dr. Singh about our...fertility problem.”

“Oh my,” said Father Karl. “That’s awkward, isn’t it.”

Alan was concerned about Jessie. "There's another side to this, Father. The police have been very thorough, and apparently they've worked out all the details for themselves. It's possible they could...arrest...Miss MacNair. I, for one, would not like to see that happen."

Father Karl brought a hand to his face and tapped a finger against his lips. "It has been my experience, Alan–particularly when I was headmaster at St. Francis–that whenever individuals who have deep emotional problems get involved with the law, the authorities tend to be quite understanding. That is, as long as appropriate action is taken. Perhaps our Catholic Social Services can be of help here. I'd like to see the Church make the effort. We didn't succeed with Joanne Brown, but maybe we can do better with her sister."

Throughout the conversation, Elaine had felt herself stirred by a feeling she couldn't quite pin down. But it had to do with the difficult relationship she'd had with Father Karl, her sense of loss at the departure of her beloved Father Edward, and now the change she'd observed in the old priest.

"Father," she said tentatively, "if I might presume..." Her words faltered.

"Please, Sister..." Father Karl said, gesturing for her to continue.

"Father, there's been something about this series of events that has had an unexpected effect on you. All of us have been touched by what's happened, of course, but... *you*...especially..."

"I once observed to you, Sister, how we can all be caught up in the circle of evil." He looked at her with a wise smile. "Evil is very seductive...in a strange sort of way. We tend to want to wallow in the pain it causes. Perhaps I've done enough wallowing."

Elaine felt her eyes moisten.

"Isn't it so often the case," Matt said, "that the greatest evil flows from the loss of innocence?"

"Better the millstone, as the Lord put it, Reverend," said Father Karl. "Here were young people deeply wounded, stripped of innocence, and left with nothing but pain, distrust and hate."

Pastor Matt thought of his father–his holy, hateful, innocent, wounded, wonderful father. "But then," he said, "the Bible teaches us about innocence...and evil...and holiness. With God's grace...good can come from suffering...redemption can come from sin."

Father Karl nodded his head. "That is our hope, Reverend. That is our hope."

Epilogue

Father Karl insisted on dealing with the authorities on behalf of Jessie. He and Chief Zubeck consulted with the district attorney, who decided that because of the general confusion over responsibility in questions related to abortion, the state would be satisfied if Catholic Social Services could arrange for a program of therapy and Jessie would agree to participate.

Alan and Sister Elaine were able to convince Jessie to submit to a psychiatric evaluation. She entered therapy, and it was revealed that she and her sister had experienced extreme and prolonged physical punishment and sexual abuse at the hands of an uncle and a male cousin with whom they had lived after the early deaths of their parents in an auto accident.

As the sisters had passed through puberty and entered adulthood, they each reacted differently to their tormented experiences. Joanne became extremely promiscuous and went through a series of abusive relationships and two disastrous marriages. Jessie, on the other hand, found herself in conflict between her aching need to be loved and an aversion to physical contact that paralyzed her with fear whenever she began to feel an attraction to any man.

After several months, and with the consent of her therapist, Jessie and Father Karl met for a brief conversation in which they asked for each other's forgiveness. It was difficult but helpful.

The bishop came to St. Mary's for the confirmation liturgy–during which the choir did a credible job on the special song which had been requested. After Mass, the bishop took Alan aside to thank him for his help with Father Karl. Interestingly, at one point, looking down from the choir loft, Alan had noticed that

Chief Zubeck was in the congregation.

Kyle Warner asked Father Karl if he would do the radio interview on the anti-abortion postcard campaign. Father suggested that Pastor Matt participate in the discussion to broaden the focus beyond just the Catholic Church's position and demonstrate interfaith unity on the abortion issue. Both clergymen were concerned when the demonstrations continued on the courthouse lawn for several weeks during St. Mary's Masses. But fewer people showed up for each session of picketing, and eventually, the project petered out.

Sister Elaine agonized for some time over whether she should tell Minnie Johnson about her nephew, Howard's, nocturnal activities in service to Drs. Fowler and Singh. Knowing Minnie's devotion to the Church, she finally decided she owed it to her. Aunt Min was not pleased, and she gave her industrious relative "the fear of God." The price of his continued residence in her home was quitting his night job immediately and going to confess his transgressions to Father Karl. The fact that Howie was not actually Catholic made no difference to Aunt Min.

Tamar's role in securing abortions for her counselling clients was made especially vivid to Elaine by seeing the redheaded girl in the van with Jessie. Their relationship became more strained. Still, the nun was determined to influence procedures at the counselling center, and she wasn't about to give up on her friend. She was encouraged that the board accepted her suggestions about how to promote adoption more aggressively. After some months, Tamar shared with Elaine that the number of abortion referrals had gone down.

English teacher Randy Burke was called to a meeting in the school district administrative offices, attended by Superintendent Adolph Schloesser, Principal Marty Casten and the teachers union building representative for the high school. It was decided that it would be best for all concerned if Randy resigned from the faculty at the end of the academic year. Since the union never leaves its people without benefits, a position was created for Randy at the state Education Department, in which he would be responsible for developing student publications and communication programs–a task eminently suited to his unique gifts. He was given a raise in salary and use of an official car.

State Senator Ben Dillard announced that he would vote against the private school voucher proposal, which spurred several of his legislative colleagues to declare their opposition as well. The measure was defeated. Subsequently, Dillard declared his candidacy for governor. He received the early endorsement of the teachers union.

About the Author

Bill Kassel is a writer with an eclectic career. He has been a journalist, advertising copywriter, public relations consultant, and media analyst, and has held staff positions in companies as varied as Dow Jones and *Guitar Player* Magazine. In addition, he has experience as a liturgical musician, Christian singer-songwriter, and playwright. Mr. Kassel has a commentator's understanding of current issues. Writing under his own byline or as a ghostwriter for others, he has authored articles appearing in *The Wall Street Journal*, *The New York Times*, *Los Angeles Times*, *Chicago Tribune*, *USA TODAY*, *Newsweek*, *National Catholic Register*, *Catholic Faith & Family*, *American Legion Magazine*, and numerous other publications. He is married with two grown children, and resides in Michigan.

Graphic Design and Production........................ Myers & Associates

Cover Photography................................ Todd Lancaster

Digital Image Enhancement.......................... Jonathan Shroyer

The typeface used for the text of this book is Garamond Light Condensed; titles are set in Swordsman Regular.

Company Publications, Inc.
www.companypublications.com